A Reluctant
WITCH'S
Guide to
MAGIC

BY SHIVAUN PLOZZA

CLARION BOOKS
AN IMPRINT OF HARPERCOLLINSPUBLISHERS

ISBN: 978-0-358-54127-1

Typography by Stephanie Hays

22 23 24 25 26 PC/LSCC 10 9 8 7 6 5 4 3 2 1

First Edition

To Ashlyn

✦✦✦

CHAPTER ONE

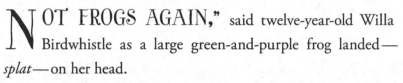

NOT FROGS AGAIN," said twelve-year-old Willa Birdwhistle as a large green-and-purple frog landed — *splat* — on her head.

It was early morning in the city of Bad Faith. The sun was rising, the birds were singing, and the frogs had begun to rain. A small blue specimen landed by Willa's feet. Then another. And another. *Splat, splat, splat* they fell, dotting the dirt lane.

Willa poked at the frog squatting happily on her head like a slimy, warty, green-and-purple bonnet. "Off you hop," she said. "I haven't got all day."

"Croak," said the frog.

"It's not *my* fault. Come on, I have to get to the mill."

"Croak!"

"Oh, please! I'm late for work and I'll get in trouble."

"Croak."

"Fine! If you enjoy sitting up there like a bonnet I'll sew ribbons on you. And buttons. And lace. And—"

The frog leapt from Willa's head and vanished into the reeds.

"Thank you!" called Willa, as yet more frogs rained down around her. She frowned. "I should have brought an umbrella."

While it was true the city of Bad Faith received more than its fair share of frog rain, this wasn't because amphibious precipitation was a naturally occurring phenomenon. In the same way that Mr. Nibler's pig walked on two legs, the bees in Weeping Meadow breathed fire, and Mrs. Tewksbury's rosebushes turned carnivorous on Tuesdays, it was all because of the war.

The Witch War.

You see, the Isle of Dreary was divided into three provinces: Gomerim in the east, home to the Silverclaw witches; Miremog in the west, home to the Irontongue witches; and squeezed between them both was the Wild, where Ordinary Folk like Willa lived.

The two witch covens had been at war for as long as anyone could remember. At least once a week, Irontongue witches gathered on the western border cliffs to cast spells at the Silverclaws, who cast equally nefarious spells right back. Most spells sailed high across the Wild, nothing more than an irritating buzz far above the heads of Ordinary Folk. But sometimes they flew astray and landed in the Wildian city of Bad Faith, where they'd cause a terrible hullabaloo. Spells to make ropes turn into snakes, to make slugs grow the size of houses, to make the hair on your head turn into spaghetti, to make mirrors laugh at the sight of you, and, of course, to make it rain frogs. Nowhere was safe — the wayward spells slipped through windows, shimmied down chimneys, and slunk through pet flaps in doors.

People in the Wild were not fond of magic.

"At least it's not cows again," said Willa as she continued her walk to work, careful to avoid stepping on the frogs.

She was equally careful to avoid glancing at the children playing Ditch-a-Witch outside the school—stomping and shrieking and being terribly, horribly *wild*. Looking would lead to wanting—wanting to join in, wanting to be . . . Willa rolled back her shoulders and marched on.

I don't have time for silly games, she scolded herself. *I have to get to the mill.*

It wasn't unusual for Ordinary children as young as ten to leave school and work, but Willa needed her job more than most: to put food on the table *and* to escape being bundled off to the Home for Lonesome Children Who Have Lost or Temporarily Misplaced Their Guardians. So she didn't have time for games or friends or school or fun. Besides, bad things happened when you were terribly, horribly wild.

She waved good morning to Mrs. Tewksbury, who was shooing frogs out from under her prized rosebushes with a broom. (It was Monday, so the old woman was quite safe from being bitten.)

"Good morning, Willa," said Mrs. Tewksbury. "You mind yourself, now. The blue frogs give you a beastly shock if you touch them."

"Thank you," said Willa. She glanced over her shoulder. "Did you hear that, Talon? Don't play with the blue ones."

Talon, a black-and-white cat with one eye missing, ignored her. He trotted at a distance behind Willa in a manner that said, *I am not following you. I am merely headed in the same direction, which is a total coincidence.*

At least today it was *only* Talon.

Irontongue witches liked to magic up strange and wondrous creatures, such as frog rain and fire-breathing bees. And not long ago an Irontongue witch had magicked up an army of cats—one hundred of the little beasts!—and commanded them to charge the Silverclaws, to scratch their ankles and bite their fingers and claw out their eyes. But the cats were feeling contrary—as cats are wont to be—and instead had found their way to mooch by Willa's front door.

"I can't keep you all!" Willa had gasped.

But the cats had stayed. And now they followed Willa wherever she went. *There goes that Willa Birdwhistle,* people whispered, *her and that army of cats.*

It was the sort of thing her father would have clicked his tongue at. "What will the neighbors think?" he'd have said. "It's not *proper.*"

Willa quickened her step. Usually she kept thoughts of her parents locked up tight. Memories were horrible things, with sharp edges to cut your hands should you examine them too closely. They were better locked away.

But this morning the echo of her father's disapproval bounced stubbornly around her heart. It left her bruised and tender. Perhaps it was because today was her birthday and she had no one to celebrate it with. Or perhaps it was because today was also the one-year anniversary of the wayward *Clouds-away!* curse that had stolen her parents. Though it sounded harmless enough, the *Clouds-away!* curse was truly unpleasant: it liquified you, evaporated you, then turned you into a cloud. And one year ago today, Willa had watched, powerless to intervene, as her parents had drifted away on the wind, misty white clouds she feared she would never see again.

And it had all been her fault.

The bruise on her heart throbbed painfully, but she was late for work and didn't have time to wallow. Instead she gathered up the escaped memories—carefully, so as not to cut herself—and shoved them back where they belonged. Hidden, forgotten, ignored.

"Watch out!" cried Mrs. Tewksbury.

Willa looked up to see a puffy orange cloud zipping like a bumblebee toward her—a Silverclaw curse. It pranced and it danced, looping and leaping. With a startled cry, Willa flung up both hands, cowering as she waited for the spell to turn her into a slug, or flatten her like a pancake, or make her bark like a dog. But nothing happened.

Willa lowered her arms and saw that the curse had taken a sudden left turn and crashed into the wall of Mr. Nibler's barn—and into his chicken coop.

"Oh dear," said Willa. "That can't be good."

In the coop, the puffy orange cloud began to pirouette. Faster and faster and faster it spun until *poof!* it collapsed into a thousand tiny rainbow sparkles that rained all over the chickens. "Bok, bok, bok," they clucked, dashing out into the lane. Then, slowly, one by one, the chickens began to dance.

"Oh, this isn't good at all."

Willa had seen this curse before: *Dance-till-you-drop!* It made you dance until you had ground off your feet and your legs, all the way up to your neck. Willa watched in horror as the chickens flapped their wings and danced on their spindly legs, unable to stop themselves. Most wayward spells were irritating but harmless; this one, however, was as evil as a *Clouds-away!* curse. Seeing it brought back a most horrible feeling of helplessness and a strange sort of tingling in her bones.

Mr. Nibler tumbled out through his front door in his pajamas. "What is it *this* time?" He startled as his pig came hurtling out of the barn (on two feet, of course) to jig in the middle of the lane with the chickens. "Not my pig! Not my chickens!" he moaned.

Willa searched the Gomerim border until she saw a Silverclaw witch balanced on the edge of the cliff, arms still raised in spell casting.

Silverclaw witches never cut their hair, nor did they cut the nails on their fingers and toes. Consequently, their hair swept the ground as they walked and their nails grew long and yellow and curled. They were short, pretty, hairy things with a serene but vague look in their eyes, as if thinking about a pleasant sandwich they once ate twenty years ago at a family picnic.

The witch peered down at the cursed chickens with a hazy smile. She didn't cast a counter-curse. She didn't seem to care at all.

Willa's blood ran cold. *How can the witch not care?*

But no matter her dismay, all Willa could do was stand by and watch, utterly, *utterly* powerless.

The bruise on Willa's heart throbbed until a strange feeling unfurled in her: a breathless, bubbling, blistering feeling. A familiar feeling, buried long ago. It was like being a soda bottle all shaken up and ready to explode. A tiny voice whispered in her mind: *You're not powerless. You can stop it.*

Before she could think twice, words bolted from her like wild horses: "You there!"

The witch turned her vague smile toward Willa.

Silverclaw witches rarely spoke, at least not in the way that Ordinary Folk did. They spoke through dance. If you ignored the fact that they were likely to turn you into a banana split if you so much as looked at them wrong, they were quite lovely to watch. Their bodies swayed with liquid grace as they fluttered their fingers and jiggled their legs and swung their hips and spun in circles. It was how they spoke to one another and it was how they cast their magic.

The witch inclined her head as if to say, *Go on. I'm listening.*

"You fix these chickens this instant," demanded Willa, brimming with that breathless, bubbling, blistering, *bold* feeling. She hadn't felt this way in such a long time. She was surprised how easily she slipped back into it, like a dress she hadn't worn for years that somehow still fit perfectly. "And the pig. You can't go about cursing anybody and anything. Accident or not, it's *wrong*."

The Silverclaw witch stared at Willa for a long time, long enough to make Willa's boldness wilt.

"Oh dear," she said as the witch began to dance. "I'm about to be turned into a banana split, aren't I?" Willa took several hurried steps back, almost tripping over a large brown toad. *Nothing good comes from being bold . . .*

The witch crossed her arms, shimmied up and down, and then twinkled her fingers. A puffy purple cloud shot from her hands and pranced toward the chickens. Willa ducked as the cloud spat out thick, shimmery, butter-yellow sparkles. When the cloud had vanished, not a single chicken was dancing; instead they clucked quietly, pecking the dirt for worms. Percival the pig was still standing on two legs, but at least he was no longer dancing.

The Silverclaw witch nodded once, then turned away, refocusing her efforts on her battle with the Irontongues.

Willa's hands trembled. Had she really confronted a *witch?* And *lived?*

She took off down the lane. If she was quick she could leave behind all trace of that horribly bold feeling—it might fit her *perfectly,* but she knew all too well it was a disaster waiting to happen. Mr. Nibler shouted his thanks, but Willa didn't turn back, not even once.

She was breathless and trembling all over by the time she arrived at the mill for her job spinning wool into yarn. "You stay outside," she instructed Talon—the master weaver despised cats—before she burst through the heavy wooden door. "What a horrible morning. At least things can only get bet—"

The factory was in chaos.

A wayward curse had charmed the long threads of yarn to life. They unwound from their spools and slithered like thin woolly snakes, chasing the poor workers, who bumped into looms and tables and one another as they battled to evade capture. Those who were too slow were quickly wrapped up from head to toe.

The master weaver wriggled on the floor, wrapped in wool like a big hairy blue caterpillar. "Someone get me out of here!" he cried.

Willa moved to help him, but a thick green thread burst out from underneath a loom and looped around her ankles.

"This can't be good," said Willa for the second time that morning.

CHAPTER TWO

WILLA TEETERED ON THE SPOT, arms flailing like a dancing chicken. As the cursed thread pulled tight around her ankles, wrapping all the way up her calves, she lost her balance and tumbled to the floor.

"Cheese and rice!" she cried.

Miss Pickwick, the head spinner, screeched as she collapsed against the cutting table. A charmed measuring tape snapped at her like a cobra. "Get back, you beastly thing!" The sour-faced spinner was a tall and willowy bag of bones with nostrils that flared like an angry horse. "Get back!" She kicked the tape and ran, trampling on Willa's hand as she hurried past.

Willa hissed in pain and collapsed onto her stomach. The cursed thread had wound all the way up to her middle, squeezing until she was breathless.

She rolled onto her back, and something hard and sharp dug into her spine. She shuffled onto her side and saw that she had landed on a pair of shiny silver scissors.

"Perfect!" She grabbed the scissors with her throbbing hand and snipped the thread down to her ankles; it fell away in lifeless fragments. "Ha! Take that!"

Willa scrambled to her feet. Around her, snake threads slithered and screams pierced the air. Her coworkers ran to and fro, faces twisted in fear. *Oh, if only I could make these scissors fly!* thought Willa. Her stomach fizzed and zizzed. *I could—*

With a puff of lilac smoke, the scissors leapt out of Willa's hands and hovered in the air an inch from her nose. Silver wings had grown on either side of the blades, flapping rapidly.

Willa stumbled back, bumping against the cutting table. *Another* wayward spell? Where had it come from?

The scissors suddenly zapped into the center of the room. Quick as a hummingbird they flew, snipping threads in half, chopping the measuring tape into pieces, and hacking through the cocoon of hairy blue wool encasing the master weaver.

At least this spell is helpful, thought Willa.

Soon the floor was cluttered with scraps of lifeless wool, and the scissors had landed back on the cutting table, wings vanishing with a *pop!*

Willa narrowed her eyes, daring to prod the scissors with her finger. *How odd! I wonder if—*

She gasped as a pair of work-rough hands grabbed the back of her neck and spun her around.

"What have you done to my wool?" growled the master weaver, the owner of the hands.

Though Willa was grateful to have found work as a little spinner at the mill, the master weaver was as charming as a regurgitated prune and took great delight in blaming Willa for *everything*—a stubbed toe, an unexpected rainstorm, a splinter, a sneeze.

"I never did a thing," said Willa.

The master weaver snorted. "All my stock has been snipped to pieces and it's *you* standing next to the scissors. Caught red-handed, I'd say."

"It was a curse!"

"A curse? *Pft!*" He looked back at his workers. "Who saw this troublemaker cut up all my stock?"

The dazed workers shuffled nervously in place, eyes darting side to side and hands wringing. Not one of them uttered a word.

Willa stuck out her chin. "See? I never—"

"I witnessed the troublemaker doing it!" cried Miss Pickwick, pushing to the front. She pointed a bony finger at Willa— Willa fought the urge to bite it. Miss Pickwick would shove her own grandmother into the path of fire-breathing bees if it meant impressing the master weaver. "I saw her grab the scissors and cut *all* the threads in the room!"

"That's a lie!"

"It's *you* who are lying," crowed the master weaver, fingers digging tighter. "Miss Pickwick *saw* you, so there's no denying it. You'll face rough music for this."

Willa gasped. *Rough music?*

The workers cheered—"Oh, goody! Haven't had a good public clanging in ages!"—as a terrified Willa was dragged into the frog-filled street outside. She tried to dig in her heels, but nothing could stop the master weaver as he set off down the lane, with workers and curious onlookers and Talon trailing behind. Her ribs squeezed as a wave of awfulness surged through her. Her first birthday alone? Awful. Blamed for something she didn't do? Awful. Rough music? The awfulest awful of all.

"Where are you going with the child?" asked a farmer as they passed his paddock.

"Rough music," said the master weaver with a glint in his eye.

The farmer hurried to join the crowd.

"What are you doing with poor Willa Birdwhistle?" asked Mrs. Tewksbury as they passed her frog-filled front garden.

"She destroyed my stock," said the master weaver. "The little troublemaker must pay!"

Mrs. Tewksbury gasped, dropping her broom. But she, too, joined the crowd. As did Mr. Nibler and his pig. And the baker. And the schoolchildren. Willa felt powerless again, and so very afraid.

Suddenly a blast of fiery Irontongue magic came zigzagging toward the crowd. Unlike the delicate, dancing puffs cast by Silverclaws, this spell was all sharp edges and lightning bolts. It hurtled like a runaway horse and cart, and instead of being shaped like a cloud, it was shaped like words, the same words the spell was screaming over and over: "Cruggity speebitty!"

The master weaver flung Willa to the ground and landed in the dirt beside her; screams rang out as everyone dived out of the way. *Boom!* The spell hit and the earth shook. *Boom! Boom! BOOM!*

Once the dust had settled, Willa opened her eyes and found herself face-to-face with a wide-eyed frog.

"Fart," said the frog.

"I beg your pardon," said Willa.

"Burp," said another frog.

"Puke," said a third.

"How rude!" said Willa. But it wasn't the frogs' fault. They'd been hit with a *Naughty-talky!* curse. It was truly a bad day for wayward spells.

The master weaver grabbed Willa's arm and hauled her to her feet. "We don't have time for this," he grumbled. "Can't they take their war somewhere else?"

Willa's heart stuttered as they set off again, followed by a chorus of frogs croaking rude words. Eventually, the master weaver marched Willa through the high-arched gates that led to the Inner Circle.

Bad Faith was a city of two halves — or, rather, two circles. The Inner Circle was where you found the royal castle (and other assorted royal buildings), the merchant houses, the main market, the Rest-a-Spell Tavern, the Academy of Ordinary Studies, and the Holy Sanctum of Everyday Wisdom. The Outer Circle was where you found everything — and everybody — else.

A high stone wall separated them.

Willa lived in the Outer Circle and had never in her twelve years stepped through the royal gates into the Inner Circle. Until a year ago, she'd hardly ever left her house. Willa's parents had insisted on homeschooling her and had been of the opinion that people and things outside the house were not to be bothered with.

"Quit dragging your feet and gawping like a cursed frog," scolded the master weaver.

But Willa couldn't help it.

A mishmash of buildings soared above her—three, four, and five stories tall, each one blasted, zapped, and cracked by magic, patched up willy-nilly over and over again. Ordinary Folk bustled along the cobblestone streets, wheeling carts overflowing with apples, shouting, "Bit early for a battle, don't you think?" to a friend across the street. "Worst one we've had in years!" There were sparkling dresses and fine suits, and people of every size and shape and skin color. There were horses and carriages and shops and—oh dear, was that a magically talking dog?—and it was all so wondrously, chaotically *new*.

Willa was dragged into the market square, where, in the very center, sat a solid metal box with a thin rectangular eyehole. Though she'd never seen it before, she knew exactly what it was: the Rapscallion's Cage.

Willa's stomach sank like a rock.

By the letter of the law, someone accused of a crime ought to go before the royal clerk, but that involved filling in a great many forms and waiting a great many months for the case to be heard. So Wildians preferred to deal with legal matters on their own. All you needed was a witness and an accuser.

Willa struggled as she was shoved into the cage. A large crowd gathered around her, their faces twisted, their voices jeering. The people of Bad Faith loved a good punishment — it was the best entertainment they had.

"Lock her up!"

"Punish her good!"

"Puke! Fart! Burp!"

The cage door slammed shut behind her.

"Gather round, everybody," said the master weaver.

Willa peered through the peephole and trembled as pots and pans and wooden spoons and lead pipes and sticks and hammers were handed throughout the crowd. However, if she angled her head just right, she could see the sky. Spells sailed far overhead — colorful, dancing, puffy clouds and screeching lightning bolts shaped like words. But beyond the spells were the *real* clouds. Big and billowy and white.

Willa searched for the two that looked most like her parents. If she squinted, she could almost convince herself she saw them, and it made her heart swell and ache at the same time.

"I'm sorry," she whispered. She had tried so hard to fit in, to be the daughter her parents had wanted, but trouble followed her like an army of cats.

Willa's eye was drawn to the master weaver as he climbed onto a box in the middle of the crowd, puffing out his chest grandly. "I hereby convict Willa Birdwhistle of the following crimes: unlawful destruction of property and blatant lying. Miss Pickwick, you are the witness. What say you?"

"Guilty!" cried Miss Pickwick.

Willa let out a whimper.

"Then I, the accuser, hereby sentence the child to ten minutes of rough music!"

The crowd raised their pots and pans with a splintering cheer. Inside the cage, Willa's knees knocked together as she trembled in fear. She covered her ears.

Rough music was the standard punishment in the Wild. It went thus: The convicted was placed in a thin metal cage while the crowd bashed makeshift instruments against the sides. The sound this caused inside the cage was the most horrible cacophony you could imagine. The cage shook and the clanging of metal rattled your bones and your ears rang and your head pounded and you'd see stars for days.

"Now!" shouted the master weaver, wielding a hammer above his head. "Do it now!"

Boom! Bang! Bash! Willa cringed as the ringing, clanging, earsplitting noise filled the cage. How would she survive ten minutes?

But as quickly as it had started, the noise stopped when a puffy orange cloud zipped like a bumblebee into the market square.

A spell.

It bounced off Willa's cage, knocking it to the ground. The door swung open, and Willa tumbled to the cobblestones.

"Cheese and rice!" she cried out.

"Are you all right?" asked a voice behind her.

"I'm—"

Everyone screamed, throwing their instruments to the

ground, as the cloud began to pirouette in the middle of the square.

Rainbow sparkles of magic shot everywhere. The owner of the voice gripped Willa and pulled her out of harm's way. She found herself peering up into the face of a boy, thin as a beanstalk with scruffy brown hair and brown skin and ears that stuck out fabulously.

"Oh," said Willa. "Um . . . Thank you."

The boy bowed deeply with an elaborate flourish of his arms. "Gish Huckabee at your service."

A thundering *thump-thud thumping* turned Willa's head. It seemed as though the master weaver, Miss Pickwick, and some other Ordinary Folk—and quite a few frogs—had been caught up in the puffy orange spell: another *Dance-till-you-drop!* curse.

"Help me!" cried the master weaver, his legs a blur as they kicked and skipped and jumped on the spot.

The witch who'd cast the curse, a hairy Silverclaw perched on the Inner Circle wall, heard the cries for help and, to the surprise of all, cast the counter-curse immediately.

"Oh, thank heavens!" puffed the master weaver, doubled over and sucking down air. "Thank you, thank you!"

Willa's tongue tingled with the urge to shout: *You didn't deserve to be saved, you cruel-hearted regurgitated prune!* But she swallowed back the bitter-tasting words. *Good girls don't shout,* said her mother's voice in her head.

"Look out!" cried the gangly boy.

A blast of Irontongue magic came screaming toward Willa from the west. "Vompity dabbity!" screeched the spell, the words themselves a streak of red lightning. Willa ducked out of the way and the spell hit the stonemason. The color drained from his face as he gripped his stomach and promptly began to vomit up daisies.

Willa spied the source of the spell: an Irontongue witch was crouched on the west side of the city wall, a crow perched on her shoulder.

Irontongue witches were hairless, warty, and green. They were also tall and knobby and hunched, like the hollowed-out trunk of an ancient tree. They never smiled (only sneered or smirked or sniveled), and they had a sharp look in their eyes, as if thinking about a difficult jigsaw puzzle they'd rather spit on than solve. This particular Irontongue witch wore a tattered black robe that rippled like a coat of snakes.

Ordinary Folk dived for cover as the witch shrieked, "Stabbity liberty-jig ab stabbity!" She poked out her tongue, waggling it like a dying fish, before glowing orange words shot from her mouth and screeched through the air.

The Silverclaw witch twirled out of the way and the words flew by him. He began to dance. With a jiggle of his leg and a hop to one side, a green cloud shot from his hands and flew across the market square. The spell landed in the vegetable stall, making a table full of apricots turn into bats. The vegetable seller fainted as the bats took off in a swarm, their leathery wings

19

beating heavily. The swarm hovered above the Irontongue witch before, all at once, they began to poop apricot pits.

On and on raged the battle, right in the center of the city.

Willa was frozen in shock. She had only been this close to a battle once, one year ago exactly. It was so frighteningly familiar: the zaps, the screeching, the colorful clouds, the lightning. She scrunched her eyes shut, trying to ward off the horrible memories making another dash for freedom.

But she remembered: A field. The squelch of mud under her feet—bare feet. "It's not proper!" Laughter. "You can't catch me!" Her father's face, purple with anger. "Come back at once, you unruly girl!" A fizzing, zizzing feeling bubbling up inside her. *Freedom!* Until . . . what's that? Something blue. Coming fast. Breathless fear. "Out of the way, Willa!"

No, no, NO! She didn't want to remember this. *Get back where you belong!*

She opened her eyes as another lightning bolt zapped past: "Boompity bobajagg bibobobit!" The gangly boy dragged Willa behind an upturned horse cart.

"This is horribly exciting," he said.

Willa shook her head. The breathless, bubbling, blistering feeling was growing inside her again. Like adrenaline or fear or . . . something. "I'm sorry, but who are you?"

"Gish. I'm the royal dogsbody. I do all the odd jobs around the castle." He waved a stack of envelopes under her nose with a cheeky grin; his front tooth was chipped. "Supposed to be delivering these, but, well." He shrugged. "And who are you? A master criminal?"

"I'm nobody."

"They don't put *nobody* in the Rapscallion's Cage. You must be *some*body."

Willa shook her head and turned away.

The battle raged on. With a gasp Willa spied Talon, sitting in the middle of the square, licking his tail and paying no mind to the chaos around him.

"Talon!" she cried. "Get away from there! It's dangerous!"

The cat ignored her, rolling onto his back to groom his tummy. Suddenly an Irontongue curse was hurtling directly toward him. Willa watched in horror.

Not again. Please not again.

Before she knew what was happening, the breathless, bubbling, blistering feeling had pulled Willa to her feet. She was so full of fizz she thought she might explode. *You're not powerless!* The whisper had become a shout: *You can stop it!*

"Stop!" she shouted.

And the spell stopped.

It hung in the air—icy blue and in the shape of words: *Duggity quabbity.*

Everyone in the market square watched as the words disintegrated into ash and floated away on the wind.

Willa fizzed all over, as if her veins had been filled with

orange soda. What had she done? All eyes were on her; even the two witches were staring.

There was a pause. A long, aching, terrifying pause in which nobody spoke and nobody moved; not even the wind blew.

Then . . .

"Witch!" cried the master weaver, jabbing his finger at Willa, his eyes large with terror. "She's a witch!"

CHAPTER THREE

I KNEW IT! I always said she was trouble! I always—" The
color leached from the master weaver's face. He took off running through the sea of pots and pans.

"Why are you running?" cried Willa. The other Ordinary
Folk ran too, diving behind upturned tables and chairs and rubble. Even Gish ducked behind the overturned horse cart. Willa
quickly stamped down the fizzy, zizzy, orange-soda feeling,
burying it good and deep and proper   it always led to trouble,
always! "I'm not a witch! I'm not going to hurt you!"

But it wasn't Willa they were running from.

The Irontongue witch swooped from the city wall and
landed in front of Willa, her tattered robes billowing. She licked
her lips with a tongue made of iron. It wriggled like a thick, gray
slug with every word she uttered.

"Mm. Fear tastes yummy!" she said. Her bald head was
painted with golden swirls, and a wonderfully giant wart was
perched on the end of her nose, almost big enough to have
eyes and a nose and a mouth of its own. She smirked at Willa.
"There you are, my dear. What impressive magic you have. You
must come with me to Miremog."

Willa backed away, heart thundering. "Th-th-there's been a
mistake. I'm not—"

The Irontongue witch cackled and stalked forward, crooked fingers reaching for Willa. But, in a flutter of crepey white robes, the Silverclaw witch landed between them.

Willa froze, fear turning her blood to ice. She had never been this close to a witch. *Two* witches.

The Silverclaw had golden-brown hair so long his bare feet trod on the ends with every step. His arms were silver from his elbows to the tips of his fingers, where the nails grew long and curling and yellowed. He folded his arms and jutted out his chin: *Back off, Irontongue scum!*

"Scram, you chicken-hearted fustilugs!" hissed the Irontongue. "You're too late! The girl is mine!"

Mine? Willa gulped.

"Eh, excuse me? Witches?" The master weaver poked his head around the corner of an upturned table. He bowed deep enough to kiss the cobblestones when both witches turned to glare at him. "Um. That is to say . . . Are you, eh, taking the girl with you and, ah, leaving? If she's, um, magic, she can't stay here. So, eh, you could just take her and go. We wouldn't mind a bit."

"But I'm *not* a witch!" said Willa. Tears of frustration welled in her eyes. No one born in the Wild had magic. Willa was Ordinary. She never played Ditch-a-Witch; she ate all her vegetables; she said please and thank you and *Lovely weather we're having today, Mrs. Tewksbury, though it's sure to rain frogs later.* She was as dull and as sensible and as Ordinary as her parents had always hoped she might be. She'd made sure of it; she had *promised.* "Truly, I'm not!"

But the Irontongue witch hissed at the master weaver. "Well, good *sir,* I am Ferula Crowspit, wolf-tier witch of the Irontongue coven, and I claim this girl as mine."

Mine. There it was again, that awful word that made Willa's knees knock and her teeth chatter and her heart go *ka-boom!*

The Silverclaw witch blew a raspberry, sending spittle flying everywhere. "She is Silverclaw!" he said. He blinked in surprise at the sound of his own voice, so unused to speaking with words. "She must come with me, Eladar Moonshine of the Maithwood Circle."

Ferula wheezed with laughter. "Prittle-prattle! She already has a familiar!" She pointed a crooked finger at Talon, who was rubbing against Willa's shins. "Thus she is Irontongue!"

In response, Eladar swirled his arms like lassos until a lilac cloud burst from his fingertips. A bucketful of glittery slime rained down all over Ferula.

Ferula spat slime on the ground. "*Ptooey!* You meddlesome gobbermouth! I ought to—"

A trumpet blared, followed by the *thump-thump-thump* of a hundred pairs of boots stomping across the cobblestones. The Royal Guard, in their forest-green uniforms, filed into the market square.

Gish poked his head up from behind the cart. "Uh-oh. It's the royal clerk." He stood to attention, straightening his rumpled shirt.

The Royal Guard parted to let through a small, round woman with light-brown skin and a dark-brown pantsuit clutching a briefcase. Her brow was lined with worry wrinkles and her eyes darted constantly, like a fly unable to contain its glee at a banquet of cakes.

"Do you have a permit for this gathering?" huffed the royal clerk.

Both witches blinked in confusion.

The clerk spied Gish. "You! Dogsbody! Get over here!" Gish ran, and skidded to a halt at her side. She shoved a handful of papers at his chest. "Any type of gathering of five or more people not listed on the Approved Gathering list requires a Permission to Loiter form submitted in triplicate. Hand these out, boy." She pointed a finger at all those around her, including the master weaver, who had once again poked his head out from behind the table. "First I hear reports of yet more unsanctioned rough music, and now whatever this is!"

Willa noticed how quickly the clerk's eyes darted from one object to the next. Was that why she didn't realize she was addressing two *witches* and was currently one insult short of finding herself turned into a banana split?

While Gish ran around handing out forms, the clerk went on. "What's this gathering in aid of, *hmm?* If it's a protest, you need to fill out a Permission to Make Unfounded and Untrue Comments Against the Royal Family form, and those take ten years to process and never get approved. They are pretty to look at, though. So many little boxes to fill in." The clerk dug into her briefcase. "I have one here, I think. But I might have spilled my tea on it."

Ferula sucked on her gums, eyes roaming up and down the clerk as if pondering which bit of her to eat first. "I am Ferula Crowspit and I am here to claim an untamed witch. *That* untamed witch," she added, pointing a spindly green finger at Willa.

Willa stumbled back as though the finger had jabbed her in the chest.

Eladar shook his head, flourishing a dainty silver arm at Willa and then back at himself: *Mine.*

Ferula bared her teeth. "The girl must choose," she sneered, and poked the clerk's shoulder roughly. "Tell the girl she must choose a coven."

Finally the clerk looked up at the witches, one after the other. She blinked slowly. Then she turned to settle her gaze on Willa, squinting. "Oh," she said. "I haven't got a form for that."

"It's somewhere here," said the clerk, voice muffled. Only her derriere, clad in brown suit trousers, was visible as she rummaged through a stack of papers. "Give me a moment."

Having been whisked through the winding, crumbling halls of the royal castle, they were now in what the clerk had called the records room. Two witches, a one-eyed cat, the royal dogsbody, and Willa, all crammed into a corner of the room and told to wait.

Between all the waiting and being declared a witch and the rough music and the anniversary of her parents' *Clouds-away!* curse, Willa had cycled through a dizzying merry-go-round of emotions but had finally settled on *extremely, very cross.* What a horrible birthday!

"It's probably hiding somewhere behind *The Long and Thoroughly Ordinary Tales of Pearl B. Purcep, an Explorer of Little Note.* A *Mischief-maker!* curse once hit that book, and now it hides my records all over the castle. And the king's socks."

Willa looked at Gish, who grinned at her. He leaned in close and whispered, "The royal clerk would make you fill out a form just to breathe and then deny it with her rubber stamp. But you get used to it."

"I have no plans to get used to any of this nonsense," she whispered back. "The sooner they realize I'm not a witch, the better."

Gish shrugged, still grinning.

Beside Willa, Ferula muttered furiously but had so far refrained from cursing anyone. Eladar smiled dreamily at a feather quill before picking it up and nibbling on it.

"Aha!" cried the clerk. She held her arm aloft, a bunch of old, yellowing papers scrunched in her fist. "*The Rules of Magic for Ordinary Folk,*" she said. She hummed as she read. "Yes, yes. Of course. Yes. Hmm. *Oh.*"

"Well?" sneered Ferula impatiently. "What does it say? It says she's Irontongue, doesn't it?"

Eladar flicked his long hair, *accidentally* poking Ferula in the eye with the ends.

"You did that on purpose, you lubberwart!" spat Ferula. "I ought to curse you bald!"

"What do the rules say, Madam Clerk?" asked Willa.

The clerk looked up, fixing Willa with a troubled frown. "The king will want to hear about this."

But the king did not want to hear about it.

Once they had been dragged into the throne room next door, the king had immediately hidden behind his throne. "Witches?" he'd whimpered.

King Teebald was a dull man. The second Willa stopped looking at him she immediately forgot what he looked like. She stared hard at him and determined that he was sort of pinkish with muddy brown hair and small eyes and a weak chin. But she forgot all that when she noticed a boy, one or two years older than her, leaning against the throne.

He was not forgettable.

He was sharp—edges to gouge out your eyes—with ghostly skin and long black hair. The one thing he shared with the forgettable king was a pair of small, beady eyes. "You can't bring witches in here," said the boy.

"Forgive me, Prince Cyrus." The clerk nodded tersely as she stood before the throne. "But this is an urgent matter."

Prince Cyrus sneered at her.

The clerk cleared her throat and proffered the yellowing parchment to what little could be seen of the king, hiding behind his throne. "Your Majesty?"

"Are the witches gone yet, Florestine?"

"No, Your Majesty," said the clerk. "They're here because the girl has magic."

"I don't," called Willa.

The sour-faced prince narrowed his eyes at Willa and scoffed. "Just what we need. *More* witches."

"But she's Ordinary," said the king, poking his head around the side of the throne to stare beadily at Willa. "Look at her!"

Everyone turned to look at Willa.

"He's right," said Willa. "I'm Ordinary."

Are you? whispered the now-familiar voice.

I thought I got rid of you! hissed Willa. *Of course I'm Ordinary!*

"She was seen conducting magic by no less than fifty witnesses." The clerk snapped her fingers at Gish until he hurried to her side and handed over the list. He shot an apologetic shrug at Willa on his way past. "And there is precedent for this."

"Twice before," said Ferula, jabbing a finger into Willa's shoulder. "Once with the"—she paused to spit: *ptooey!*—"Silverclaw queen and once again seventy years ago. And we all know what happened to *that* one."

The king gasped and hid behind his throne again. Ferula cackled, Eladar smiled dreamily, the prince scowled, and the clerk clutched her parchment tightly. Even Gish shifted uncomfortably from foot to foot. It seemed everyone but Willa knew "what happened to *that* one."

"What happened?" asked Willa, but no one answered her.

"The girl must choose," said Ferula, and waggled her tongue in glee.

Eladar blinked vaguely.

The clerk nodded. "It's the law." She held up the parchment and read: "Should an Ordinary child exhibit magical powers, they must choose a coven to join before their thirteenth birthday *or else.*"

Another jab in her shoulder sent Willa stumbling forward. "How old are you, child?" demanded Ferula.

Willa wanted desperately to give the witch a swift kick in the shins. "Today is my twelfth birthday," she said.

"Happy birthday!" said Gish.

The clerk scowled at him. "That means she has exactly one year to decide."

"She will choose Irontongue," said Ferula.

"Silverclaw," said Eladar, giggling.

"But I'm not even a witch!" said Willa. Frustration was building like a summer storm inside her. But she wouldn't let that fizzy feeling return—she had stamped it down, locked it up tight with all her bad memories, and thrown away the key.

King Teebald peeked out from behind his throne. "Eh,

perhaps you could come to a decision among yourselves. No need to involve me. It's magic business. Where are the girl's parents?"

"Cursed. And I'm afraid it *is* your business, sire," said the clerk. She held the papers aloft once more and read: "'It is the royal responsibility to house and educate the magical protégé in both Irontongue and Silverclaw magic so they may be guided to make an informed decision.' These are the laws of Queen Arabella the Second, of course."

The king clicked his tongue.

"We can't have a witch living in the castle." Prince Cyrus flicked his curtain of shimmery black hair from his shoulder. "She'll curse us in our sleep. Make us barf up frogs and grow monkey's tails. I don't care who made the law, especially not if it was my silly great-great-great-grandmother."

Willa bristled. *Live* in the castle? She thought of her small, ramshackle cottage on the edge of the Outer Circle. It wasn't much, but it was home. It was familiar. And if one day a miracle occurred and her parents came back, how would they know where to find her if she wasn't there?

"I'm afraid the law *is* the law," said the clerk. "It's written that the girl *must* be taught the theory of magic by an independent guide, and when she's thirteen she'll choose a coven or—"

"Or what?" snapped Willa.

Everyone went quiet. Willa looked to Gish for help, but he inspected his scuffed boots, refusing to meet her eye.

"Or what?" said Willa. This time her voice was small and uncertain.

"Or," said the clerk. For once her dancing gaze landed squarely on Willa, and there it stayed. "Or you'll explode."

CHAPTER FOUR

WILLA BLINKED. She couldn't have heard the clerk correctly—was there a frog in one of her ears? "I'm sorry, but did you just say I'll *explode?*"

"Ha!" laughed the prince. "Of course you'll explode. How do you think the Desolation was formed?"

Willa gulped.

The Desolation was a desert in the north of the Wild, a wasteland brimming with dangerous monsters and dead things. It was forbidden to enter, but who would dare try? If you so much as glanced at it, your eyes melted out of your head.

"Do you mean," said Willa, whisper-small, "that *that's* what happened to *that* one?"

The clerk nodded, cradling the parchments to her chest. "Poor little Rab Culpepper. Couldn't decide in time, so his magic went *ka-boom!* and all that was left was cursed land and monsters."

Ferula smacked her gums. "Nasty little scamp. Should have chosen Irontongue."

Eladar plucked a dust mote out of the air and ate it.

"The point is," continued the clerk, "you have no choice— *all* young witches take the coven initiation on their thirteenth birthday to avoid magical combustion. It's the only way to permanently tame magic before it grows too wild. And because you weren't born into a coven, you have to choose one to join or . . . *boom!*"

Confusion settled over Willa like a wet blanket. Wouldn't her parents have told her if she was a witch?

They'd called her bold and unruly and headstrong. They hadn't let her go to school because it was better to "keep our eye on you at all times, you wild thing." They'd clicked their tongues and shaken their heads and said, "Why can't you behave?"

Her mother used to say, "You're naughty because you've got a bad imp in you, Willa," but Willa thought of it as the fizzy, zizzy orange-soda feeling. That's what it felt like, bubbling up inside her right before things would go wrong. That's why she'd made a promise to her parents. Or, rather, to the clouds that had once been her parents. She had promised: *If I'm good, if I bury the fizzy, zizzy orange-soda feeling deep, deep down, you'll come back, won't you? You'll come back and I won't be alone.* And she *had* buried it—for a whole year.

But none of that made her a witch!

The whisper laughed. *Are you sure?*

Of course I am! Now hush, you! She squashed the unwelcome voice beneath her thumb like a bug. *Take that!*

"Are you listening?" The clerk snapped her fingers in front of Willa's nose. "Pay attention! I said the dogsbody will show you to your room. Hurry along now."

Gish arrived at her side, an apology in his smile.

It had to be a joke, Willa decided as she and Talon trailed

35

after him. It was the master weaver, no doubt, or Miss Pickwick. Any second now they would jump out from behind a statue and shout, *Ha-ha! What a jolly good laugh! We made you think you were a witch!*

"... not all bad here," Gish was saying. He nudged her side and Willa blinked at him, as though waking from a long nap. "Good food, comfortable beds, a few cursed potted plants and walls and vases, but that's normal."

He took Willa and Talon on a looping journey through the castle. Everywhere Willa looked, there were painters and builders and stonemasons and cleaners buzzing away at their jobs, patching up years of spell damage. But no one jumped out from behind a statue to tell her it was a joke. And there were far too many soldiers guarding doorways for her to escape.

Willa was out of breath by the time Gish had led her up a narrow, winding tower. All the way to the top they climbed until, panting and doubled over, Willa found herself in a small, round bedroom.

At least, Willa *hoped* it was a bedroom—she couldn't see a bed for all the junk stacked high. *Magical* junk. Potted plants that burped lullabies, paintings that laughed at you, chairs that sat with their legs crossed, tables that wept uncontrollably, a wardrobe that added extra sleeves to everything placed inside it, and doors that shouted, "You can't come in!" It seemed as if every permanently cursed object in the castle had been crammed into this one room.

"Well, good night," said Gish, bundling Willa inside. "I reckon it'll be fun having a witch in the castle."

"But it's not even lunchtime," said Willa. The door closed in her face and the tinkle of a key in the lock was her only answer.

Willa wiped her eyes with the backs of her hands. "I won't cry," she told herself sternly. Talon rubbed against her shins. "I will *not* cry."

Instead of crying, Willa crawled under a weeping table and began to search for a bed. She found one tucked away on the far side of the room, a single with an iron frame that creaked when she sat on it.

"I'll stay *one* night," she said, giving the top of Talon's head a scratch. "In the morning, when everyone realizes their mistake, I'll leave. And if they keep insisting I'm a witch, then . . . then . . . then I'll find a way out myself."

Talon purred.

The painting of a milkmaid at the head of Willa's bed pointed at her and laughed.

Willa hoped that wasn't a sign of things to come.

Early the next morning, before the sun had peeked over the cliffs of Gomerim and while the sky was blessedly free of spells, Gish beat against Willa's bedroom door and announced, "Breakfast!"

Willa was awake on account of being unable to sleep (*you*

try falling asleep when you've been told you're a witch and must choose a coven in one year or else *explode*), so she leapt up and rushed to the door.

"Good morning, Gish Huckabee," she said. She was wearing a dress with five sleeves and two neck holes, courtesy of the cursed wardrobe. She was also wearing her best smile. She had been out of sorts yesterday. The incident with the rough music had no doubt given her a wild look in her eyes—all those horrible memories that had resurfaced. If she could only *show* them how Ordinary she was, Willa was certain she could go home. "Have they realized yet that I'm not a witch?"

Gish snorted. "Unlikely," he said, and led Willa and Talon on another winding journey through the castle, this time all the way to a fancy dining room. She was bustled to the far end of a long table, past paintings of former kings and queens, and red velvet chairs, and servants with food-laden trays and pitchers of juice and water.

"Tea?" asked Gish. He pushed Willa into a chair.

"Oh. Um. Yes? Please and thank you."

With a flourish, Gish poured tea into Willa's teacup. "Here you go, madam."

"Dogsbody!" cried the clerk. "Where are you? I need you!" Her arms overflowed with papers as she hurried into the room. She was wearing another pantsuit—beige this time—and a scowl. Gish dropped the teapot on the table with a clang and chased after her, catching any forms that fell from her grasp.

"Quit slacking off and get to work," she scolded him, settling into a chair halfway down the table. Gish stood to attention behind her, shooting Willa a wink and a cheeky smile.

Others soon arrived: the scowling prince, a smiley gentleman in an elaborate maroon cloak (he plonked down beside Willa with a wink), eight lords and ladies wearing fine robes and snooty airs, and a girl Willa's age with wire-rimmed spectacles and a mouse sitting on her shoulder. The girl looked at Willa, head tilted and nose scrunched, as though trying to determine what sort of creepy-crawly she had just discovered and whether or not she should stomp on it with her boot. Willa slunk down in her seat.

"Where's King Teebald?" asked the clerk. "His crumpets are getting cold."

The prince slumped into place at the head of the table. "Hiding from *witches.*"

As if summoned by the word, Ferula and Eladar swept into the room, causing a great deal of pearl clutching and gasping. Willa froze.

What in the Wild are they *doing here?*

The room held its breath as the witches took their seats, one opposite the other. Ferula sucked on her gums. Eladar drummed his fingernails. The air sparked with tension.

"Well, isn't this marvelous," said the smiley gentleman in maroon, nudging Willa with a pointy elbow. He was quite old, thought Willa, perhaps twenty-eight or even twenty-nine.

Foppish hair, laugh lines, creamy skin, and bushy brows. He helped himself to a large scoop of eggs and grinned at everybody—he never stopped grinning.

"Yes, *marvelous*," sneered the prince. He turned to the bespectacled girl on his left. "As marvelous as a bag of farts. Pass the sausages, Marceline."

The girl—Marceline—fed cheese to her mouse and gave the prince a *what creepy-crawly is this and should I stomp on it?* look. The prince stared hard at her. He glanced pointedly at the sausages, then back at Marceline.

She ignored him.

The prince rolled his eyes. "Honestly, you let *witches* into the castle and suddenly everybody's a Disobedient Dora. *I'll* grab the sausages myself, shall I?"

The witches ignored him too. Eladar stabbed berries with his long, sharp fingernails and sucked them down. Ferula shoveled bacon in her mouth until her cheeks puffed like a chipmunk. Neither of them cursed him silly, which Willa secretly found disappointing.

The smiley gentleman bent close to her. "Have you heard?" he whispered theatrically. His teeth were very white. "The covens have agreed to a cease-fire for a whole year, just so you can concentrate on your studies. You must be *very* powerful. They must want you *very* much."

They'll be disappointed when they discover I'm not a witch, thought Willa.

"Could someone please pass the toast?" she asked. She smiled politely at everyone around the table. No one moved, so Willa reached for the toast rack herself, but the prince snapped it up and piled all of it onto his plate.

"Sorry, *witch*," he said. "None left."

Willa frowned at the limp extra sleeve attached to the front of her dress like a deflated elephant trunk. Perhaps it was her clothes? How could she look Ordinary in a dress with so many sleeves!

"And, of course, these two insisted on sticking around," continued the smiley man. He jerked his chin at the witches. "To keep an eye on your magical studies and to make sure the other doesn't influence your choice. Neither coven would agree to the truce without it. The king fainted when he heard he'd be sharing his home with *three* witches!"

"Lovely weather we're having today," said Willa loudly, "though it's sure to rain frogs later."

"*Pft!*" said the prince. "Frog rain. Yet another abomination foisted upon us by witches." He jabbed his fork at Willa. "And now we're forced to educate a dangerously untamed witch, who will no doubt grow up to curse us with *more* frog rain! What a joke! I think . . ."

As the prince droned on and on about witches and Willa and wicked magic, Willa's skin tingled all over. *I do wish someone would shut him up,* she thought, as the tingle grew into a fizz.

". . . and if she turns out like *that one* and blows up the castle? Then what?" The prince sneered and shook his head. "What we need is—"

A platter of scrambled eggs leapt into the air.

"My word!" A regal lady swooned as it flew over her head.

The smiley gentleman ducked, the clerk gasped, and the mouse squeaked as the platter swooshed up the table.

"Who's doing this?" cried the prince. "Stop it! There's a magical cease-fire. Stop it at once!" But the platter flew to the head of the table, where it hovered above him.

"Oh dear," whispered Willa. She fizzed and zizzed all over.

The plate upturned itself, and gooey eggs slopped down the prince's hair and face, dripping from the point of his chin into his lap.

There was silence.

And then . . .

Marceline erupted with a single "Ha!" Ferula threw back her head and cackled; Eladar's shoulders twitched. The smiley gentleman grinned. The snooty men and women gasped and tittered. Gish hid his smile behind his hand.

The prince stood, hands slamming against the table. "There is a truce!" he shouted, glaring at the witches. Scrambled eggs slid down his face. "No magic allowed. From either of you!"

"Don't look at me," said Ferula with a smirk, feeding toast to her crow. "Did you hear me utter a spell?"

The prince turned his glare on Eladar.

The Silverclaw witch poured mustard into his mouth and said nothing. But he hadn't danced, so . . .

The prince frowned.

And then . . .

His eyes went black with rage as they settled on Willa.

She shrunk back in her seat. "It wasn't . . . I didn't . . ."

The smiley gentleman threw his napkin onto his plate and stood. "I think that's my cue," he announced with a toothy grin that swept the table. It landed on Willa, where it stayed. "Come on then, young Willa Birdwhistle. It appears we have much to learn."

Willa leapt up immediately, more than happy to follow the man out the door. Perhaps, she lamented, getting out of this mess would not be as simple as a polite smile and a conversation about the weather.

With a sigh, Willa hurried after the strange man, but not before she heard the prince sneer, "You'll pay for this, *witch*. Just you wait."

The smiley gentleman led Willa up another narrow, winding tower. At the top of this one was a sparsely furnished classroom. The window was too high to see anything more than blue sky and clouds; on the teacher's desk sat books like *Tongue Twisters Untangled: Irontongue Magic Made Easy* and *Dance Your Way to Understanding Silverclaw Magic: A Beginner's Guide.*

The gentleman shucked off his robes and tossed them over the back of a chair. Underneath he wore a peach suit that appeared to have shrunk in the wash. A green handkerchief poked out of his breast pocket, along with a spotted feather pen. He swirled to face Willa. "My name is Gaspard Renard," he said grandly, "and I am here to teach you magic."

"But you're Ordinary," said Willa. It was true—his skin was not green and his tongue not iron. His arms were not silver and his hair had clearly been trimmed. "What do *you* know about magic?"

Gaspard chuckled. "Oh, a great deal. I'm the professor of Magical Understanding at the Academy of Ordinary Studies. Just because Ordinary Folk can't cast spells doesn't mean they can't know how magic works. Sit and I'll show you."

Willa sighed. "All right," she said. "But I think you should know I'm not—"

"For instance!" Gaspard clapped his hands. "Did you know there are only two types of magic, Irontongue and Silverclaw? Oh, there's wild magic, of course, but that's just what you're born with. If you don't tame it into one type or the other, it . . . well, they've told you what happened to *that one,* haven't they?"

Willa nodded, squirming in her seat.

"Once you're initiated, you can *only* cast that coven's magic. Very powerful witches *might* be able to override the initiation spell and cast willy-nilly, but it takes a great toll on the body and results in a *severely* reduced life span. Interesting story about that: There used to be one big book of spells that all witches used. But the two covens had a bit of a tiff over it and ended up tearing it in half, and that's how it was decided which spells belonged to which coven. Fascinating, yes?"

"Well, a little but—"

"*But!*" cried Gaspard, spinning in a circle. "Did you also know there are a finite number of spells and no more can be invented? All possible spells were recorded in the book by the Original Witch. Until it was torn in half, obviously. Some curses can last seconds while others can last a lifetime—like this excellent *Switcheroo!* pen." He took the spotted feather pen out of his breast pocket and tickled Willa's nose. She sneezed. "If I've made a mistake, all I do is write over the top and it simply replaces the words underneath. How wonderful is that!"

"That does sound helpful, but—"

"*And* did you know that when one of the Ordinary Folk is born with magic, they are more powerful than any coven-born witch? Only the strongest of magical genes can thrive in someone so otherwise Ordinary."

Willa shook her head. When would he stop and *listen?* "I didn't know that, but—"

"Let's see how powerful you are, shall we?" The odd man arranged a pile of ribbons on the floor. "A simple *Bow-knot!* charm should do." When he was done arranging, he stood back. He waited. He glanced at Willa and then back at the ribbons. "Go on," he said, grinning.

Willa stared at the ribbons too. They remained unknotted.

"I'm sorry, Mr. Renard," she said, "but I'm not actually—"

45

"Most odd!" cried Gaspard. "I'd been led to believe you could already cast a few charms. The incident at breakfast, certainly—but let us not dwell on that. I'll teach you the spell, shall I?"

"But, Mr. Renard, I'm not—"

Gaspard retrieved the large *Dance Your Way to Understanding Silverclaw Magic: A Beginner's Guide* from his desk, then flipped a few pages in. He clicked his tongue against the roof of his mouth as he scanned the page. "Ah! Here it is! You twirl both your arms in figure eights *three* times. That's very important: *three times.* The left hand goes clockwise and the right goes counterclockwise."

Willa screwed up her nose but did as she was told. *If he won't listen to me, I'll show him.*

Willa twirled both her arms. She made fine figure eights in the air. Her left hand swished clockwise and her right hand swooshed counterclockwise. She repeated the movements three times.

The ribbons did not move. Willa smiled, smug. *See? Not a witch.*

"I don't understand," said Gaspard.

Willa sighed. "I did try to tell you. I'm not really a witch. It's all a horrible misunderstanding."

Gaspard eyed her with the sort of frown one directs at the lid of a jar that is refusing to budge no matter how hard you twist it. He shook his head as Willa plonked herself down again. "But, Willa, I *saw* you do magic this very morning."

46

"That wasn't me! I didn't make those eggs fly."

"Then who did? Ferula never spoke and Eladar didn't dance."

"Neither did I," said Willa, shifting in her seat. "And, anyway, I expect the eggs simply got fed up listening to his insufferable ranting and decided to do something about it."

Gaspard threw back his head and laughed. "What a wonderful thought," he said, "but that's wild magic. It's unpredictable and untamed and can burst out of you simply because you thought, *This boy is very annoying! Wouldn't it be a treat to see him with egg on his face?* Sometimes all it takes is a single word or a stomp of your foot. But magic like that overpowers you. It grows wilder and wilder and wilder until . . . Not to worry. We'll soon have you casting like a proper witch. There must be some kind of block . . ." He walked away, rubbing his chin and muttering.

Willa squirmed in her chair. Why did no one listen to her? Did she still look too wild? Willa would have to bury that breathless, bubbling, blistering orange-soda fizz even deeper, so deep it could *never* escape again.

She glanced out the small classroom window at the clouds: *I promise.*

CHAPTER FIVE

D ESPITE ABSOLUTELY DEFINITELY *not*
being a witch, Willa had to endure more magic lessons
with Gaspard. She'd been certain that after the disappointment
of her first lesson the tutor would give up, declare her exception-
ally Ordinary, and send Willa home to her cats. No such luck.

"You might think that because of the war, all witches are
trouble," he said one morning when Willa was refusing to even
pretend to cast magic. (What was the point? Nothing ever
happened when she tried.) "But have you ever wondered what
started the war?"

Willa frowned. There had always been a war; everybody
said so. The sun rose in the east, people lived and people died,
and the witch covens fought each other in a never-ending magical war. "It's just the way things are," she said.

Gaspard shook his head. "It's actually because Ironton—
gah! . . . Well, you see . . . some witches are mo—*oh!* . . . It's
about how mu—*argh!*" Strangely, the tutor couldn't finish a
single sentence; his lips kept fixing together like sticky bubble
gum. He kept trying: "What I mean to say is that not all—
hmph! But Ironton—*oomph!*" Gaspard wiggled his jaw side to
side, loosening his uncooperative mouth. "I'm supposed to give
you an impartial magical education, Willa. You are to learn the

basics of both forms of magic without any bias — I signed a very strict magical contract that forbids me from doing otherwise. So I'm afraid I can't tell you about the war without the contract stopping me. It literally sticks my lips together should I attempt to say anything negative about either coven. And telling you about the war requires me to say some very unflattering things about— *mmmm! Hmm-mm-hm!*"

Thankfully, there was a knock on the door.

"Perfectly on time!" announced Gaspard, leaping to his feet. He flung open the door, and there stood Eladar Moonshine.

The breath caught in Willa's throat.

The Silverclaw witch was shoeless, of course, and the length of his curling, yellowing toenails caused him to lift his feet high as he entered the room, marching like a puppet through mud. He smiled vaguely, a rubber chicken cradled in his arms and real live spiders for earrings as he approached the front of the classroom. His long, golden-brown hair swept the stone floor as he walked, stirring up dust and making Gaspard sneeze.

"Welcome—*achoo!* Thanks so —*achoo!*—much for coming and—*achoo!*—helping today. We appreciate it—*ah-CHOO!*—very much."

Willa avoided looking directly at him. Being close to the witch gave her an itchy, squirmy feeling, like catching sight of the broken vase you shoved under the couch so your parents wouldn't discover it.

Perhaps she could make an excuse and leave?

She opened her mouth but was startled into silence by the

sticky-raspy sound of a throat clearing nearby. Ferula Crowspit stood in the doorway.

"Ah! And you've made it too, Ferula," said Gaspard. "Splendid!"

The Irontongue witch glowered at them all. The frayed strips of her long black cloak writhed. The crow on her shoulder cawed as Ferula took a step inside. And another. And another.

Willa gulped. Make that *two* broken vases shoved under the couch.

Ferula stomped past Gaspard to lean against the far stone wall and mutter about stinky Silverclaw witches. Talon hissed from his perch high up on the windowsill.

"Oh, but not enough chairs," said Gaspard, stroking his chin. He was right: there was only Willa's chair and the teacher's chair. "Perhaps if I —"

Undulating his arms like an octopus gliding through water, Eladar swirled and bopped and wiggled until a puff of blue cloud burst from his fingertips. The cloud did a jig in the middle of the room before — *poof!* — it vanished and in its place were two chairs. Each chair was purple velvet, had six legs and red trim, and was very, very squishy. Eladar climbed onto the left-most chair, squatting on top of it like a frog.

"I'm not sitting on *that*," said Ferula with an imperious sniff. "Thebbity-joop ab chabbity ib thebbity!" she said, then licked the tip of her nose three times with her long iron tongue. The words shot from her mouth as purple lightning bolts. "Thebbity-joop ab chabbity ib thebbity!" screeched the spell as it careered toward the remaining squishy six-legged chair. After it hit, the chair erupted into flames that spat and sparked and shimmered before vanishing, leaving behind a black chair made of interlocking bones and black velvet and spikes and four furry legs. Ferula plopped herself smugly into the chair, arms folded. "Much better," she said.

"Well," said Gaspard. He ran his hand through his hair. "I'm sure Willa is wondering why I've gathered you all here."

He grinned at Willa. Willa did not grin back.

"I've invited Mr. Moonshine and Ms. Crowspit to help us learn about witches and — more specifically and *most* excitingly — to tell us about their wonderful covens! A bit of theory, as it were, while I work out what's going on with Willa's, eh, magical block thingy."

It's not a block *if you don't have magic to begin with,* thought Willa.

"Don't know why that — *ptooey!* — Silver*bore* is here," sneered Ferula. "It's pointless when the girl is obviously going to choose Irontongue."

In response, Eladar picked his nose and flung the booger at Ferula.

"Why, you fustering ninnyplunk! I'll show you!" Ferula picked her nose and flung an even bigger booger back at her rival. Willa gagged when the Silverclaw witch caught the booger in midair and popped it in his mouth.

"Now, now!" said Gaspard. "Eladar, why don't you tell Willa about the Silverclaw coven?"

Ferula narrowed her eyes. "Why does *he* get to go first?"

Gaspard's tongue flapped and floundered. "I'm not . . . ah, it's just that . . . I'm sure it doesn't actually . . . Oh dear. Let's just start, shall we?"

Eladar smiled vaguely into the distance, idly picking his nose. He didn't say a word.

"Eladar?" said Gaspard. "It's your turn?"

Instead of opening his mouth, the Silverclaw witch suddenly swung the rubber chicken in circles. He dipped forward in a deep bow, almost falling off his chair, then leapt on top of it and marched on the spot. He twirled once before returning to a frog crouch. His body rippled with a single hiccup before the vague smile settled on his face and he was still once more.

Ferula snorted.

"Ah," said Gaspard. "I think what Eladar just said is that the Silverclaws live in seven smaller covens, which they call circles. For example, Eladar is from the Maithwood Circle. They have a queen—her name is Opalina Starbright—but otherwise Silverclaw witches are considered equal and live together as one big, happy family."

Eladar bit the head off the rubber chicken.

"Eh," said Gaspard, and coughed into his fist. "You might also like to know that Silverclaw witches have a varied diet, are fond of music, and settle inter-circle disputes with friendly leap-frog competitions."

"Enough, enough!" said Ferula, snapping her teeth. "Such boring whiffle-waffle! The child's brain will melt and trickle out her ears if you utter another word!" Ferula licked her lips with her wriggly iron tongue and settled her beady black eyes on Willa.

"What you need to know, my dear, is that Irontongue witches live in strict tiers, from least to most powerful, slug tier to dragon tier. I am a wolf-tier witch; that makes me the third most powerful kind. Our leader is Mortus Dragonstink; he is smelly and rude and I hate him. We would rather lick a hot poker than spend more than five minutes in one another's company, and we kick our children out of our homes to fend for themselves the second they can walk. We abhor music, eat worms and sprouts and raw meat, and settle our disputes with a tongue-twister battle to the death." She leaned back in her chair, lips twisted into a smug smile. "Now, doesn't that sound like a coven you'd wish to join?"

Willa blinked up at Gaspard and found him equally slack-jawed.

"Eh," he said. He scratched his head until his hair stuck up like a peacock's tail. "I think we'd best move on to the demonstrations."

Willa slunk low in her seat. The itchy, squirmy feeling grew. *If I was a witch,* she thought, *I don't think I'd like to join either coven.*

She was very glad she wasn't a witch.

Between classes, Willa was instructed to make herself useful by helping around the castle.

Her first job was to bring order to the records room.

"*The Long and Thoroughly Ordinary Tales of Pearl B. Purcep, an Explorer of Little Note* has been up to all sorts of naughtiness in here," said the clerk, flinging open the door.

Willa's jaw dropped at what she saw.

She remembered the records room from her first day in the castle. It had been messy then. Now it appeared as if a tornado had ripped through it. The shelves were bare, and forms had been flung every which way; piles and piles of teetering books were a whisper away from tumbling; thick folders lay — *splat!* — on the floor like spilled pancakes, their insides spewing out in paper fans.

"Your job is to tidy up this wretched space," explained the clerk. "The filing system is simple. First, forms are sorted into one of four categories: animal, mineral, vegetable, or magical. Then they're sorted according to mood — anger, frustration, sadness, or jealousy — then by paper color — white, off-white, cream, or off-cream — and, finally, by neatness of handwriting, from least to most. *Any* form asking permission to criticize the royal family goes into *that* filing cabinet." She pointed to a trash can. "Simple."

Willa stared at the clerk, slack-jawed and speechless.

"Just get on with it. And *no* making trouble." The clerk spun on her heel and slammed the door behind her.

"I never make trouble," Willa muttered. "Well, not *intentionally.*" She sighed as her gaze swept the messy room. Where would she start? "What does *animal, mineral, vegetable, or magical* even mean?" she wondered aloud. She picked up a handful of forms. "'Notice to Prevent Cows from Mooing before Sunrise,'" she read. "I guess that's animal. But where do I file 'Permission to Burp Discreetly During Sunday Lecture in the Holy Sanctum of Everyday Wisdom'? And what about 'Permission to Sing in the Shower Despite Having No Musical Talent'? And why are my feet so cold all of a sudden?" Willa frowned down at her toes, her *bare* toes. "Hey! What happened to my shoes and socks?"

Willa looked around. Piles of papers, boxes of books, and stacks of scrolls lay everywhere, but there were no shoes and no socks. "I swear I was wearing them a moment ago."

Willa spied a book with a familiar title sitting atop the desk that had been crammed into the corner of the room: *The Long and Thoroughly Ordinary Tales of Pearl B. Purcep, an Explorer of Little Note.*

She narrowed her eyes. "You! You hide papers and steal socks, don't you?"

The book, of course, said nothing.

By now Willa's toes were turning blue from the cold. She marched up to the book and waggled her finger at it. "Now, you listen here, book. You give me back my shoes and socks *at once.*"

Again the book said nothing.

But a pair of green lace-trimmed socks and brown leather

55

loafers sprang up from behind a stack of forms, hurtled through the air, and smacked Willa square in the face.

"Ouch!" Willa pinched the socks between her finger and thumb and raised them to eye level. "These aren't my socks. And those aren't my shoes."

Four sets of balled-up socks — none of them hers — were flung at Willa from all corners of the room. She ducked out of the way. "This isn't funny!" she cried.

The book jiggled. The cover flapped open and closed again as if to say, *I think it's* very *funny.*

"Well, it's not," said Willa. "It's *your* fault I have to clean up this mess in the first place, and now I have cold toes, thanks to you. So if you don't . . ." A tower of forms beside the desk trembled, tilting back and forth. "Oh dear," said Willa, inching away. "Please don't—"

The tower came crashing down as hundreds of socks flew out from behind it, flinging themselves wildly at Willa. She dived under the desk, away from the hail of socks and shoes and pens and keys and all the things *The Long and Thoroughly Ordinary Tales of Pearl B. Purcep, an Explorer of Little Note* had stolen from around the castle.

When the pitter-patter had ceased, Willa poked her head out from under the desk. A large pile had formed in the middle of the room, reaching halfway to the ceiling. At the very top were Willa's lilac socks and black buckle-up shoes.

"Finally!"

Willa crawled out from her hiding place. *The Long and*

Thoroughly Ordinary Tales of Pearl B. Purcep, an Explorer of Little Note sat innocently on top of the desk. She scowled at it.

Willa teetered on her tiptoes as she reached for the top of the pile. Her fingertips brushed the smooth, shiny leather of her shoes, but she couldn't get a firm hold. "Just a bit more," said Willa.

But as she stretched higher, Willa lost her balance and fell face-first into the pile of stolen things.

"Cheese and rice!" The pile crumbled, taking Willa with it. Her fall was cushioned by the abundance of socks, but her pride was battered and bruised. She sat up, head spinning. In her hands were her shoes, her socks, and a piece of scrunched-up paper. "Aha! I win!" She was just about to toss away the scrunched-up paper when a word, visible in the top right corner, caught her eye.

Culpepper.

Rab Culpepper? Wasn't that the name of the last Ordinary child to be a witch? Willa was just about to unscrunch the paper when a thought struck her. "It's quite a coincidence that this particular scrap of paper should end up in my hands, isn't it?" She looked up, eyes narrowed. *The Long and Thoroughly Ordinary Tales of Pearl B. Purcep, an Explorer of Little Note* sat on the edge of the desk. It did not jiggle. It did not flap. "Is this another of your practical jokes? If I open this, will a sock come shooting out and boof me in the nose?"

The book said nothing, but Willa detected the smallest shimmer of its pages. She looked down at the ball of paper. "I suppose I *would* like to know more about him. Just to see what all the fuss is about."

Willa carefully unscrunched the paper. It was a partial diary entry, with scratchy handwriting.

Rab Culpepper continues to be a difficult student. He simply will *not* tame his magic, despite knowing that failure to undergo the coven initiation will result in a thoroughly unpleasant death-by-explosion. This morning he turned the castle's water supply into chocolate mousse and refused to turn it back, threatening me with a Nose-knotting! curse if I tried to make him. "There's no such spell!" says I. "Ha!" says he. "There is because I can improve spells by smooshing two together!" "Preposterous! Abominable! Heresy!" I shouted at him until I was blue in the face but all he did was insist that a witch like him doesn't need to choose a coven! "There's another choice," he says, but won't tell me what it is. I must do more to keep him away from

"I wonder why he was such a troublemaker?" said Willa. "And why did you even give me this, you silly book?" She looked up, but the book was no longer sitting on the edge of the desk. It wasn't anywhere she could see.

How strange!

She read the entry again, eyes lingering over the words *doesn't need to choose a coven* and *there's another choice*. It did seem harsh for witches to be forced into one clan or the other (or else explode!). What if they didn't find either agreeable? What if they liked their current life and didn't want to change a thing about it, thank you very much?

But it didn't matter to Willa—she wasn't a witch. And she hadn't even fizzed or zizzed in *ages!*

She was about to toss the paper away when the clerk appeared in the doorway again. "Just thought I'd—*Argh!* What have you done?" she shrieked.

"I can explain," said Willa, quickly balling up the diary entry and stuffing it up her spare sleeve. "It wasn't me! It was—"

"This is why nobody trusts witches," wailed the clerk. "Fix this at once! *Or else!*"

"Or else what?" muttered Willa. "Or else I'll *explode?*" But she did as she was told. She always did as she was told.

CHAPTER SIX

A WEEK SHUFFLED BY, each day longer and more tiresome than the last.

Every morning the prince sneered, "Sorry, *witch!* The toast is all gone."

Every magic lesson Willa failed to conjure so much as a button or a butterfly or a baby elephant, and no one in the castle listened when she explained it was because "I'm not a witch, actually."

And every night she tossed and turned while cursed objects wept, shouted, and laughed at her.

"Which is why today we're going home," announced Willa, sitting up in bed on the eighth morning. Talon purred in her lap. "We're sneaking out. I don't care if it's against the law. It's time for this nonsense to end."

Willa was now in possession of a Permission to Make One's Own Way to Breakfast Independently of Supervision form, so she leapt from her bed and opened the wardrobe. Once she was dressed in trousers (three legs) and a dress (four sleeves), she hurried downstairs, Talon trotting after her.

She had no intention of going to breakfast, however.

Instead, Willa and Talon headed to the kitchens. Yesterday she'd spied a small, unassuming back door there, which she planned to sneak out of. The cooks would all be too busy preparing breakfast to notice her slipping by them. It was the perfect plan.

But once she stepped into the kitchens, she bumped straight into Gish, who was shooing two stray cats out a window. One cat—a tabby with half its tail missing—had a fish fillet wedged between its jaws.

"Beat it!" Gish told the cats. "If Cook Krige sees you, there'll be cat casserole on the menu." He latched the window shut behind the thieving cats and turned, smiling brightly when he noticed Willa. "Aren't you supposed to be at breakfast?"

"There's never any toast," she muttered, distracted. She glanced at the rickety wooden door in the back corner. It was slightly ajar.

"Can't you just"—Gish waggled his fingers—"magic it?"

There were many things Willa liked about Gish. She liked his sticky-outy ears and his exuberant bows. She liked the faces he made behind the clerk's back and the winks and the smiles. She liked the way he purposefully mispronounced the words *Wednesday, cupboard,* and *probably.* But suggesting she could waggle her fingers and make toast appear was *not* something she liked *at all.*

"I am not," said Willa, "a witch."

Gish gripped his belly and laughed, great big honks like a startled goose. But when he saw that Willa wasn't laughing with him, he stopped. "Seriously? You *really* don't think you're a witch?"

Willa shook her head. Gish's eyes grew wide in disbelief.

"I'm not," she insisted. The kitchens were so warm; Willa used an extra sleeve to fan herself. "Honestly, I haven't got a drop of magic in me. Which is why I'm leaving."

"Leaving?"

Willa nodded. "I'm escaping the castle." She nodded at the back door. The longer she stayed, the more she itched and squirmed. And if she picked at that itchy-squirmy feeling . . . well, she didn't want to *think* about what she'd find underneath. "So I guess this is goodbye."

Gish slipped from the bench and stood before her, tugging his earlobe. "Oh," he said. "That's a shame. I think it might be quite boring here without you."

"Don't be silly. Without me, things can go back to normal. I, for one, can't *wait* to get home and see all my cats and the spiders and . . . and . . . and . . . well, that's it, really." Willa took a deep breath. "But one day my parents will be uncursed and they'll come home. And I'll be waiting for them."

Gish frowned but didn't say anything.

Willa stood as straight as she could. There was a lingering dullness in her chest, a strange feeling of heaviness. Perhaps she was coming down with a cold. "Goodbye," she said, and held out her hand.

Instead of shaking it, Gish started grabbing every piece of food he could reach. "In case you get hungry on your way home," he explained, stuffing muffins and biscuits and cakes into a tea towel. He tied the corners into a knot and shoved the bundle at her. "But you can't go out the back door. Guards out there. *Loads.*"

"Cheese and rice!" Willa stomped her foot. "I guess I'll think of something else . . ." She glared at the back door. "I can't stay in this castle a moment longer."

With that, she turned and hurried from the kitchen.

"Goodbye!" called Gish. "Come back and visit!"

How would she escape now? The front door? She had to try *something*. But when she heard voices outside the breakfast room, she quickly ducked behind a nearby statue of King Teebald riding a fierce stallion. "Hide!" she told Talon. The cat plonked himself in the middle of the hallway, licking his coat clean.

The first voice belonged to Ferula. "I expect the girl has mastered standard-level Irontongue spells by now," said the witch. "We have high hopes for her to reach dragon tier. After she chooses Irontongue. Which she will."

Willa peeked around the corner of the statue: Ferula had crowded Gaspard up against a wall.

"I wouldn't say *mastered*," replied the tutor, grinning politely. "It's only been a week, and her magic is a little, um, on the brink, you might say. So I rather think—"

Ferula eyeballed Gaspard like dinner. "Well, then, good *sir*, pray tell what progress she *has* made."

"Oh, um, well, lots of theory, of course."

Willa snorted. Yesterday he'd handed her a thin book— *The ABC of Witches!*—and instructed her to read it for homework. "I think you'll most enjoy the entry for *W*," he'd said.

"'*A* is for *age*,'" Willa had read to Talon in bed last night. "'Did you know that witches live for hundreds of years? The average life span of a witch is eight hundred years, though it is said that Mortus Dragonstink, the High Witch of Irontongue, is over a thousand! Can you imagine?'" Willa had tossed the book aside. "I can't imagine, and I won't even try." Talon had purred in agreement.

And that was the extent of her "theory."

Gaspard rubbed his chin, smile faltering under Ferula's sharp glare. "Er, and, um, lots of demonstrating and, er . . ."

Eladar glided into view. He cradled a garden gnome in the crook of his arm and wore a lampshade for a hat. "Good morning," he singsonged, "to everyone *except* Irontongue witches." He bopped Ferula on the nose, then disappeared into the breakfast room.

"Why, you simpering mumblecrust!" She chased after him.

Gaspard straightened his tie and fanned himself. "Golly," he said, then hurried after Ferula too. "Remember the magical truce!" he called.

"Between you and me, Talon," said Willa, "those two are one booger fling short of going back to war." But that didn't concern Willa, of course.

She was escaping.

64

Unfortunately, every exit she knew of was teeming with guards. She tried to sweet-talk her way past, but each guard explained, in a trembling voice, that they were under strict instructions *never* to let the untamed witch out of the castle without the correct forms.

"Clerk's orders," said one, then hid behind a statue of Prince Cyrus wrestling a bear.

Willa swallowed down the urge to scream. She no longer felt like a twelve-year-old girl—she was a bag of firecrackers one match away from exploding. Her skin tingled.

She stuffed her face with muffin and angrily marched through the castle, searching every corridor and peering through every door, but there was no way out. Near the library, she paused in front of a large wall hanging of a pretty white cottage with a thatched roof and climbing white roses draped over the door.

If only that door was real, thought Willa. *If only I could reach into the tapestry, open the door, and run.*

A fizzy-zizzy tingle danced up and down her spine, and it seemed for a moment—just a second—that the tapestry glowed. Slowly, hardly breathing, Willa reached for the wool-spun door and gasped as her hand sank all the way into the tapestry and closed around the handle. When she turned it, the door opened into a small, square courtyard *outside* the castle.

The fizzy-zizzy feeling grew . . .

"No!" She stomped her foot. "It's not fizzy *or* zizzy. It's barely a tingle. More like an itch. I pushed that silly feeling so far down it will never see the light again. I'm sure this tapestry was already cursed. Right?" She looked down at Talon.

The cat meowed.

Willa shook her head. It didn't matter. This nonsense would be over soon and she would be home. She stepped outside; the breeze tickled her skin.

At the end of the courtyard, underneath a high arch that opened onto the market square, sat three familiar cats: a gray cat, a white cat, and a calico kitten. It seemed Willa's army of cats was determined to follow her wherever she went.

Talon ran to greet them, and all four cats slunk off toward the market square as if on important business.

Well, supposed Willa, escaping the castle *was* important business. She took off after the four cats and into the bustling market. Stallholders laughed and bartered, and no one scowled at wayward curses buzzing overhead, because there were none. Willa's heart beat to the rhythm of *home, home, home.* But there was also a familiar whisper dancing underneath, running counter to her heart's drumbeat: *What a coincidence the door opened after you wished it to!*

Go away!

She quickened her step. At the Rest-a-Spell Tavern, Willa hurried around the corner and bumped into someone coming the other way. "Ouch!"

She rubbed her head and looked up. It was the master weaver.

"You!" He dropped an armful of apples in his haste to stumble away from her. "B-b-but they locked you up good and proper!"

His raised voice drew the attention of those around them; one by one they turned to see what the fuss was. News of the untamed witch had obviously spread; gasps of recognition echoed through the market. "It's her! It's the witch!"

"There was a mistake," Willa hurried to explain. "I don't have magic."

"Witch!" The master weaver's eyes bulged, froglike in fear. "Don't make me dance again! Oh, please don't!" With a cry he heaved an apple at Willa.

"Ouch!"

"I should never have given you a job," he wailed, throwing another apple. "Once a troublemaker, always a troublemaker!"

Willa ducked and weaved, but soon her dress of many sleeves was weeping fruit juice. Humiliation burned raw.

"No doubt it was *you* who cursed your mother and father!"

Willa reeled, as though the words had been flung at her too. "That's a lie!" she cried.

And it was. It *was* a lie.

But the master weaver's words were sticky — she couldn't shake them off. Because she might not have cast the spell, but it *was* her fault. A wave of guilt crashed through her, dragging her memories with it.

She remembered everything: Eleven-year-old Willa running through the Weeping Meadow. The squelch of mud between her toes. "It's not proper!" cried her father, but Willa only laughed. It was her birthday and she wanted to run. They never let her outside — they never let her have any fun — so she'd snuck out. "You can't catch me!" she cried. "Come back at once, you unruly girl! It's dangerous outside! Why must you be so *bold?*" The fizzy, zizzy, orange-soda feeling bubbled up inside her, urging her to run faster, farther.

She had loved that feeling. Wonderful things happened when it bubbled inside her. Her boring schoolwork caught fire. The icky sprouts on her dinner plate turned into chocolate cake. The spiders in her room danced when she was lonely. How could it be wrong?

So Willa had run and fizzed and zizzed. She ran and ran and ran until over the hill spilled the sounds of battle. Witches cackling. Hissing curses. So close. "Watch out!" cried her mother, skirts hoisted up to her knees as she gave chase. But ahead of her, Willa saw blue: a wayward spell. So fast! She heard her father's breathless voice: "Out of the way, Willa!" His hands pushed her out of the way, and she was tumbling forward. Suddenly there was mud under her fingernails and a sharp pain in her side. And then . . . and then . . . and then . . .

No, no, *no!* She didn't want to remember this! The fizzy-zizzy feeling was trouble — if she pushed it down, if she ignored it, she could make everything okay again. She could undo her mistake.

An apple splattered at her feet. She startled. "Someone call the Royal Guard," said the master weaver. He reached for another apple. "Quick! Before she—"

There was a loud *pop!* and then a flash of yellow-green lightning. A *thing* wrapped around the master weaver's legs— sparkly and sizzling and ropelike. Was it hissing? Suddenly it vanished.

The master weaver opened his mouth to scream but no sound came out. What *did* come out was a shimmery clear bubble the size of a watermelon. It flickered golden before it shot into the air and disappeared. The master weaver's eyes bulged as he opened his mouth again—his lips moved and his tongue waggled, but no sound came out. He gripped his throat with one hand and pointed wildly at his mouth with the other.

"Is he choking?" asked someone.

"He's lost his voice!" said someone else.

The master weaver nodded vigorously—*yes!* He pointed at Willa, jabbing his finger over and over.

Willa stumbled back.

Another coincidence? laughed the whisper.

Yes! she wanted to scream.

But the fizzy, zizzy, orange-soda feeling had returned, bigger and bolder than ever. It bubbled inside her: *You couldn't keep me locked away forever, Willa. You know what I am. You know what you are.*

She shook her head. She didn't want to know! If she couldn't make the fizzy-zizzy feeling go away, how would she keep her promise to her parents? How would they ever come back?

A freckled young man pointed at her—his arm shook. "She stole the master weaver's voice!"

Cries of "Witch!" pierced the air, followed by a chorus of trumpets: the Royal Guard was coming.

"Stop! Please!" she begged. But the fizzy, zizzy, orange-soda feeling grew and grew and grew. It was huge, too big to fit inside her.

All at once every pot and pan and every fork and knife and spoon flew out of the Rest-A-Spell Tavern's window. They hovered in midair.

Willa let out a whimper.

There wasn't another witch nearby, not a single wayward spell.

There was only Willa.

There was only Willa, who could make tapestries come to life and scrambled eggs fly through the air. Willa, who could burn schoolwork and turn sprouts into chocolate cake and make spiders dance. There was no denying it, no burying it deep, no forgetting. The truth had broken free.

It was magic.

Wild magic.

And she couldn't hold it back any longer.

"Oh dear," said Willa, and the air erupted with a banging, clanging cacophony as a hundred pots were banged by a hundred spoons. The crowd tried to run, but the pots followed them. Willa closed her hands over her ears and crouched. It was just like rough music.

But not even the banging cacophony of pots and pans could drown out the voice in Willa's head: *I'm a witch.*

I'm a witch.

CHAPTER SEVEN

THE CLERK DRAGGED Willa through the castle, giving her a tongue-lashing so sharp it left Willa's heart stinging like lemon in a paper cut. "This will require an Unauthorized Use of Untamed Magic, Subsection E: Excessive Use of Silverware in a Threatening and Unsanctioned Manner form. And *mountains* of paperwork for willfully stealing a fellow citizen's voice—Oh! I'll run out of ink!"

Willa opened her mouth to argue, but all that came out was a pathetic croak. Her voice hadn't been stolen like the master weaver's, but the words refused to leave her mouth. They stuck to the tip of her tongue, one word stickier than the rest: *Witch!*

Had her parents known? Was that why they'd hidden her away? Why they'd thought her too loud, too wild, too bold, too *everything*?

Outside the throne room, the clerk shoved Willa to one side. "Wait here until we're ready for you. And try not to steal *more* voices," she said. She vanished inside.

Willa sniffed, all too aware her cheeks were damp and her vision was fuzzy. "I will not cry. I will *not*. Even though I have lots to cry about."

Her ears still rang from the accidental rough music—or

perhaps from the shock. She looked down at her trembling hands. They looked so Ordinary.

But they weren't. And she wasn't.

Willa added *you're not who you thought you were and you never were* to the many bruises that littered her heart.

There were raised voices inside the throne room—was that Miss Pickwick? And the prince? She couldn't focus long enough to make out their words.

"My, my!" crooned a voice behind her.

Willa whirled around, almost taking a tumble in her haste.

Ferula.

The witch crept up the hallway, black robes wafting around her. "It seems our little untamed witch is quite the troublemaker."

Willa stumbled back until she hit the stone wall with a slap. "I—I—I didn't mean it," she said.

"Let's not dilly-dally any longer," said the witch, inching closer. Her iron tongue peeked between her lips, licking up the spittle that had gathered in the corners. "There's no point muddying your pretty head with all that 'both covens are worthy' gobbledygook." Ferula ran a blunt nail along the edge of Willa's jaw. "Come with me back to Miremog. We Irontongue will gladly squeeze the troublemaker out of you."

"Th-th-that's very k-k-kind of you to offer," stuttered Willa, "but I'm n-n-not sure—"

"Bah!" snapped the witch. "Don't tell me you want to join Silver*snore?* If you think *Smel*adar is awful, just wait till you meet the rest of them. Ha!"

It hit her like an apple: she really *did* have to choose a coven or explode. She would have to join the war. Cast magic with the intention to harm. Some of her spells might fall astray. They might make chickens dance or pigs walk on two feet or turn parents into clouds . . .

She couldn't meet Ferula's eyes, so she lowered her gaze. There was a bracelet—chunky and sharp and white—dangling loosely around Ferula's thin wrist, rattling as the witch stroked Willa's jaw again. There was something not quite right about it . . .

Willa blinked several times before she realized the sharp white chunks were teeth and bones. Fangs, knuckles, toe bones, wishbones, and molars. "B-b-bones? *Teeth?*"

"For added magical potency." The witch shoved her wrist under Willa's nose for a closer look. "Gifted to an Irontongue witch at initiation. I'm sure you can't wait for—"

"Ahem!"

Willa could have wept with joy to turn and find Gaspard outside the throne-room doors. He gave Willa a comforting smile.

"What's going on?" asked the prince, appearing beside the tutor. He narrowed his eyes at Willa and Ferula. "You two better not be conspiring."

"Of course not! Willa and I were just having a little chinwag," soothed Ferula. She patted Willa's cheek: *pat, pat, pat.* "Weren't we, dearie?"

"Well, I think your little chin-wag is over," said Gaspard. His eyes darkened as they met Ferula's.

Willa took that as her cue to duck under Ferula's arm and rush to Gaspard's side; she was tempted to hide underneath his swaths of tartan robes and never come out again.

Ferula hissed, baring her teeth. "Heedless jackanapes," she muttered, and hobbled away.

"I'm afraid you're not quite out of the woods yet, Willa," said Gaspard, turning and placing a hand on her shoulder. His look was full of commiseration. "You still have to face the king."

Willa gulped.

"And I suggest you don't keep him waiting," snapped the prince.

"Are they very mad at me?" Willa asked Gaspard as they followed the prince inside.

Gaspard assured Willa that no, no, they weren't mad. Not *very* mad. Just a *little* mad.

Which, of course, was a no-good, horrible lie.

The crowd waved pots and pans and yelled, "There she is! There's the witch who steals voices!" as Willa was ushered inside the throne room. Gaspard guided her through the chaos until she was standing before the king. (Technically, the king was hiding behind a potted plant, so Willa was standing before a trembling potted plant.)

On the low dais at the head of the room, a guard was bent on all fours, the clerk using him as a temporary desk while she filled in a mountain of forms. Willa's heart squeezed as she spied the master weaver beside the clerk, weeping silently.

"I'm still not sure what's going on," said the trembling potted plant, "and I rather wish it would go away and leave me in peace."

"Go on, Willa," whispered Gaspard, nudging her forward. "Tell the king what happened."

Willa opened her mouth, but the words still clung to the tip of her tongue so they came out all sticky and wrong. "I—you see—it wasn't—I didn't—"

"Here comes the royal healer," interrupted the clerk. "She needs to examine the victim."

The crowd parted as a short woman with gray hair, a pug nose, and deep brown skin pushed her way through. The name tag on her lapel read: HEALER BERWIG. The healer peered down the master weaver's throat, poked his cheeks, tapped his temple, and harrumphed. She turned to face Willa. "What did you do with it?" she said. "Put it in your pocket, no doubt. Has anyone checked this girl's pockets?"

The prince, who was by now lounging on the throne, snapped a hand at the guards in a *well, go on and check the witch's pockets* kind of way, and the guards looked back at him in a *we're not stepping anywhere near that witch* kind of way.

"This dress doesn't even have pockets," said Willa. "Plenty of sleeves, but no pockets."

With a sigh, the healer turned to the trembling potted plant and explained that the master weaver had been hit with a

Cat-got-your-tongue! curse. "A mostly harmless Irontongue spell that traps the voice in a bubble, which floats around for a bit before returning to its owner."

So that's what that strange bubble was, thought Willa.

"But as it was untamed magic," continued the healer, glaring at Willa, "the spell will wear off quick as a wink. These untamed spells are always short-lived."

Willa sighed in relief.

"Excellent!" said the king from behind the potted plant. "We can all go home now. I'm so glad that's over."

"But she can't get off scot-free," said the prince. "*I'll* decide her punishment. Just give me time to think up something really, *really* nasty."

"But you haven't heard my side yet!" said Willa. "I didn't mean to do it! I don't even know *how* I did it."

The crowd booed.

"Take her away," said the prince. He flicked his hand at her. "This inquiry is *boring.*"

Gaspard grabbed Willa's arm and steered her away from the dais. "Don't worry, Willa," he whispered. "A little burst of wild magic here and there is a natural part of being untamed. I'm sure Eladar and Ferula could tell you no end of hilarious stories about the untamed witches in their covens and all the mischief they got up to."

His words didn't help. Willa buzzed all over.

"Come on," he said. "The important thing is we get it under control soon."

As he led her away, every person they passed covered their mouth. As if *that* would stop Willa being able to steal their voices and stuff them in her pockets.

"This dress doesn't even *have* pockets," she said again, this time through gritted teeth. She was just *so* angry. She felt like she was full of bees. Or firecrackers. Or orange soda . . . Orange soda? Oh dear.

Sparks erupted from her fingertips and blue smoke swept around her. Folk screamed and ran, dropping their pots and pans. The king fainted, taking the trembling potted plant with him.

When the smoke cleared, five pockets had appeared willy-nilly all over Willa's floral dress. "Cheese and rice!"

Gaspard sighed. "Come on, Willa Birdwhistle. We have work to do."

"It's a simple spell." Gaspard's tartan cloak had been tossed over the back of his chair, but his dazzling smile remained in place. "Can't go wrong."

The simple spell that could not go wrong was called *Light-and-shine!* and was an Irontongue spell.

To cast Irontongue magic:

1. Say the spell in Ibbity Jiggity Joop, the Irontongue

language. For a long-lasting spell, screech the words at the top of your lungs; for a curse that's over in a jiffy, a mere whisper will do.

2. Make the right tongue movement to bring the spell to life. For instance, rolling your tongue in a clockwise circle is the movement for the *Spaghetti-hair!* spell.

"Just say, 'Libbity-jig bibuggity,'" explained Gaspard, "and then undulate your tongue three times like so." He demonstrated with his own tongue, like a kitten licking up milk. Talon watched from the windowsill, silently judging. "Then—*ta-da!*—the candle will magically light up. Now that you've accepted that you're a witch, I think the block on your magic will have lifted."

Willa eyed the unlit candle in the middle of the classroom. She wasn't sure *accepted* was the right word. Her denial had been dragged kicking and screaming from her until she'd had no choice but to let it go.

Despite the way her stomach heaved, Willa began the spell.

"Libbity-jig bibuggity," she said in a voice as clear as a bell.

She poked out her tongue and undulated it once, twice, three times.

Her skin prickled and orange soda fizzed through her veins. Two small, spluttering sparks shot from her fingertips, as weak as a mouse sneezing. And then . . .

Gaspard's sleeve caught fire.

"Oh dear," said Willa.

Gaspard danced up and down, waving his burning arm. "Put it out! Put it out!"

All Irontongue spells could be reversed by the caster—and the caster alone—by undertaking the following:

1. Say the counter-spell command: *Stoompity nag!*

2. Open your mouth wide—as wide as it can stretch—poke out your tongue, and say, *Ahhh!* while flopping it about like a dying fish.

But as Willa hurriedly performed the counter-curse, the fire *grew* in size, jumping from Gaspard's sleeve to the robe slung across the back of his chair.

"Never mind," said Gaspard, shaking free of his burning jacket and stomping on it. "All part of the learning process." He smiled as he tossed a cup of tea at the flaming robe.

Willa collapsed into her seat. "Are you sure I'm a witch?" She worried her bottom lip. "It could be a mistake."

Gaspard shook his head. "No mistake. You're very much a witch."

"I'd rather I wasn't," Willa admitted. "I promised my parents, you see. Well, I promised their clouds. I promised I'd be good, and stealing voices isn't good *at all*. How do I make my magic behave? My parents tried to scold it out of me, but that only made me naughtier. I tried pretending it didn't exist, but that made it erupt like a volcano. It's so contrary!"

"Magic is about control, Willa," said Gaspard. "You're right to fear wild magic. It's nasty stuff. But once you tame it, once you learn coven magic and take the initiation, that's when you'll be in control of it. And what better way to keep your promise to your parents?"

Willa supposed that *did* sound good. She didn't want to be wild. She didn't want to explode. She didn't want to get in trouble all the time.

But did she want to join a coven? Did she want to leave everything she knew behind to be lonely in a faraway city? Did she want to fight in a war and cast wayward *Clouds-away!* curses? Couldn't she tame her magic and just . . . never use it again?

"Why didn't Rab Culpepper choose a coven?" she asked. "Why did he explode rather than choose?"

Gaspard's smile disappeared from his face. "Forget you ever heard his name. You're *nothing* like him. He was evil, Willa. The very worst kind of witch. And he had a knack for corrupting those around him. Yes, he started out Ordinary, like you, but that's where the similarities end."

Willa nodded. She supposed it made sense—if she wanted to avoid exploding, she had to control her magic. But the thought of joining a coven made her feel itchy and squirmy all over again. *Like being forced to eat sprouts when you'd rather gobble up chocolate cake?* said the whispery voice.

Listen, just because I'm not hiding you anymore doesn't mean I want to hear your snarky comments, okay? huffed Willa. Was all magic so rude? Honestly!

"You will get better at magic," said Gaspard. He knelt before her. "Trust me. Anyway, it's my fault our lessons haven't gone well — I get so excited by magic, and you have so much potential, that I've skipped a few steps. Tell me, what does it feel like when you cast a spell?"

Willa glanced down at her hands in her lap. "Like I'm a soda bottle that someone shook up."

Gaspard nodded. "That's wild magic. That's what it feels like: all fizzed up and ready to explode. Close your eyes, if you'd be so kind."

Willa let her eyelids flutter shut.

"I want you to picture a box," said Gaspard. "Picture it right in the center of your chest."

Willa scrunched her eyes shut extra tight and pictured a box. For some reason, she saw the Rapscallion's Cage.

"I want you to imagine pouring all that fizzy magic into the box. Do it now. Are you doing it?"

Willa nodded. The fizzy stream sparkled — a liquid, glimmering rainbow — as she poured it into the make-believe Rapscallion's Cage. It was just like before, when she'd locked it all away and pretended it didn't exist.

"When every last drop is in the box, close the lid. Snap it shut. Quickly!"

Willa snapped the cage shut, trapping the fizzy magic

inside. An odd feeling came over her—an emptiness, a chill, a loneliness.

"Isn't this like when my magic was blocked?" she asked. "Isn't it dangerous to keep the wild magic locked up?"

"Not quite," said Gaspard. "Take a closer look at the box, Willa. It has a very narrow, very thin spout in one corner. When you cast a spell, I want you to picture a thin stream of fizzy soda trickling out of that spout—just the smallest trickle, like a lovely babbling brook that pitter-patters to the tips of your fingers."

Willa tried to picture the spout, but all she could visualize was the long rectangular peephole of the Rapscallion's Cage. The gap was too big, and out gushed the fizzy soda. *Get back!* she told it. *You're supposed to be a trickle!* But her magic was contrary and instead poured free and—*bam!*—shot out of her fingertips.

"Oops," said Willa, blinking open her eyes.

The teacher's desk had caught fire.

Gaspard grinned and stood. "Never mind. Just need a wee bit more practice. And a fire extinguisher." He whistled as he flung tea over his burning desk. "Truly, Willa, you're going to love being a witch."

Willa doubted that very much. Because even if she successfully tamed her magic, she still had to join a coven. And join a *war*.

What a silly choice that was—choose a coven or explode! There ought to at least be an alternative. A choice to live a quiet, uneventful life as a witch who would rather stay home than go to war. A choice that would have made her parents happy.

Willa sat bolt upright.

Because there was! Rab Culpepper had said there was.

The worst part is he keeps insisting he doesn't need to choose a coven, the diary had said. *"There's another choice," he says.*

"Back in a jiffy," said Gaspard with a panicked grin. "Just have to, eh . . ." He waved the empty water pitcher; beside him the desk continued to burn.

Willa watched her tutor rush from the room, her whole body tingling with possibility. He'd said to forget about Rab, but if there was another choice . . .

The idea sang to her. The most beautiful music she had ever heard.

Wasn't it worth looking for?

CHAPTER EIGHT

B Y THE FOLLOWING DAY, the master weaver's voice had not returned. Nor the day after that. Nor the day after *that*. Search parties scoured the city for the missing bubble, but they all came back empty-handed.

Most people covered their mouths and ran when they saw Willa. "She's so powerful," they hissed. "We're all doomed!"

"Actually, it's impossible for an untamed witch to cast such a long-lasting spell with wild magic," Gaspard told anyone who would listen. "I rather think she isn't to blame after all." But no one, as it turned out, would listen.

Willa had known loneliness all her life; it was her constant companion, her oldest friend.

It had been lonely to gaze out the window at schoolchildren filing past, never able to join them.

It had been lonely to watch her parents float away as clouds.

And it had been lonely living in a house filled only with dust and spiders and cats.

But it was loneliest of all to be feared.

"You'll clean my supply room and not utter a word of complaint," barked the pug-nosed healer as Willa arrived in the hospital wing. Over breakfast the prince had declared that her punishment was working for Healer Berwig. *What could be so awful about that?* she had wondered.

Willa was led through an office and into an anteroom, where she found herself face-to-face with a large hairy spider in a glass jar. The spider blinked all eight of its eyes. Willa blinked back.

The healer's supply room was crammed full of creatures that crept and crawled, bit and sucked, stung and slithered. Everywhere Willa looked she saw jars of scaly, hairy, slimy critters with altogether too many legs, eyes, and wings. There was also a bitter stench that stung her nostrils.

"Insects go here," explained the healer as she bustled through the room. "If you see any dead ones, do not open the jar. Just put them on this cart and I'll deal with them. Arachnids on this shelf. Amphibians on this one. Animal bones here and here. Teeth have their own place—here. Hair and animal skins go here. Eyeballs here and liquids there—if it's bubbling, try not to look at it, but if you *must,* at least cross your eyes first. Wear gloves if you need to touch anything green, and do not go near *that* cauldron unless you want the skin to melt off your bones. Questions?"

Willa gulped. *Now* she understood the prince's smirk when he'd announced her punishment.

"What's all this for?" she asked.

"Medicine, of course." The healer disappeared into a side

room and returned with a vial in her hand, purple and hissing. "Like this Muscle-magic!, which your master weaver needs to keep his throat from seizing while his voice is missing. Four tablespoons of rat vomit, one crushed spider's leg, three gray-wolf hairs, five and three-quarters butterbeetle wings, and six drops of viper venom. Yummy!"

Willa's stomach rolled. "Mr. Renard thinks I might not have cast the voice-stealing spell," she muttered.

"Of course you didn't."

"*What?*"

The healer snorted. "No untamed witch can cast a spell that long-lasting. Obviously it was another witch."

"Then why didn't you tell the prince that?"

"Because I needed my supply room cleaned, obviously. I'll tell him once you've finished." She patted Willa on the head as she hobbled away, calling over her shoulder, "Remember: if it's green, wear gloves!"

"Unbelievable!" cried Willa.

With nothing else to do, she rolled up her sleeves (all four of them) and set to work.

"I'm sorry," she told the spider, carrying its jar to the middle shelf. "I wish I could set you free, but I think that'd only get me into more trouble."

Willa worked for hours. She didn't go near the skin-melting cauldron (though she did determine it was the cause of the bitter stench), she crossed her eyes whenever she looked at a bubbling liquid, and she diligently wore gloves that reached her elbows whenever she touched anything green—and blue and yellow, just in case.

"Mr. Renard says it was definitely an Irontongue spell, but the other witch couldn't have been Ferula," she told Talon. "She was squabbling with Eladar over breakfast when the spell stole the master weaver's voice."

Talon gazed at the jars of mice, licking his lips.

"And both covens are banned from the city on account of the magical truce. So who was it?" Willa shook her head. "I'm sure Mr. Renard will figure it out—he's an expert on magic, so the prince has him on the case." She blew the hair out of her eyes. "Which gives me time to uncover what Rab Culpepper meant when he said there was another choice."

The more she had thought about it in bed last night, the more it had made sense: a choice to be her own kind of witch. No war, no wayward spells. No one would fear her then. She wasn't sure why Rab had exploded rather than take the mystery choice, but . . . that was a worry for later.

She was sweating and aching and cursing the prince's name by the time she placed the last jar of pickled lava worms on the shelf. She stood back and admired her work—every worm, spider, and rat in its rightful place. "At least I can do some things right," she told Talon.

"You've done it wrong," said a voice behind her.

Willa turned.

Healer Berwig scowled at her from the doorway, arms folded, brow heavy.

"No, I haven't," said Willa. "I put everything exactly where you told me to."

"Then where are my crickets? There should be one full shelf of them. Spiders and snails, too. And my toads—where are all the purple toads?"

"There weren't any purple toads." Willa seethed.

The healer shuffled up and down each aisle with a hawklike eye. "Then where are they? Did you steal them?"

Willa turned out the pockets in her trousers. "Empty," she snapped. "Where do you think I could have hidden a bunch of purple toads?" How intolerable to be accused of stealing *again!* She was always getting in trouble when she hadn't done anything, not on purpose. It made her skin itch and her blood boil. It made her all tingly and fizzy and — "Oh no!" Willa scrunched her eyes shut tight. *Pour the magic into the cage. Close the lid. Oh, stay inside, won't you? Don't fizz to my fingertips like a blast of orange soda!*

The magic erupted from her, her fingers burning with lightning sparks—*zip zap zoop!* She lurched backwards with the force.

When she opened her eyes, smoke was clearing, Healer Berwig was coughing, Talon's whiskers were twitching, and the healer's long white robes were covered in pockets.

"Not again," moaned Willa.

The healer looked down at her robes. "Actually, these pockets will come in handy. Just scram before your wild magic causes *real* damage."

Willa didn't wait to be told twice, backing out as quickly as her legs would carry her. "I am sorry," said Willa, but the healer ignored her.

"If it wasn't the girl, then who was it?" muttered the old woman, frowning at the shelves.

Who wants purple toads and creepy-crawlies? wondered Willa. *And what would they do with them?* But she didn't fancy staying to find out.

Even after the healer had announced Willa wasn't to blame for the voice-stealing spell, folk still ran from her.

"Aren't *you* worried I'll steal your voice?" Willa asked Gish after a week had passed with still no sign of the master weaver's voice. The pair were crowded under a table in the Royal Portrait Hall to split three still-warm blueberry muffins between them. The dogsbody had finally been given a break from delivering the prince's anti-magic notices around the city and had "borrowed" the muffins from the kitchens in celebration. Willa had been surprised to be invited. Only Gaspard and Gish smiled at her these days; she supposed Gaspard had to, seeing as he was her teacher, but she wasn't sure what motivated Gish.

He scrunched up his nose and hummed. "Nah," he declared finally. He shoved half a muffin in his mouth. "I'm not worried."

She blinked at him in surprise. *He trusts me?* It was a warm feeling, a little campfire in her heart. She added *doesn't think I'll curse him* to her list of things to like about Gish and felt a little less horribly, awfully lonely.

Another thing to like about Gish was: there wasn't a room in the castle that he didn't have a key to. He wore a large silver ring loaded with keys clipped to a loop in his belt. It had given Willa an idea.

She shoveled the last of her muffin into her mouth and asked, "Do you want to sneak into the records room on a secret mission with me?"

He very much did.

"We're looking for *The Long and Thoroughly Ordinary Tales of Pearl B. Purcep, an Explorer of Little Note*," explained Willa, peeking into the familiar room after Gish had unlocked the door. It was neat for once: papers perfectly stacked, folders folded away, and books in beautifully aligned towers. In fact, it was *too* ordered, *too* perfect—it was most suspicious. Willa poked around but the cursed book was nowhere to be seen. "I want to ask it about Rab Culpepper."

"But he blew up half the province!" spluttered Gish. "I wouldn't go around saying his name too loudly. Or folk might think you're looking to end up just as wild as him."

Willa's step faltered. She turned and found Gish fiddling with the hem of his shirt. The campfire in her heart dimmed. Would he understand?

"Can you keep a secret?" she asked.

Gish crossed his heart and nodded.

"I know Rab Culpepper was a rotten sort, but he said there was a way for witches like me to not choose a coven. A different choice. I don't want to join a coven, you see. I don't want to be part of the war or be responsible for wayward spells. I want to be an Ordinary witch. I want to stay in Bad Faith and only cast spells that are helpful or not cast any at all. And that can only happen if I uncover his secrets."

Gish frowned and took a long time to weigh up Willa's words.

Finally, he grinned. "That would be *brilliant!*"

Willa exhaled, matching his grin. She knew Gish would understand. She *knew* it.

"Then you could stay in the castle," he said. "It's dead boring around here — or it was until you showed up. There's no one my age. Except for the prince and Marceline. He's a horror and she's . . ." He scrunched up his nose "Odd. But if you stay, we can be friends."

Friends?

The idea of having a friend had always been out of reach, a hidden treasure with no map. First her parents hadn't allowed it, and then Willa herself. But Gish was handing her a map, and Willa wondered: Would it be so bad? If she'd been wrong about being a witch, could she have been wrong about not needing friends? She was tired of being lonely.

Willa found it hard to contain her smile.

"I'll help you find the book," said Gish with a firm nod.

They searched the room, every nook and cranny, but the book was nowhere to be found.

"What would some silly cursed book know about Rab Culpepper anyway?" said Gish. Suddenly a whizzing sound cut through the air as a balled-up sock smacked him square on the jaw. "Hey!" He rubbed his chin. "I only meant because that book is about some boring explorer. So why would it know—" Another sock smacked Gish on the chin. "Fine!" he snapped. "I'll shut up."

Willa bounced on her toes. So the book *was* here. "It's temperamental," she explained in a whisper. "You have to speak nicely to it." She cleared her throat and stood in the middle of the room. "Oh masterful *The Long and Thoroughly Ordinary Tales of Pearl B. Purcep, an Explorer of Little Note*," she said. "Could you kindly bestow upon us more diary entries about Rab Culpepper? Or any information about him would do. Please and thank you." She ducked on instinct, but no socks cannonballed toward her—just silence. "Cheese and rice! Where is it?"

Behind his hand, Gish whispered, "You could always use *M-A-G-I-C*." He waggled his fingers. "Make it come floating out or something."

Willa didn't think that sounded like a sensible plan *at all*. Even though she had no better ideas up her sleeve (and she had *five* sleeves today), she knew that using her temperamental magic was a bad idea.

"I'll just have to find another way," she said.

"You could always try the library," suggested Gish. "They have a gazillion books about—"

A commotion on the other side of the wall startled them both. Muffled voices. *Lots* of muffled voices.

"Is that the throne room?" asked Willa. It sounded as if half the city was in there. "What's going on?"

Gish shrugged. "Let's find out."

They ran next door and found it bursting with Ordinary Folk, yelling and pointing fingers. And in the middle of it all was a boy, a scrawny, sniffly boy with legs as thin as a chicken's and a pale face smeared with grime.

"Who can tell me what happened?" snapped the royal healer from beside the boy.

The butcher stepped forward, twisting his hat in his hands. The crowd grew quiet.

"This here's my delivery boy," explained the fair-haired man. "I was giving him a telling off on account of him being late back from his deliveries and the little rascal was spinning some yarn about cursed tulips belching so loud he fainted but I didn't believe a word of it on account of there being a magical truce and that's what I says to him, I says, 'Don't you be lying to me, you little moppet,' but then he's got his mouth open only no words are coming out. 'Ha!' says I, 'cat got your tongue because you've been lying to me,' but then he points to his mouth and I can see he's trying to speak but nothing is coming out so I says, 'This is just like the master weaver, it is.'"

The healer bent over the child, opening his mouth and peering inside. She humphed and aahed and tsked. "It's true," she announced. "His voice has been stolen."

The crowd gasped.

Willa turned to Gish. "Another voice?"

Gish gulped like a guppy. "B-b-but . . ." He tugged on his earlobe, eyes wide. "If it happened again, then it wasn't an accident."

The crowd was quickly herded out of the room by guards. The healer led the boy toward the hospital wing. "Got a lovely potion to make you feel better," she told him. Willa and Gish ducked behind a statue of Old King Fustus and watched as the prince, the clerk, and the royal entourage gathered in an urgent circle once the room had been cleared. The king, no doubt, was hiding.

"I think we can all agree this voice-stealing business is disturbing," said the prince.

"We're doomed!" gasped the royal entourage. "Who will be next? What can we do?"

"The spell is Irontongue, but Ferula was arguing with Eladar over a rubber duck in the billiards room all morning," continued the prince, "so it *must* be the untamed witch."

"I'm afraid that's impossible, Your Highness," said the clerk. She dropped her papers as the prince turned to glare at her. "She was in class all morning, and her magic isn't tamed yet," she hurried to explain.

The prince sniffed. "I suppose she *is* rather awful at magic."

He rolled back his shoulders. "Then it has to be a rogue coven witch, someone from Irontongue with a score to settle. Or . . ." He paused, narrowing his eyes. "Or it's one of us."

"Us? We would never!" cried the entourage.

"Not *us* us," snapped the prince. "But a witch in disguise, a rogue coven witch pretending to be Ordinary. Somewhere in the city. Haven't you noticed the influx of cats around the castle? Those disobedient beasts are *always* a sign of trouble."

There was a wave of gasping.

"How will we uncover the truth?" cried one of the lords. "Guide us, Your Magnificence!"

Willa scoffed. She wondered what the royal entourage did all day other than parade about in jewels and furs, pandering to the prince's every word fart.

The prince puffed out his chest. "I propose the formation of a special committee, the Very Sensible Committee for the Protection of Ordinary Folk from Evil Witches and Witchlike Behavior, of which I will be president," he said. He waggled his finger at the clerk. "Take a note of that name, Florestine."

"An excellent name, Your Highness." The clerk scribbled furiously.

The prince preened. "The royal clerk will distribute an Official List of Ordinary-like Conduct throughout the city. Anyone who behaves in a manner contrary to this list will be considered suspicious."

"Very sensible!"

"So wise!"

"A true leader!"

The prince led his adoring fans from the room.

Once the door closed behind them, Willa and Gish crept out from behind the statue. She had a terrible feeling the prince was about to cause a lot of pain.

"Why would an Irontongue witch deliberately attack the city?" said Gish. "A witch has never cast spells against us on purpose. They were always accidents. Why would they want to steal our voices?"

"And the voices are supposed to come back after a bit," said Willa. "That's how the spell works. Why aren't they coming back?"

Gish didn't have an answer. Neither did Willa.

"Come on," she said. "I could do with another muffin."

CHAPTER NINE

NEWS OF THE SECOND STOLEN VOICE spread fast, a monsoon of gossip that raged from one end of the city to the next. There was even talk of a third, a fourth, a fifth stolen voice. People wore buckets on their heads to shield themselves from the spell. An enterprising young carpenter offered to cut eye holes in the buckets for "a small fee" and made a fortune.

Then he had *his* voice stolen too.

Gaspard's smiles became strained as he worked to uncover how the spells were being cast, why the voices didn't come back, and who was behind it all.

"Nothing for you to worry about," he told Willa over the breakfast table. He glanced nervously at Ferula, who was watching them both with narrowed eyes. "I'll figure it out."

Willa tried three more times to find *The Long and Thoroughly Ordinary Tales of Pearl B. Purcep, an Explorer of Little Note,* but she could only endure being smacked in the face with socks for so long. Eventually she got so angry she accidentally vanished every sock in the castle. (She was still awaiting a fitting punishment for *that* incident after the socks reappeared in the prince's bathtub, while he was in it.)

She needed another way to uncover more about Rab Culpepper's mysterious alternative choice. She didn't even have Gish to help her brainstorm, as he was being run ragged by the clerk, zipping all over the city to stick up notices of the prince's Official List of Ordinary-like Conduct. So Willa took to wandering the castle, hoping the repetition of movement would jiggle an idea out of the deepest, darkest corners of her brain.

While on one such walk, Willa stumbled across an odd sight: a long line of Ordinary Folk that disappeared into the throne room. Before the crowd could shriek and cover their mouths, she ducked behind the nearest potted plant.

She spied between the plant's leaves. *What in the Wild are they doing?*

"I've been waiting two hours," complained the cobbler. "What's taking so long?"

"I've been waiting as long as you," argued the tailor. "And I have *valuable* information. I should be taken to the head of the line."

"Are you saying *my* information isn't valuable?" scoffed the cobbler. "I'll have you know my neighbor has pointy shoes *and* a pet cat *and* he told me that if I didn't stop spying on him my eyes would fall out of my head and today my eyes are *very* itchy. He's cursed me! He's the rogue witch!"

Ah, thought Willa. This was the line for the first meeting of the Very Sensible Committee for the Protection of Ordinary Folk from Evil Witches and Witchlike Behavior. It seemed half the city had turned out to accuse someone or other of witchlike behavior.

"How ridiculous," hissed Willa. "Don't they know—"

"*Psst!*" said a voice.

Willa glanced around, but no one was behind her.

"*Psst!*" hissed the voice again.

"Who's there?" whispered Willa.

The potted plant she was hiding behind ruffled its leaves. Willa lurched back—was it the king? Hiding again?

"It's me," said the plant, for it was indeed the plant speaking. "And it's rude to spy on people, don't you know?"

Willa's cheeks burned hot. "I wasn't . . . I didn't . . ."

"I'm going to tell on you," singsonged the potted plant. *Cheese and rice,* thought Willa. It's been hit with a *Dibber-dobber!* curse. The plant ruffled its leaves and began to shout: "Hey! You over there! Yes, you! There's a girl hiding behind me and she's—"

Willa ran away before anyone could accuse her of cursing them.

She continued to wander.

Eventually Willa found herself in front of the library. She stood before the tapestry, frowning at the cottage door. Talon suddenly joined her—wherever he had been had earned him something tasty to eat, judging by the way he licked his whiskers.

"I hope you haven't stolen anything from the kitchens," said Willa.

Talon flicked his tail. He looked up at the tapestry.

Willa's fingertips tingled. "Even if the door still worked, I don't think escaping is the answer," she said. The answer, she hoped, was in the diaries about Rab Culpepper. But the cottage door draped in roses still made her skin tingle. She wasn't sure why.

"It's White-Rose Cottage," said a voice to her left.

Willa spun around and found Marceline eyeing her curiously.

The young girl stood—shoulders back, chin lifted—beneath the high stone arch of the library entrance. She wore her hair coiled into a nest atop her head, with the white mouse curled in a sleeping ball in the middle of it. Her face was all odds and ends: sharp nose and puffy cheeks, pointed chin and lumpy brow, warm golden skin and cold black eyes. She blinked at Willa in silence before eventually she motioned to the tapestry with her pointed chin. "It's where Rab Culpepper lived before . . . well, *before*."

Willa had never heard Marceline speak; she had a nice voice, like early-morning birdsong. Willa had often wondered who the girl was. A cousin? A servant? A daughter of one of the lords or ladies who followed the prince around, licking his boots with their praise? Willa supposed she could have asked, but people tended not to answer her questions: they usually ran away the very second Willa opened her mouth.

Willa cleared her throat. "Are you looking for a book?" she asked.

Marceline's nose twitched, but she didn't run away. "I'm the librarian. Well, *junior* librarian."

"Oh."

More silence. More blinks. Willa wondered if she should ask about the weather.

"Does your mouse have a name?" she asked instead.

"Huggin. What's your cat's name?"

"Talon. Do you like being a librarian?"

"It's all right. Do you like being a witch?"

Willa's mouth stuttered. What could she possibly say in answer to *that?*

"I guess I . . . I never had a choice."

Not even her parents had been able to scold it out of her —she was a witch: magic ran deep within her and always had. If she'd had a choice, she would have been someone her parents could have loved unconditionally. But her choices were Silverclaw, Irontongue, or explode.

She shook her head, and finally an idea jiggled free. It landed with a thump that rocked Willa on her feet. "You could always try the library," Gish had said. "They have a gazillion books . . ."

Willa wasn't sure how many a gazillion equaled, but it was definitely more than a hundred and that was *a lot.* Could one of the library's books tell her about *the mysterious other choice?*

She wasn't entirely convinced books were helpful. Last night she had read in *The ABC of Witches!* that

L is for *law!* Did you know there are over five thousand Irontongue coven rules? From "Always spit on the host after a meal to show your appreciation" to "Never eat another witch's toenail clippings no matter how appetizing they look," there is a rule for every aspect of Irontongue life. Punishment for breaking these laws

ranges from foot stomping to beheading, so be sure to
follow the rules!

Willa didn't think she was any better for having learned
such nonsense.

On the other hand, Rab had obviously gotten his ideas from
somewhere—and where else did you get ideas from, if not books?

"Do you have any books on Rab Culpepper?" she asked.

Marceline narrowed her eyes. "He was evil, you know."

"I know. But there's something I need to find out about
him. Nothing evil. It's very boring, actually."

Marceline continued to stare at her with narrowed eyes.
Sweat trickled down Willa's back.

"It's difficult to know for sure," said Marceline finally.

Before Willa could ask what she meant, the young librarian
had swiveled on her heels and was marching into the library.

Unsure what else to do, Willa followed. "Come on, Talon."

The library was a cavernous hall with row after zigzag row
of giant bookshelves, thick and long and yawning all the way
to brush the ceiling. Each shelf was double-stacked with dusty
books; at the end of each aisle teetered yet more piles. Books,
books, and more books.

So this is what a gazillion looks like, thought Willa.

Marceline weaved through the stacks, pointing out various
features. "That section is about cheese. Over there is a lovely
painting of a horse. This wall weeps raspberry jam—an old

curse, but very fine jam. Watch where you walk! That pile of books will tell you lies. That vase belonged to Queen Arabella the Second. On your left is a rather unfortunate painting of King Teebald as a child. Oh dear, I think you've stepped in raspberry jam."

Willa wiped her feet on a rug before scurrying after Marceline.

She found the girl behind a large desk at the far end of the library, running her finger down a roll of parchment.

"The problem is," said Marceline, glasses slipping to the tip of her nose, "that the master librarian, the Fastidious Keeper of Words, vanished a year ago. I think a wayward curse got him and he was sucked into one of the books. I've been reading them all, trying to find him, but I haven't had any luck so far. So I'm a bit behind with my cataloging and—" Suddenly Marceline cried out, "Aha!"

Willa startled, knocking over a lamp.

"The good news," said Marceline, ignoring the crash, "is that we *do* have a book: *The True (and Explosive!) History of Rab Culpepper.*"

Willa grinned as she righted the lamp. That *was* good news.

"The bad news," said Marceline, "is that it's in the haunted section."

Willa waggled a finger in her ears until she was certain there was nothing stuck inside. "I'm sorry, did you say *haunted?*"

Marceline nodded, face blank. "Section G."

"But I didn't think ghosts were real."

Marceline scoffed. "Of *course* they're made-up. But years ago a *Get-real!* curse hit a number of books, including *The Giant Book of Ghostly Bedtime Stories,* so all the ghosts came to life. Now they haunt section G."

Willa sighed. Why did it have to be so difficult? Couldn't the book she wanted be found in the whipped-cream section, next to the scone section? Then she could wander by the weeping-jam wall and have herself a pleasant snack by the end of it.

But she *really* wanted that book.

"The author's name is Amaryllis Youngblood," explained Marceline. "That means the book will be at the far end of the aisle, somewhere on the bottom left. Come on, I'll show you."

Willa sucked in a deep, steadying breath, then set off as Marceline led her toward section G. The closer she got, the less brave she felt.

At the top of the aisle there was a sign:

— SECTION G —

(G IS FOR *GHOST,* IF YOU DIDN'T KNOW, BECAUSE THERE ARE GHOSTS HERE, WHICH MEANS *YOU* SHOULDN'T BE.)

(WHAT ARE YOU STILL DOING READING THIS SIGN? I SAID THERE ARE *GHOSTS!* LEAVE NOW! YES, *NOW!*)

That's encouraging, thought Willa. She peered down the

aisle. Beyond the first few rows were flickering shadows, then nothing but darkness.

She gulped. "How far to the end?"

"*Very* far. We have *so* many books." The young librarian's eyes sparkled as she gazed into the middle distance. "I expect you'll run into a great many ghosts," she said dreamily. "It will be quite an adventure. Like in this book I know: *Horrifically Extraordinary Adventures for Young Girls Who Should Know Better than to Leave the House.*" She bit her lip. "Perhaps I should go with—"

Willa shook her head. "It's far too dangerous."

The glittery, far-off glaze in Marceline's eyes vanished in a blink. She humphed. "I didn't want to go anyway," she said. "I abhor adventures."

Willa summoned all her remaining bravery (about a teaspoonful) and announced, "You stay behind too, Talon." The cat was licking jam from his coat and did not look up.

Marceline shoved a lit candle at Willa. "Try not to get eaten by ghosts," she said, mouth pinched.

Willa grasped the candle tightly and stepped into the cool of the aisle. The shelves loomed high on either side, casting thick, oily shadows that bullied the candlelight. *You've no business being here!* the shadows sneered. The light cringed, pulling back into a feeble circle around Willa. *Oh, let's leave,* said the light, *pretty please?* When Willa glanced over her shoulder, the darkness had closed around her and she could no longer see Marceline or Talon.

Her teaspoon of bravery was all sucked dry.

She pressed on.

The deeper she crept into the aisle, the more her imagination played tricks. *Are you sure that's the sound of your footsteps? Are you sure it isn't a ghost sneaking up behind you? Did your hand brush a book or was it a . . . GHOST!*

"You're a witch!" she scolded herself. "Witches aren't afraid of anything."

Eventually she spied a thick stone wall ahead and she whooped with glee. She hurried the last few steps and knelt, running the candle along the rows, searching for *Youngblood*.

She saw *Yarsley, Yelder, Yockins,* and *Yoxon,* but no *Youngblood*. There was, however, a gap between Yockins and Yoxon where Youngblood *should* have been. Willa huffed. "Maybe there's a spell that will call the book to me. I should—"

Something hard slammed between her shoulder blades. She lurched forward with an *oof!*, dropping the candle. It landed on the stone floor, its light flickering out as it rolled out of reach.

Willa turned to find a book on the floor. Her heart beat fiercely—had her wild magic performed a useful spell for once? But when she drew the book close, the spine declared it to be *Not the Book You're Looking For* by A. Nony-Mous.

Willa dropped the book with a thump. "What use is this?" she huffed.

Another book came hurtling toward her and smacked her hard on the shoulder. "Ouch!"

Someone giggled.

Or, rather, some*thing* giggled.

Willa grasped for the fallen candle, but a flying book knocked her hand out of the way; then a wisp of smoke swept past and scooped up the light.

Three ghosts materialized in front of her: an old man in rags and chains, a little girl with ringlets and missing front teeth, and a tall, willowy woman in a wedding dress, cradling her decapitated head in the crook of her elbow. The old man in rags held the candle, wafting it back and forth, rattling his chains as he moved.

"Woo!" howled the man. "Woo!"

"I only wanted a b-b-book," stuttered Willa, backing away. She knocked into the shelf behind her. "I didn't mean to dis-t-turb you."

"Our little corner of the world is popular recently," moaned the bride. She waggled her severed head, veil skimming the stone floor. "We let the last visitor leave with her prize because we liked her bird; she'll be cooking up all kinds of trouble by now. But what shall we do with this one?"

"Eat her!" squealed the little girl, clapping her hands, ringlets bobbing. "Oh, *please* can we eat her?"

"Woo!" agreed the man, and rattled his chains.

"I'd rather you didn't," said Willa. Her knees wobbled in fear.

"Woo! Woo! WOO!" howled the man as the three ghosts advanced on her. His chains rattled like rough music, all knotted and twisted and— Suddenly Willa had an idea.

She twirled both her arms in figure eights. Her left hand swished clockwise and her right hand swooshed counterclockwise. She repeated the movements three times. *If I could knot those chains around all three of them . . .*

The fizzy, zizzy, orange-soda feeling lashed at the walls of the Rapscallion's Cage. She tried to visualize a gentle trickle through a spout, but instead there was a whirlpool. Tiny puffs of baby-pink smoke shot from her fingertips before—*poof!*—the old man's chains transformed into ribbons.

"That's not right!" said Willa.

His raggedy cloak turned into ribbons too. The little girl's ringlets glowed pink then—*poof!*—suddenly they were long, curly ribbons. The bride's veil transformed, then her dress, too. *Poof!* All ribbons.

"What's happening?" cried the little girl, pulling at her ribbon hair in horror.

"My beautiful veil!" cried the bride.

"Woo?" said the old man, frowning at the ribbons twisted around his arms and waist. He tried to shake them, but they didn't make a sound.

"Sorry," said Willa. "I'm still learning, so my magic is a bit wonky."

The beheaded bride sneered, ribbons flapping around her face. "We can still eat you!"

But the spell hadn't finished misbehaving. All the ribbons began to knot. *All* of them, in one tangled ball. The little girl's once-golden ringlets knotted with the old man's ribbon chains. What had once been a veil knotted with the old man's cloak.

"Get off me!" cried the little girl.

"You're standing on my foot!" shouted the bride.

"Woo!" howled the old man, tugging on his ribbon chains until all three ghosts tumbled to the floor in a knotted ball.

Seizing her chance at escape, Willa ran. She stumbled through the dark, three ghostly voices calling after her: "Come back! Untie us! Woo!"

She ran and ran and ran. When her lungs were one wheeze away from exploding out of her chest, Willa tumbled into the light at the end of the aisle and collapsed at Marceline's feet.

"No book? How boring," said Marceline, who was cross-legged on the floor, eating a scone with jam and cream. She licked a blob of cream from her top lip. "Would you like a scone? The jam is fresh."

Willa shook her head, panting hard.

Right now she didn't care about scones or jam. All she cared about were the bride's words: *Our little corner of the world is very popular of late . . . We let the last visitor leave with her prize because we liked her bird . . .*

Bird.

That meant Ferula.

That meant *Ferula* had taken the book.

But what did Ferula want with a book about Rab Culpepper?

CHAPTER TEN

STEAM SPEWED from beneath the lids of bubbling pots and pans on the stove. The head cook's booming voice bounced from one end of the kitchen to the other: "Hand me the sugar. Stir clockwise at a medium pace. Medium! Are the whelks ready? Why does this cake look like it's been sat on? Is that a paw print? I said, *medium!* Oh, just give it to me, you useless dillywomp!"

Tucked away in a corner, Willa was perched on a crate, a small knife in one hand and a potato in the other. She had already peeled a gazillion potatoes and there were a gazillion more to go. A lumpy red sore had formed on her finger where the knife handle rubbed over and over.

"There you are!" Gaspard poked his head around the corner, grinning as usual. He plonked himself down on a bag of potatoes next to Willa. "How's the punishment going?"

For vanishing the socks *and* making them reappear in his bathtub (while he was using it), the prince had set Willa to work in the kitchens.

"I never want to see another potato again," said Willa.

Gaspard laughed. "Cheer up. Did you know that slug-tier witches in the Irontongue coven have limited magical powers but get to do all sorts of exciting jobs? Like wading through mud to gather worms for the other witches to feast on and sweeping up the dragon dung and pulling animal teeth for jewelry and, well, that's mostly it. If you get assigned slug tier, that could be you! Wouldn't that be fun?"

"But you said I was powerful," gasped Willa. "Ferula said I could be dragon tier." Not that Willa had plans to join Irontongue, at least not unless it was either that or exploding.

Gaspard's smile held firm as he patted her shoulder. "Of course you're powerful. It's just, if you can't control your magic, then . . . Well, not to worry. Worms are great. They're wriggly and slippery and a little bit slimy. What's not to love?" He slapped his thigh. "Anyway, I've got a surprise for you. You looked glum this morning, so I've organized something to cheer you up."

Willa *had* been glum.

All night she'd tossed and turned, wondering what Ferula wanted with a book on Rab Culpepper. She'd tried to ask over breakfast—smiling politely, all her teeth on show: "Read any good books lately, Ferula?"

"Books? *Pft!*" Ferula had licked grease from her fingers, reaching for more bacon. "Reading is for sniveling bumfuzzles. I'd rather sit on a scorpion than read a book."

Well, Willa had thought with a sniff, *I guess you won't mind if I steal it, then.*

But later when she'd chanced to sneak away for that very purpose, she'd instead spied the witch casting a spell on her bedroom door.

Hidden around a corner, Willa had watched as words shot from Ferula's mouth. Before the spell could hurtle through the air in search of someone or something to curse, the witch had trapped it in a shimmery bubble. Carefully balancing the bubble on her fingertips, Ferula had placed it in front of the door. If Willa hadn't already known Ferula had alibis for each of the voice-stealing incidents, she'd have assumed then and there the witch was guilty—the bubbles were *very* similar. "Hibity-jig bobajagg noompity!" Ferula had spat, and the bubble had instantly vanished.

Willa had gasped. *What in the Wild was it?*

After casting several more strange bubble spells, Ferula had hobbled away, muttering, "That ought to keep out busybodies." The crow on her shoulder had cawed in agreement.

Willa sighed at the potato in her hand—she didn't know what that bubble thing had been, but she knew Ferula's room was off limits. How was she supposed to uncover Rab's mystery choice now?

"What kind of surprise?" she asked, wary.

Gaspard grinned and stood, beckoning Willa to follow.

Willa quite liked her tutor, but she wasn't sure if she trusted his surprises. But what else could she do? Willa threw down her knife and half-peeled potato and followed him out of the kitchen.

He led them to the front entrance of the castle. "It's quite all right," he told the guards who moved to block their exit. He handed over Willa's long-sought-after Permission to Leave the Castle form. Willa gasped. She could leave? Whenever she wanted?

"Just around the castle gardens," whispered Gaspard, as if reading her mind. "Best to avoid the city."

Willa had not been out of the castle in weeks. As they stepped through the doors, she sucked down fresh air and grinned at the warming touch of sun on her skin. Almost like a mother's hand cupping her cheek.

Almost.

"So you're still interested in the Irontongue coven?" asked Gaspard as they strolled through the gardens. Willa spied half a dozen familiar cats sunning themselves in the flower beds, ignoring the guards trying to shoo them. "That is, if you're thinking about which tier you might be." He grinned down at Willa, but it was a strained sort of grin, the kind that was tight around the edges, the kind that spoke of sleepless nights and pulling out hair over a puzzle he couldn't untangle. Willa feared Gaspard was burning the candle at both ends, trying to uncover why the voice bubbles weren't returning and teaching Willa as well. The pressure was wearing on him. "I would have thought after the whole voice-stealing thing . . . but of course! We can delve into more Irontongue magic. I admit I get carried away teaching Silverclaw spells—so elegant! So refined! But of course, Irontongue magic has its . . . um . . . good spells. There's *Bug-belch!* Which is elegant-*ish*. And *Tentacle-arms!* Excellent for those long, arduous battles. A good set of battle spells is imperative for a witch."

Willa frowned at her hands. She preferred when they were used to create, not destroy. "Can't I be a witch who doesn't fight?" she asked.

Gaspard's jaw worked as he tried to find the words. Was the contract preventing him from speaking freely or did he just not know what to say?

"Are you still reading *The ABC of Witches!*?" he asked eventually.

Willa nodded.

"Such a helpful book," said Gaspard. "My favorite entry is *W.* Have you read it?"

Willa shook her head. What did any of this have to do with her question?

"Pity," said Gaspard. "Such a good entry. *Very* enlightening."

They ducked through an open archway that led into a courtyard.

"Ah! Here we are!"

Butterflies and bees buzzed around kaleidoscopic flowers, and fat slants of afternoon sun toddled between the high, open arches of a walkway to the courtyard's east. It was beautiful.

Which was why the sight of Eladar dancing in the mud stuck out like a pus-filled pimple.

The witch flapped his arms like an angry bat, pointing and stomping and twirling. He was singing, too. Or more like howling.

"Ah!" said Gaspard, lowering his voice to an excited whisper. "Silverclaws are at one with nature, as you know, so here you can see Eladar communing with the butterflies." Gaspard shook his head in wonder. "You're so lucky to observe a real Silverclaw ritual."

Willa wrinkled her nose as Eladar slapped mud to his cheeks and danced as if he was hacking up a fur ball. "Is this my surprise?" she asked.

"No! This is an unexpected cherry on top." Gaspard guided her into the garden and to Eladar's side. The witch did not stop dancing. "Eladar! How are the butterflies?"

In answer, Eladar picked his nose and rubbed the finger down Gaspard's cheek. Willa gagged behind her hand.

"Ah!" Gaspard grinned down at Willa. "Eladar says the butterflies are happy today but the bees are perturbed by the influx of cats."

Eladar continued to dance, undulating his arms, wriggling his legs, and twisting his body into all kinds of shapes.

"Your surprise," said Gaspard, "is a one-on-one lesson with Eladar. I figured one-on-one was best after the last debacle. And I know you want to learn more about Irontongue, but this will be good too, won't it?" He tapped the side of his nose. "Just don't tell Ferula. You know how jealous she gets."

Willa tried her best to look pleased. She worried it looked more like she'd stubbed her toe.

"I'll leave you to it, then, shall I?" Gaspard clicked his heels.

"Wait!" cried Willa. "You're leaving me? Alone? With *him*?"

"Of course!"

Willa watched her tutor leave, disappearing through the

archway. As she turned back to Eladar, she tugged nervously on the collar of her blouse (which had the correct number of sleeves but fifty pockets).

The witch had stopped dancing and was staring at Willa.

"The bees like you," he said. He smacked his lips and frowned, as though speaking words out loud tasted like bitter lemons on his tongue.

Willa swallowed over the dryness in her mouth. "Thank you?"

Eladar smiled vaguely at Willa for what felt like an age. Discomfort grew, making Willa unsteady on her feet. She focused on the hum of the bees and the whoosh of the wind, the tittering of birds and the faint gurgle of the River Disappointment in the distance. Slowly, it eased the lump of worry in her throat.

"Exactly," said Eladar with a nod.

"I'm sorry, what?" asked Willa.

Eladar tilted his head to one side, so far Willa worried he would tumble. "You feel magic inside you. What does it feel like?"

"Like I'm a bottle of soda all shaken up," answered Willa automatically.

Eladar hummed. "Interesting," he said, and then paused to blow kisses at a particularly fat bee hovering over a violet.

Willa racked her mind for an excuse to leave. Her cat needed feeding? Her hair washing? Honestly, she would rather peel potatoes.

"Sunlight," said Eladar. He wiggled his fingers, nails clacking together.

Willa opened her mouth but shut it immediately. She didn't know what to say.

"My magic feels like beams of sunlight," explained Eladar.

"Oh. Well, that must be nice. Nicer than fizzy soda."

"Soda is nice. Except when the bubbles go up my nose. It makes me sneeze."

Willa tugged again at her collar.

"But magic is not just inside you," continued Eladar. He waved his arms in sweeping circles. "Can't you feel it?"

Perhaps this is a lesson after all, thought Willa. "Feel what?"

"Magic."

Willa looked down at herself. Now that she was no longer blocking it completely, the fizzy, zizzy thrum was always inside her. Sometimes a whisper, sometimes a shout.

Eladar shook his head, poking a long, curling nail at Willa's chest. "Not there." He swung his arm in an arc, as if to mean the garden, the sky, everything. *"There."*

Willa wrinkled her nose. "Do you mean magic is everywhere?"

Eladar smiled. "Yes!"

A bee buzzed around Willa's head. Eladar nodded as if it was saying something.

"I felt you. Before. You drew on nature to calm yourself. The bees and the wind and the birds and the river. I felt your magic reach out, and it tickled. The butterflies laughed and laughed."

Willa frowned. She *had* done that, but . . .

"You cannot be a Silverclaw witch without understanding that you are one with nature. You are mud. You are a spider. You are a fat bee sucking pollen from a sunflower. You are a worm. Each time you cast magic, you must remember this."

Eladar smiled vaguely at Willa, so Willa smiled back and nodded.

"Wonderful! The bees approve of you." Eladar bent and scooped up a handful of mud.

"I'm not sure—" said Willa before the gluey, gooey sensation of mud down her cheeks cut her short. Eladar had just slapped a handful of mud on her face.

"Pretty," said Eladar. "Now we cast a spell."

Willa stood still in shock as Eladar began to dance.

He looped his left arm in a wide circle. He rolled his right arm back and forth. He bent his head and flicked his hair side to side. He jumped in the air. Once. Twice. Three times. He shivered from head to toe.

Puffy yellow clouds shot from his fingers, whooshing toward Willa. Before they hit her, they changed course, twisting ninety degrees to shoot straight up into the air. The clouds joined, weaving into the shape of a helix, hovering above Willa's head.

It began to rain. A downpour of thick drops. Willa was drenched in seconds.

Eladar, however, was completely dry.

Willa looked up. A gray cloud hovered overhead, raining down on her and *only* her.

"Hey!" cried Willa in protest. She stepped to one side, away from the cloud. But the cloud followed her, the rain refusing to let up.

Eladar laughed, a high-pitched honk.

"Not funny," said Willa. She tried to run, but the cloud followed her everywhere, even when she ducked under the covered walkway. The cloud poured and poured and poured, and all the while it shrank. Eventually, it was nothing more than a wisp, and all that Willa felt were tiny droplets, like tears.

They stopped and the cloud was gone.

Willa was soaked to the bone. She stomped over to Eladar, face like thunder.

"The bees are amused," said Eladar.

"But I'm not."

"No," agreed Eladar. "You are wet."

Magic surged in Willa, waves of it crashing against the Rapscallion's Cage. It fizzed and it zizzed. It wanted to burst free: *Let me out! Let me out!*

Willa was inclined to let it.

Eladar smiled, twirling the end of his hair around a fingernail. "Your turn," he said. "Remember: let nature guide you. The butterflies will sing you to your best self."

Dripping wet and seething, Willa looped her left arm in a wide circle. She rolled her right arm back and forth. She bent her head and flicked her hair side to side. She jumped in the air. Once. Twice. Three times. She shivered from head to toe.

Willa closed her eyes and focused on the trickle of magic

flowing from the peephole in the imaginary Rapscallion's Cage. *Just a little bit,* she willed it.

The magic burst from her fingertips—yellow clouds spiraled toward Eladar.

They made the same ninety-degree turn and shot up into the air. Instead of a helix, the clouds wrapped together in the shape of an angry blob. It smoked and sizzled.

A cloud began to form, not just over Eladar's head, but the entire courtyard. The world grew dark as the cloud blocked out the sun.

And then it began to pour.

As well as rain there were bolts of lightning; they zapped from the cloud and burned holes in the earth.

She ran to the undercover walkway. This time, luckily, the cloud did not follow. Eladar calmly skipped after her, and together they watched the storm drench and singe the courtyard until the cloud had shrunk to the size of a pea.

With one final burst of lightning that cut the head off a sunflower, the cloud vanished.

Eladar rung out his hair. "The bees are unhappy with you," he said.

Willa winced. "My magic is a bit wonky."

"The word I would use is *wild*," said Eladar. He looked sidelong at Willa, and for once his gaze wasn't far-off and hazy. It was as sharp as a lightning bolt. Willa felt herself wilt under the weight of it.

She gulped.

Just as the sun appeared again, Eladar's face bloomed with a smile.

"The bees forgive you," he singsonged, then waltzed into the courtyard, where he sat in the middle of a flower bed with a squelch. Willa watched the Silverclaw witch giggle to himself as he bathed in mud.

"Will I ever get better at magic?" muttered Willa. Each of her fifty pockets was full of water. She pressed her hand to one and the water spurted out, dribbling down to her feet.

Her *bare* feet.

"That horrible, no-good book!"

CHAPTER ELEVEN

T HAT HORRIBLE, NO-GOOD BOOK" was Wil-
la's last hope. With *The True (and Explosive!) History of
Rab Culpepper* hidden behind the cursed door to Ferula's room,
her only remaining option was to entice *The Long and Thoroughly Ordinary Tales of Pearl B. Purcep, an Explorer of Little
Note* into giving up more diary entries.

But how?

How could she convince the most ill-tempered book in the
Wild to do *anything*?

She tried walking again, hoping she might jiggle free an idea.
For days she wandered the castle, thinking, thinking, thinking.

One morning she came across Marceline in the corridor,
Willa headed to class and Marceline to the library. "Have you
found that book you were looking for?" asked Marceline, falling
into step beside Willa. She wore a fussy purple dress with a lace
collar so high it tickled her chin. She regarded Willa sidelong,
a look like a magnifying glass hovering over a bug. Willa had
not spoken to Marceline since the incident with the ghosts but
had, more than once, felt the burn of the librarian's gaze aimed
at her.

Willa shook her head. "I'm looking for a different book now.
A cursed one."

"Oh?" The magnifying-glass gaze intensified. "I suppose you'll need my help."

"No!" said Willa in a rush. "I mean, no thank you."

"Good." Marceline raised her chin. "Because I'm too busy to help you." She marched away.

"What a strange girl," said Willa, then returned to racking her brain.

"Is there a spell for making cursed books behave?" she asked Gaspard in class later that same day.

The tutor rubbed his chin. "Not *behave,* as such," he said. "But you could cast *Freeze-frame!* A cursed book that can't move can't misbehave, can it?"

What an excellent idea, thought Willa.

The following day she cornered the book in the records room.

"If you'd only be nice I wouldn't have to do this," she said. She flapped her arms and wiggled her hips, letting the smallest trickle of magic ooze from its imaginary cage. It felt like squeezing the last globs of toothpaste from the tube. But the spell worked and jade-green clouds burst from her fingertips.

The book leapt out of the way—a backflip, a somersault, a pirouette! The spell flew by, hitting the wall behind instead.

"You're a book! Books don't fly," said Willa.

With a haughty flick of its pages, the book looped through the air and took off out of the room—very definitely *flying.*

"Get back here!" cried Willa.

She chased the impossible book through the castle, casting

the *Freeze-frame!* spell over and over. But each time the jade-green clouds shot from her fingertips, the book jumped out of the way. Soon Willa had frozen three guards, a bowl of soup, a potted plant, a bee, and the clerk's feather pen, but not *The Long and Thoroughly Ordinary Tales of Pearl B. Purcep, an Explorer of Little Note.* And because her magic was still wonky, the three guards, the bowl of soup, the potted plant, the bee, and the clerk's feather pen were *literally* turned into ice (luckily, it took only seconds to melt and everyone was fine except for a bit of brain freeze).

"I'm so sorry," Willa told a dripping-wet guard outside the throne room, ice crystals glistening on his uniform. "I didn't mean to. It was the book!" But the book had vanished.

"You look like you need help to me."

Willa startled to find Marceline suddenly next to her, chin tilted, arms folded. Today her dress was black but equally lacy and fussy.

"Well, I don't," said Willa churlishly. *Drip, drip, drip* went the guard.

"Good," said Marceline with a snort. She marched away. "Because I'm still too busy."

A week later, Gish found Willa in the kitchen courtyard, an empty food bucket in her hands and an army of cats sunning themselves on the cobblestones, bellies full.

"Cats sure are fond of you," he said. A tabby weaved between his ankles, then flopped on the ground, displaying her tummy. Gish reached down to pat her.

"I wouldn't if I were—"

"Ouch!" Gish jerked his hand back, a thin line of blood marring his palm. "That wasn't very nice," he scolded the cat.

The cat rolled onto her side, eyes half closed, content.

Willa turned the bucket upside down and sat on it. She heaved a sigh. "You can't expect a cat to do what you *think* it will," she said. "A cat will always do the opposite of what you ask."

It was just like *The Long and Thoroughly Ordinary Tales of Pearl B. Purcep, an Explorer of Little Note,* thought Willa glumly.

She had tried and failed to capture the book three more times since the *Freeze-frame!* debacle.

Willa sighed and rubbed along the tabby's spine with her bare foot. "There's simply no way to reason with a cursed book," she huffed. "I'm doomed."

"Are you trying to find that awful book again?"

Willa nodded. "I've tried *everything.*"

Gish tugged his earlobe and squinted into the sun. "Have you asked a book expert?" he said.

Willa blinked and sat up straight. It felt like being boofed over the head with a bag of potatoes. "Oh," she said. The answer had been right there the entire time! Wearing fussy lace and glaring at her. "I think you're right. But I think—"

The tabby bit her big toe.

"Ouch! Cheese and rice!"

"So you *do* need my help," said the book expert once Willa had stuttered and stammered her way through an explanation.

The rough weave of the threadbare couch itched her thighs, even through long pants (four leg holes!). Marceline stared at Willa for a long time.

"Sounds like trouble," said Marceline, breaking the awkward silence. She narrowed her eyes. "Sounds to me like you're planning quite the adventure."

Willa shook her head. "No trouble! No adventure!"

Marceline stared.

Willa gulped.

Gish cleared his throat.

With a loud sigh Marceline slumped against the desk. "Oh," she said, nose scrunched. "I suppose that's good. Adventures are terrible things, or so my father says." She pouted at the book beside her hand. Willa tilted her head until she could read the spine: *Horrifically Extraordinary Adventures for Young Girls Who Should Know Better than to Leave the House.*

Oh.

Oh.

Perhaps Marceline wasn't such a mystery after all.

"I can't help you anyway because I'm far too busy," Marceline went on. "I hardly ever leave the library. Why would I? It's exciting enough for me in here. There are ghosts and jam and books about cheese and—"

"Actually," said Willa. "Now that you mention it, we probably *will* cause quite a lot of trouble."

"Really?" Marceline brightened instantly.

"We will?" said Gish.

Willa dug her elbow into his side. "Yes, *we will.*"

"Ow! I mean, oh! *So* much trouble," said Gish, rubbing his side as he finally caught on. "It will be one heck of an adventure."

Marceline's eyes lit up. "Will it be dangerous?"

"Very," said Willa.

"Will we get into trouble with Prince Cyrus if we're caught?"

Gish nodded. "So much trouble."

"Will there," asked Marceline, lowering her voice, "be dragons?"

Willa blinked several times. "Maybe?"

Marceline sighed, picking at the corner of her book with studied disinterest. "I *suppose* I could help you," she drawled. "I'm very busy and I *loathe* to cause trouble. But it sounds important that you find this diary."

Willa and Gish shared a grin.

"So you'll help?" Willa asked.

"Even though I'm a very sensible girl and my father expressly forbids me from going on adventures, I'll help."

Willa could hardly contain her excitement. For the first time in weeks, she felt hope. "Do you know how we catch a cursed book?"

"Simple," said Marceline. "You give it what it wants."

What *The Long and Thoroughly Ordinary Tales of Pearl B. Purcep, an Explorer of Little Note* wanted, of course, was socks.

"Why didn't I think of that?" grumbled Willa.

"The fluffier the better," explained Marceline, as she picked through a pile of laundry. "The king's bed socks *always* go missing."

When they had chosen the fluffiest socks they could find, Marceline led them back through the castle, explaining her plan in detail.

They would go to the location where the book was known to cause the most trouble: the records room. There they would place the socks on the floor with a box poised above them, rigged with string. And when the cursed book arrived to steal the socks, a single tug would send the box falling.

"What happens when the book is trapped?" asked Willa.

Marceline shrugged. "That's up to you."

"Magic," said Gish, wiggling his fingers.

Willa grimaced but didn't say anything.

They watched Marceline carefully set up the trap. "I learned how to do this from *Horrifically Extraordinary Adventures for Young Girls Who Should Know Better than to Leave the House.* Isn't it awful?" she said with a grin, tying the final knot.

Her excitement was contagious; it thrummed in Willa's veins, warm and sweet like honey. She wished she'd known to ask for help ages ago. But there had never been anyone she could turn to. It was a giddy feeling to realize that perhaps now, when she turned, there might be someone standing there.

"Thank you for helping me," said Willa.

The young librarian paused. Though her lips were pressed thin, there was a faint quirk at the edges. "Thank you for asking me," she said, handing Willa the string.

The three of them waited around the corner, just out of sight. Gish struggled to keep still, wriggling in place like he had ants in his pants, while Marceline read *Ten Terrifying Encounters with Dragons*. Willa toyed with the string, her mind wandering.

Perhaps she should have brought something to read too. She was up to *R* in *The ABC of Witches!*

R is for *ruler!* Did you know that just like Ordinary Folk, witches have kings and queens? Silverclaw is ruled by Queen Opalina Starbright. (Did you know she was once an Ordinary child? Fascinating!) She was fourteen when she became queen and has ruled for almost two hundred years! Her subjects call her wise and generous and pretty and hairy and horribly good at leapfrogging. She is beloved by all.

The Irontongue ruler is Mortus Dragonstink. He seized power after spitting in the previous king's eyes until he cried. He's not very nice.

Willa shook her head. The more she read of that book, the less she wanted to join either coven.

But could she go home instead?

Thinking of her little cottage lately brought on the itchy-squirmy feeling. She could no longer picture herself sitting in the sunshine-yellow kitchen without becoming restless. She had a suspicion that her home was an ill-fitting dress, the kind she had once worn without question but now thought to be the wrong color, the wrong fabric, the wrong *something*. It was a dress someone else had picked for her to wear but didn't suit her at all.

If she couldn't picture herself in her home and she couldn't picture herself in either coven, then where did she belong?

Suddenly a balled-up sock—a yellow-and-blue bed sock—hit Willa square in the face.

"Hey!" Another sock hit her, and another and another. "Stop that!"

The book appeared in the middle of the hallway, hovering in midair. The box and string had vanished.

"How did you do that?" gasped Willa.

In answer, the book sent a spray of balled-up socks at Willa. She threw up her hands and ducked as sock after sock flew at her.

When the barrage ended, Willa lowered her hands and looked up. The book opened its pages, let rip an ear-shattering burp, then shot off down the corridor.

"Don't let it get away!" shouted Willa.

The three children chased the book through the castle, up stairs and down winding corridors, until finally it flew outside, into the soldiers' yard.

They chased the book out of the yard and down a sloping field to the riverbank, where the water happily chattered to itself as it meandered over rocks.

Willa was out of breath as the book paused to let rip another burp before it shot off back up the hill.

"That way!" shouted Marceline.

The three children chased the book through gardens, past cats and over walls, around barns and outhouses and grain sheds, and into a familiar kaleidoscopic courtyard, where it promptly vanished.

"Where did it go?" asked Willa, doubled over and panting.

"Hiding?" suggested Gish.

They looked—behind shrubs, in tree branches, under the stone bench, between the green leaves of a thick bush.

As Willa bent over a patch of broad, crinkly leaves, she startled. A strange creature was hiding there. Willa parted the leaves and looked closer.

It was a purple toad, which wasn't unusual, but then it also *wasn't* a purple toad. Because it had the head of a snail and hind legs that ought to have belonged on a hairy spider and the antennas of a cricket.

"Hello," said Willa. She peered at the strange, mixed-up creature. "Are you one of Healer Berwig's missing toads?"

The creature opened its mouth, but instead of a croak, out came a spurt of sickly brown sludge. "Blergh!"

Willa jumped back. "Oh dear!"

"A jumble?" said Marceline with a deep frown as she moved

to take a closer look at the strange creature. "What's a jumble doing here?"

"A what?" asked Gish.

"A jumble. It's an Irontongue creation," said Marceline. She folded her hands behind her back and looked like a small, serious version of Gaspard, lecturing from the front of his classroom. "Irontongue witches like to splice together bits and pieces of animals to make new creatures. Sometimes as soldiers in the war but mostly just for fun."

"That's awful!" said Willa. "Look at the poor thing! It's sick."

To illustrate her point, the toad once again threw up, then hopped away.

"I guess whoever made it didn't know what they were doing," said Marceline.

Willa hummed to herself. What was a jumble doing in Bad Faith? And wasn't that the list of creepy-crawlies the healer had been missing? Purple toads, crickets, snails, and spiders . . .

"Hey! *Psst!* You over there!"

Willa turned, but there was no one behind them. All she could see was a lone potted plant in the arch of the covered walkway. It was shaking madly.

"Is that . . . is that plant talking to us?" said Gish.

"Yes! Over here!" cried the plant. "Someone is spying on you from behind my—*argh!*"

The plant tipped forward and Willa saw a flash of dark robes billowing behind a running figure. By the time she reached the arch, the walkway was empty.

Gish righted the plant.

"Ta ever so much," said the plant. "Honestly, you try and do a good deed and look what happens."

"Thanks for trying," said Willa. *I wonder who would be spying on me,* she thought. *And I wonder how many potted plants in this castle are dibber-dobbers?*

Suddenly a fluttering of black feathers caught her eye.

High up on the wall, at the very end of the walkway, was a crow.

Willa gulped.

"Caw!" said the crow, its beady black eyes burning into Willa. "Caw, caw!"

"Is that . . . ?" whispered Marceline.

Willa nodded. "I think so."

With a flutter of wings, the bird took off, a streak of black against blue sky.

CHAPTER TWELVE

THE CITIZENS OF BAD FAITH found it highly entertaining to accuse one another of witchcraft. Each morning the line for reporting suspicious conduct spilled out of the castle and twisted three times around the market, and by the afternoon half the city had rushed to the square to watch the public witch trials.

The trials comprised four tests devised by the prince to determine if the accused was a witch in disguise.

1. The Circle Test, whereby the accused must prove they can spin in a circle for twenty minutes without throwing up.

2. The Duck Test, whereby a duck is placed in front of the accused. If the duck quacks, they are a witch.

3. The Tickle Test, whereby the accused is tickled with a hundred feathers. If they laugh, they are a witch.

4. The Truth Test, whereby the accused is asked, "Are you a witch?" If they answer yes, they are a witch. If they answer no, they are trying to trick you into

thinking they're not a witch and are, therefore, a witch.

Two afternoons following the incident with the jumble, Willa stood on a castle balcony overlooking the city. She frowned at the market square below, where Ordinary Folk jostled one another for prime viewing position at the foot of the newly constructed Theater of Trials.

The theater was a hodgepodge of scraps salvaged from magic-damaged buildings—broken doors, wooden beams, window frames, and more. In the center was a throne dripping with blue velvet, where Prince Cyrus sat, inspecting his nails. Beside him, the clerk clutched a handful of forms and a feather pen. Willa was surprised to see Mr. Nibler's pig among the accused.

"How could a pig be a witch?"

"Could be a thingamajig," said Gish from beside Willa. "Like that purple toad thingy."

"Jumble," corrected Marceline. She was scowling at the prince, a look that said, *I find you more disagreeable than dog poo on the sole of my shoe.*

Willa had told everyone about the jumble over lunch yesterday, but the prince had scoffed.

"You probably made it yourself. Looking for attention as always."

Ferula had said nothing, fingers toying with the bone bracelet around her wrist. Gaspard had eyed the witch nervously, plastering on a reassuring smile when Willa caught his eye. "I'm sure it's nothing to worry about," he'd said.

"Look!" Gish pointed. "The trial is starting."

Willa was sick to her stomach as the crowd chanted "witch, witch, witch" while the accused were led to the front of the stage. How could the prince do this to his own citizens?

The trial was a mess. Every accused failed the Circle Test, splattering their lunch all over the front row of spectators. The duck ignored the accused and instead quacked at several people in the crowd (who were led away kicking and screaming and covered in vomit). Four cats ran onto the stage and bit the prince's ankles. One accused laughed so hard while being tickled she kicked a guard in the shins. And when it came time for the pig to answer the Truth Test, he merely oinked and ate the clerk's pen.

The clerk frowned at the prince, clutching her Failure to Pass the Four Ordinary Tests of Witch and Witchlike Behavior forms. "I'm not sure which box to check, Your Highness," she said in a harsh whisper. "The pig hasn't said yes *or* no. I don't have a box for *oink*. And now I don't have a pen."

"Of *course* he didn't answer!" The prince rubbed his ankles. "A non-answer is just as suspicious as an answer. In fact, it's *more* suspicious. The pig is definitely a witch. Take them all away!"

"What a farce," scoffed Marceline. "He's out of control."

But as the guards led the accused witches — pig and all — from the stage, something strange happened.

Willa heard a pop. It sounded like a balloon bursting. Then it happened again. And again. Three distinct pops.

I've heard that sound before, thought Willa. Dread made her skin prickle with goose bumps.

A flash of green—a sickly yellowy green—caught Willa's eye. What she saw was long and thin like a rope, but it glowed and sizzled like lightning. It hissed *Cabbity goompity bibyobobit toompity-jip* over and over as it slithered out from behind an apple cart to weave around the ankles of the nearest person. The glowing, hissing rope snaked up the man's leg, all the way to his head, before it vanished. On the other side of the market Willa spied another flash of sickly yellowy green, then one more on the theater stage, another rope wrapping around a guard's ankles.

Oh no, thought Willa. She had seen this before. It was just like the master weaver, right before his voice was—

"Witch!" screamed a woman. She was beside the apple-cart man; he had keeled over, clutching his throat as a glimmering golden bubble shot from his mouth. "My Henry's had his voice stolen!"

Fear rippled through the crowd, a rumble of gasps and murmurs. The sound was broken by another scream. From the opposite side of the market a man shouted, "Miss Pickwick, too! Someone stole Miss Pickwick's voice!"

Onstage, the clerk dropped all her forms. "That guard has lost his voice too!" she cried, pointing wildly.

The guard had both hands wrapped around his throat, and

he coughed until his face was shiny red, but no sound came out, just another golden bubble.

Chaos erupted.

"We're under attack! We're all going to die!" the crowd screamed as they ran, pushing one another.

"Get me out of here!" The prince grabbed two guards by their shirts, shaking them. "Protect me, you fools!"

"Come on," said Gish. He backed away from the balcony's edge. "Before the spell comes for us."

But Willa couldn't move. What she'd seen didn't make sense.

How had the spell been cast? Why had it behaved so strangely? A rope? A hiss? Why did it *pop?*

"Come on!" said Gish, urgent this time.

Marceline tugged her spare sleeve.

Willa had no choice but to follow. And no choice but to wonder: *How?*

"No cackling is allowed," said the prince, counting off his additions to the Official List of Ordinary-like Conduct on his fingers. "Anyone seen standing within two feet of a cat is suspicious. Laughing too loudly is automatic grounds for a trial. Singing, humming, or talking to yourself is un-Ordinary-like. Hair cannot reach below your waist, but if you are bald, grow out your hair *at once*. Folk who eat broccoli without complaint are definitely witches in disguise."

He paced beside the clerk's hospital bed. The clerk scribbled down each item with her newly procured feather pen while the royal healer tended to a weeping gash on her forehead.

The patient wing of the hospital was a large circular room with beds placed around the outer wall like the points of a clock. Every bed was occupied and more were needed. The stampede had resulted in countless injuries, not to mention the three stolen voices.

So there really is *a rogue witch targeting Ordinary Folk,* thought Willa, watching the chaos unfold around her. *But why?*

"See to it that the updated Official List of Ordinary-like Conduct is distributed around the city, Florestine," said the prince. He turned and waggled his finger at the injured Ordinary Folk around him. "Be warned!" he cried. "All you witches in disguise can't run from me. And as for the rest of you? Stay vigilant. Anyone could be the rogue witch. Even your mother. Your father. Even *you*." He pointed at a man holding his wife's hand; the wife was nursing a broken arm. "Actually, you *do* look like a witch," said the prince. He waved at the nearest guards. "Guards? Take that man in for questioning."

As the gentleman was dragged kicking and screaming from the hospital, the prince approached Gaspard and Willa. His entourage chased after him like baby ducklings.

Gaspard and Willa had attempted to stay out of the way by hovering just outside the healer's office. Gaspard had clearly been roused from an afternoon nap. He wore silk pajamas and one bed sock. It seemed as if everyone had been dragged to the hospital to help. Even Eladar and Ferula were there—on opposite sides of the room—along with Marceline, Gish, all the lords and ladies, every healer and apprentice, *everyone.*

"What are you still doing in bed, Florestine?" snapped the prince. "I need you to dictate what the girl says."

The clerk stumbled from her bed, trailing blood and gauze and an angry Healer Berwig.

"Right." The prince folded his arms and looked down his pointy nose at Willa. "The girl thinks she saw something helpful? I doubt it—when has a witch ever been helpful? But go on, I guess."

Willa swallowed down her fear—and annoyance—when all eyes landed on her. Gaspard urged her on with a nod. "Well, at first it wasn't what I saw but what I heard," she explained. "I heard a pop."

"A pop?" said the clerk.

Willa nodded. "Like a balloon bursting. And then I saw a glowing, sparkling rope."

"A rope?" The prince glared at her dubiously. "Not a cloud? Not lightning in the shape of words?"

"What color rope?" asked the healer.

"A sickly yellowy green," said Willa.

The healer's hands stilled.

"A sickly yellowy green?" repeated Gaspard, voice pitched oddly high.

Willa nodded.

Gaspard cleared his throat, sending a smile sweeping across the group, the kind of smile that said, *Don't panic! Everything is fine! Don't panic!* "Go on," he said to Willa.

Nerves fluttered in her belly. "The glowing, sparkling rope appeared out of nowhere," she said, "and it was hissing, 'Cabbity goompity bibyobobit toompity-jip!' It wrapped around the nearest person and weaved up his body until it reached his head. Then it disappeared. I saw it happen three times, near the people who lost their voices."

The prince snorted. "Well. That was quite the story. Complete hogwash, of course." He smirked over his shoulder at his entourage. The lords and ladies chortled appropriately. He turned back to sneer at Willa. "Everyone knows that's not how magic is cast. It doesn't just pop out of nowhere. It doesn't hiss. It doesn't snake like a rope, sparkling or otherwise."

"Quite right!" said Gaspard, nodding and tugging at the hem of his pajama top.

"What a waste of paper," grumbled the clerk, who had diligently copied down all of Willa's words.

Willa flushed, indignant. "It's true!"

"*Pft!*" The clerk scrunched up the paper and tossed it over her shoulder.

"Actually," said Healer Berwig, "it's called a magical mousetrap. A rare skill only a handful of witches possess. Both covens have the ability: You cast a spell and freeze it in a bubble. Then you leave the bubble lying in wait, and when it's popped—triggered any number of ways, from a voice command to mere proximity—the spell escapes. *Boom!* Voice stolen!"

A bubble? The hairs on Willa's skin prickled.

"Like a booby trap?" said the prince. "So the city could be filled with magical mousetraps just waiting to be stepped on? And no way of knowing who set them?"

Everyone looked to Gaspard to confirm.

He tugged at the hem of his pajama top. "Um, er, well, I'm afraid it's true," he said. There were gasps. "But it's so rare that it never crossed my mind."

Rare, but not unheard of, thought Willa.

She had seen Ferula utter a spell only to capture it in a shiny, wobbly bubble and hide it outside her door. It meant she could cast a spell in advance and be somewhere else by the time it went off, giving her the perfect alibi.

A mousetrap. A rare skill. A rare skill that apparently the rogue witch also possessed . . .

With a gasp, Willa spun around to where Ferula had been standing, on the other side of the room, only moments ago. But the witch had vanished.

"Um, Mr. Renard?" she said.

"We'll comb every corner of the city and collect them all," said the prince.

Gaspard shook his head. "Not possible. They're invisible until you trigger them. Soon as you hear the pop, it's too late."

"Ridiculous!" wailed the prince. He stomped his foot. "Who allowed magic like that?"

"Who indeed?" agreed the royal entourage. "Such an outrage!"

"Mr. Renard?" Willa tried again. She tapped his shoulder.

"But that's not all," said the tutor, flapping her hand away. "I'm afraid . . . I mean, I believe—and I could be wrong because, honestly, it *should* be impossible—though I have heard of it once—or rather, not heard, exactly, but—"

"Spit it out, man!" snapped the prince.

"I believe the voice bubbles haven't come back because the curse is two Irontongue spells joined together to make one," he said in a rush. "It's *Cat-got-your-tongue!* but it's also *Keepings-off!*—a spell that refuses to give back stolen property. This means the caster can keep the voice bubble and do whatever they want with it."

"Impossible!" cried the clerk. "I've read *The Rules of Magic for Ordinary Folk* back to front—altering spells is inconceivable."

"Mr. Renard!" said Willa. She tugged on his arm.

"Not now, Willa." Her tutor wiped the sweat from his brow and plastered on a smile for the prince. "I'm afraid the evidence points to two merged spells, Your Highness. The *Cat-got-your-tongue!* spell is bright yellow, and *Keepings-off!* is a pale blue—mix them together and you get a sickly yellowy green. And the fact that it was a rope and not word lightning? A hiss and not a shout? The rogue witch has been meddling with spells."

Two spells in one? Joined together? Hadn't Rab claimed he could do such a thing? And hadn't Ferula stolen the book on Rab Culpepper?

And she could create mousetraps . . .

"Mr. Renard!" Willa tugged so hard on his arm he cried out in pain. "I know who—"

Willa was cut off by a scream. A tray of instruments went flying as a young apprentice stumbled back from the window, pointing.

"Mo-mo-mo—" stuttered the apprentice. "Mo-mo-monster!"

Willa turned toward where the apprentice was pointing. What she saw made her legs wobble.

Peering into the hospital window was a jumble. But it was nothing like the purple toad. This was a ginormous creature that loomed tall enough to be eye level with the third floor. It had a troll's head with eight spider's eyes — were those dragon scales, wings, and a snake tail Willa glimpsed too?

"Hello, little ants," growled the creature. "Which one of you will I eat first?"

The blood drained from Willa's face.

The jumble monster's voice belonged to the master weaver.

CHAPTER THIRTEEN

PEOPLE SCREAMED AND RAN for the door; the prince shoved his way to the head of the line. Where was Gish? And Marceline? Willa couldn't see them. Her heart thumped.

Suddenly Gaspard's hands were on her shoulders, guiding her back until she hit the wall. "Stay out of harm's way," he ordered. Then he ran to help the clerk, who had fallen over in the stampede.

Willa flinched as a crash sent glass flying everywhere. The jumble had punched through the windows with thick bear claws. "Who wants to play?" it said.

Eladar shot a *Tickle-me-now!* curse, but it bounced off the window frame and hit Gaspard, who bent over double, crying with laughter.

Willa spied Marceline weaving through the crowd toward her. But where was Gish?

"What are you going to do?" Marceline was breathless as she reached Willa's side.

"Do?" Didn't Marceline know Willa was terrible at magic? It was up to Eladar, a proper witch, to save them. "I don't—"

There! Gish was running toward them, pushing against the flow of traffic. Willa sagged in relief. But it was momentary.

Because the jumble monster reached through the broken window and knocked Gish sideways with a swipe of its giant claw. Gish landed butt-first on the floor with a yelp of pain.

"Heh-heh-heh!" laughed the jumble monster.

Willa made to rush toward Gish, but the jumble whipped its snake tail at her; the tail really *was* a snake, but at the tip was a rat's head. "Got you now!" sneered the rat in the master weaver's voice. Marceline stumbled back as the rat gnashed at her.

Jumping the tail like a skipping rope, Willa ran toward Gish and hauled him to his feet.

Marceline swatted the rat's head with a bedpan. "Take that!" she cried. *Plonk!* The bedpan hit the rat squarely on the nose, forcing it to retreat.

But it didn't retreat far. Instead it swerved to wrap around Gish's middle, ripping him from Willa's grip. She cried out, fear coursing through her. The rat laughed gleefully as Gish was pulled out the window and hoisted high into the air.

"Let me go!" yelped Gish, dangling upside down in the jumble's grip.

"Such a tasty meal I've caught!" said the jumble, and stomped away from the castle.

Gish!

Willa grabbed Marceline's hand and ran, escaping the hospital and racing through the castle. The fizzy, zizzy orange-soda feeling bubbled inside her. *Stay in your cage!* she warned it. *That's the only way I'll get the spells right and save Gish.*

Willa and Marceline burst through the castle doors and out into the soldiers' yard.

"I can't see it," cried Marceline. "Where did it—*argh!*"

From behind the stables, the jumble appeared. It unfurled ginormous eagle wings and launched into the air, then landed between the two girls and the castle doors. The girls skidded to a halt and screamed as the jumble scuttled toward them on eight giant spider legs.

"Help!" cried Gish. The jumble flung him side to side.

The soldiers' yard was ringed by a high stone wall; at the north end, an arched gateway led to the market square. With the castle cut off, this was their only way out, but they needed to get Gish first.

Marceline grabbed an armful of stones and began tossing them at the jumble's head. "Hey! Leave him alone!"

But Willa didn't have stones; she had magic.

It surged inside her, a roaring wave of fizz. It *wanted* to be let out; it *wanted* to be wild. But she closed her eyes and directed the magic back into the Rapscallion's Cage. *Stay there,* she warned it. The magic thrashed at the walls, desperate to break free.

Please work, please work, please work . . .

Willa planted her feet and lifted her arms above her head. She swayed side to side. She kicked out one leg, then the other. She stretched her hands in front and wiggled her fingers. She pictured the magic trickling from the cage—just enough, just the *teeniest* amount. It fizzed as it slid from the center of her chest to the tips of her fingers.

Three tiny red clouds burst from her fingertips. They whooshed through the air and — *bam!* — the *Daisy-vomit!* spell collided with the monster's chest.

Willa held her breath.

The jumble gripped its belly and coughed once, twice, three times before a single daisy spluttered from its lips and into its paw.

"Was that it?" cried Gish, dangling upside down from the jumble's tail.

Willa frowned at her hands. The spell had *almost* worked. Had she used too little power? Was that even possible?

The monster's nose began to twitch. "Ah, ah, ah," gasped the jumble.

"What's happening?" shouted Marceline.

"Ah, ah, AH!"

"I think it's allergic to flowers," said Willa, backing away.

All eight of the monster's eyes were scrunched tight; its mouth opened wide. "Ah, ah, ah . . . Ah-CHOO!"

The sneeze blasted through the air like a rocket and nearly knocked Willa off her feet. Worse still, a wave of bright green snot shot from the monster's nostrils in an arc. Green gunk dripped down Willa and Marceline.

"Yuck!" Marceline groaned.

The jumble monster sneezed again. More rocket-force snot shot through the soldiers' yard — *splat!* It sneezed again. Finally, it sneezed so hard, Gish was flung into the air. He sailed up, up, up—so high he was just a speck against the cloudless sky. And then he started to fall down, down, down.

He screamed, arms and legs flailing as he rocketed toward the cobblestones.

Willa's heart leapt into her throat.

"Do something!" cried Marceline.

Willa shouted, "Floompity libity-jig ab buggity-joop!" She poked out her tongue and wiggled it up and down four times.

Instead of a trickle, fizzy magic gushed through her; lightning strikes of purple and screeching words shot from her mouth as the *Float-like-a-feather!* spell hit Gish square on. For a moment he was frozen in the air; then suddenly he was floating gently, like a feather.

Willa pitched forward as relief whooshed through her. "I did it," she breathed. "I actually did it." She had cast a spell and it had gone to plan.

Mostly to plan.

Because this time the spell had worked *too* well. Gish was so featherlight he stayed hovering in the air.

"Is this supposed to happen?" he asked.

Before Willa could answer, the monster coughed up three more daisies, pouting at the snot-covered flowers in its hand. Its nose twitched. "Oh no! Not again."

This time the sneeze was so violent the jumble flew backwards, crashing into the yard wall with an almighty *crack!* It crumpled to the ground, out cold. The force of the sneeze blasted featherlight Gish through the air like a popped balloon.

"Help me!"

Willa and Marceline charged after Gish as he zipped one way, zapped another, and zoomed over the high stone wall and into the market square, where he crashed into a pyramid of hay bales outside the stables.

"Are you okay?" asked Willa, helping him to his feet.

Though he looked like he'd been dragged backwards through a hedge, he was grinning. "That was fun," he said, dusting himself off.

Marceline huffed. "At least *you* didn't get covered in snot."

Suddenly a table crashed to the cobblestones next to them. They all jumped back.

"What in the Wild?" Willa looked up and gasped.

There, by the vegetable stall, taunting the grocer, was a jumble with a dragon's head on a giant rat's body. In front of the baker's shop was a troll with tree stumps for legs and snakes for arms, throwing bread rolls at the Ordinary Folk, who ran away, screaming. Smashing through the stonemason's workshop was a giant spider with eight bear's legs and three sets of raven's wings. And there were more.

Seven jumbles in total.

The city was in chaos. Eladar was in the middle of it all, flinging spells this way and that, but there were too many jumbles for him to control.

"You! Little girl! Come here so I can eat you!" cried a jumble as it flew toward Willa. It had the head of a wolf and the body of an eagle, plus two extra spidery arms, each with dragon claws.

And it had Miss Pickwick's voice.

Gish dived behind an upturned cart and Marceline ducked behind a barrel. "Use magic, Willa!" she cried.

Willa flapped her arms and wiggled her hips. The magic raged against the walls of its cage, but Willa willed it to trickle out. A series of jade-green clouds spat from her fingertips and hit two jumbles and an unfortunate horse.

It was the *Freeze-frame!* curse, but it fizzled to a gentle *zzzz!* and only the jumbles' legs were fixed in place like a statue—the poor horse's, too. The jumbles waved their arms and wings frantically. The horse neighed.

Willa stomped her foot. "Why can't I get it right?"

Her magic hissed at her: *Let me out! Let me be wild!* But what if she hurt people? What if she *exploded?* Her head hurt—she didn't know what to do!

She spied a large ball of yarn rolling out of the milliner's shop. Of course! The *Snakes-alive!* curse! Willa spun in a circle, clockwise three times and counterclockwise two times. She wiggled to a crouch and then jumped in the air, waving her arms like a juggling frog. Her wild magic lashed at the Rapscallion's Cage so hard Willa worried she would topple over. *Not too much!* she begged, but her arms quivered as magic spewed out of her. This was not a babbling brook; it was a tidal wave! Orange clouds flew from her fingers, hitting the ball of yarn and erupting into a shower of pink sparkles.

The ball of yarn unspooled quickly, then slithered across the cobblestones. It wrapped itself around all five of the remaining jumbles, plus three broken tables, a bag of potatoes, and a cow. The yarn looped and looped and looped until the jumbles were cocooned in a knotted mess. A host of stolen voices cried out: "Free us! No fair! I haven't eaten anybody yet!"

"I did it!" cried Willa. She was out of breath and shaking with effort. Should casting magic be this hard?

But the spell hadn't finished. *More* yarn, tape, and ribbons slithered out of the milliner's shop, wrapping up anyone and anything they could find. Even Gish. Even Marceline.

"What do I do?" She couldn't cast the counter-curse without freeing the jumbles, too. The spell raged on and on until the entire city was wrapped up in threads, everybody and everything except for Willa (and an army of cats looking on with amusement). "Oh dear." Her shoulders slumped. She was the worst witch *ever*.

"Not to complain," said Gish—he was tied with Marceline around a lamppost—"but do you think you could magic us out of this?"

"This is *slightly* more trouble than I bargained for," agreed Marceline.

"I'm not sure what to do," Willa admitted. "If only I could smoosh spells together too," she muttered as she sprinted toward the milliner's shop. "Maybe then I'd know what to do."

When she reemerged from the shop, she was carrying a pair of scissors. She ran back to the lamppost and knelt, then snipped the thread from Gish's ankles to his neck.

Gish wriggled, and the snipped yarn fell to the ground.

"Much obliged to you, Willa Birdwhistle," he said. "You're a true friend."

Friend. The word still felt like popping candy on her tongue. She didn't mind being a terrible witch if she was a good friend. She blushed furiously but couldn't hide her smile. That is, until she heard the worst possible sound.

Pop!

"Oh no," said Willa. She knew that sound.

"What's going on?" Marceline struggled against the yarn still shackling her to the lamppost.

A glimmering rope, sickly yellowy green, slithered out from under the upturned cart and wrapped around Gish's ankles. It wasn't a ball of yarn cursed with *Snakes-alive!* It was so much worse.

"Look out!" cried Willa, but it was too late.

The rope weaved up Gish's body before it vanished and he began to cough violently. Out popped a balloon, with hundreds and hundreds of golden words dancing inside.

"Your voice!"

Gish's mouth was still open but he couldn't make a sound. He stretched on his tiptoes, fingertips brushing the underbelly as the bubble bobbed just out of reach. Then it floated away, riding the wind toward the Inner Circle wall.

"Don't let it escape!" cried Marceline.

Willa dashed after the bubble. Left, right, left again, right, right, straight ahead.

Soon she had cleared the Outer Circle and was being led

toward the Lonesome Fields. She pushed herself to keep running. She couldn't let Gish down.

She spied the bubble heading east toward the River Disappointment. She ran, arms outstretched, but the stolen voice was far out of reach. The wind picked up, pushing it farther away — if it landed in the river, it would wash downstream, and they'd lose Gish's voice forever.

Suddenly a golden lasso whizzed by her. It wrapped around the bubble, squeezing the middle.

"Don't let it pop!" cried Willa.

Behind her, Eladar danced in smooth, elongated movements as he wound the magical golden lasso around his wrist, guiding the bubble down.

When it was bobbing just above head height, Eladar passed the end of the lasso to Willa while he conjured a glass jar. He squeezed the voice bubble inside the jar, screwed on the lid, and handed it to Willa.

"Pretty," he said. "Is it yours?"

Willa shook her head. Her heart ached as she hugged the jar tightly; the golden words squished against the side of the glass as if trying to hug back.

Oh, Gish.

CHAPTER FOURTEEN

THE CITY WAS IN RUINS: splintered wood and cracked bricks everywhere. Threads of colorful yarn dangled from awnings and lampposts; it had taken three hours and a hundred pairs of scissors to free everyone.

Now the citizens of Bad Faith gathered in front of the Theater of Trials, their clothes littered with fluff, their skin red with crisscross burns from the cursed threads that had squeezed so tightly around them. Their fear was palpable: the air sizzled with it.

Finally, the prince stepped onto the stage. "We're under attack!" he screeched. "This is war!"

Willa leaned against the fishmonger's shop and sighed. "Marvelous work!" Gaspard had said. "Not the, eh, destruction and all that jazz. But the spell work is brilliant! A touch too much power, of course. Golly, is that a horse tied to a lamppost?"

If magic was so marvelous, wondered Willa bitterly, then why did she feel so rotten?

She thought of Gish in the castle, slumped in a hospital bed, hugging the jar filled with golden words.

Ah, yes, that's why.

"Cheer up," said Marceline, hands cupped around her eyes

as she peered through the window into the fishmonger's store. A sign on the door read **BACK SOON!**, but they'd been waiting forever for the fishmonger's return. "We'll find her."

Her was Ferula.

The rogue witch.

After the jumble attack, Willa had finally been able to tell everyone what she knew about Ferula. "Why didn't you tell us sooner?" the clerk had scolded. The prince hadn't waited for Willa's answer, screaming, "Guards! Find me Ferula Crowspit! Now!"

But the guards had not been able to find her: Ferula Crowspit was missing.

Which meant no counter-curse for those who had lost their voices until she was found.

If she was found.

The prince paced the stage, yelling about war and magic and revenge. Willa pressed her lips into a tight sash. The familiar fizzy, zizzy orange-soda feeling churned deep within her. *Behave!* she warned it. The magic hissed but did as it was told. The more she stamped it down, however, the harder it fought to break free. Taming her magic was *exhausting*.

Marceline nudged her shoulder. "Don't worry about *him*," she said with a nod toward the stage. "Cyrus has been a pompous gobermouch since the day he was born. It's because of what happened to our mother."

Willa blinked. "*Our* mother?"

"Unfortunately, yes," said Marceline. "Cyrus is my brother."

"You're a *princess*?"

"Technically, yes," huffed Marceline, "but I don't like to go on about it. I don't fancy anyone knowing I'm related to *those* two walnuts. Cyrus is a bully and Father is . . . well, he can't help it, I suppose. He witnessed what happened to Mother."

"What happened?"

"Witches." Marceline sighed. "I was just a baby, but Cyrus and Father witnessed a wayward curse hitting her. An *Inside-out!* curse, do you know it?"

Willa shook her head.

"I'm sure you can guess what it does." Marceline frowned. "It is . . . unpleasant."

Willa remembered too vividly watching her own parents turn into clouds. She thought the prince was a horrid bully, but she *did* feel sorry for him — and no wonder the king fainted at the merest mention of magic.

"I'm sorry," she said. The words felt insignificant — two small words to take away such a thundercloud of pain? Impossible! "You must hate *all* witches."

Marceline scoffed. "If I hated *all* witches because of the actions of *one,* that would make me no better than my brother. I'll be very cross if you think I'm anything like him," she said. "Some witches are nice." She flicked her gaze sideways at Willa. "*Some* witches let me go on adventures."

Adventures that steal voices, thought Willa miserably.

"Out of the way," snapped the fishmonger. The little bell above his door went *dingle-dongle* as it opened. "Some of us have work to do." He ripped off the **BACK SOON!** sign before— *bang!*—the door slammed behind him.

"Excuse me," called Willa. She hurried after him but came to an abrupt stop just inside the door; her toes curled in her shoes.

Bouquets of dead fish dangled from the ceiling, suspended on large silver hooks. Buckets and barrels and baskets littered the shop floor, filled with fish gunk—tails, scales, and squidgy pink innards that made Willa's stomach heave. The stench made her see stars.

"Come on," said Marceline, tugging Willa's arm.

They followed the fishmonger to the back of the shop, passing two white cats sneaking into a basket of fish heads.

"We've been waiting for you," said Willa.

"I'm a busy man!" said the fishmonger. "Quick, quick! Tell me what you want?"

Willa was distracted by a fish tank in the middle of the table. Inside was a round, spiky fish with puffy lips that went *pop-pop-pop* at Willa in surprise.

"That's Frank," explained the fishmonger with a sneer. "Frank the Finger Eater. He bites the fingers off little girls who waste my time."

Willa took a quick step back. "Um. We need two pounds of fish eyeballs and one pound of fish scales and . . ." She checked her note. The healer had handwriting like a spider that had fallen into an inkpot and then tap-danced across the page. "Five catfi—"

"Say, aren't you that witch?" The fishmonger stumbled backwards. "The one who tied up the city in knots?"

Willa sighed.

She'd been sent to fetch ingredients for the potions Gish needed—throat-relaxing and stomach-settling and sleep-inducing. There were so many cases of stolen voices now that the healer had run out of stock. Willa had jumped at the chance to escape. The castle was *suffocating*. Everybody stared at her, awed by her powers, afraid of what she'd do next.

But it was no different out in the city.

She had tried to help, and now people feared her *more*.

Marceline marched forward. "Willa saved the city from a jumble attack," she said. "You should be saying thank you."

The fishmonger stumbled back another step. "Th-th-thank you?"

Willa took a deep breath. "Two pounds of fish eyeballs, one pound of fish scales, and five catfish whiskers," she repeated. "Please."

The fishmonger gaped at her for a long while. Eventually, he nodded. "Just don't try any funny business. Frank the Finger Eater has got his eye on you. What do you need all that for, anyway? Not spells, is it?"

Marceline jutted out her chin. "Official royal business."

Willa wondered how she'd never realized the young librarian was related to the prince.

The fishmonger quickly prepared their order. Willa noticed another tank behind him. This one was full of minnows, tiny silvery creatures swimming around and around in an unbroken dance. Like little golden words swimming around a glass jar . . .

Gish.

Willa couldn't wash away the memory of him clutching the glass jar tightly, a small lump under starchy white hospital sheets with a trembling lip and damp eyes that glistened like jewels. She'd hoped to outrun the memory, but it had followed her, sticking close like a shadow. And no one could outrun their shadow.

Willa had tried.

"That's the last of my eyeballs," said the fishmonger, handing over a bag that was damp and squelchy. "Now scram! Before I set Frank on you."

As tempting as it was to curse his hair green, Willa walked away.

Outside the shop, it had grown quiet. The stage was empty and the crowd had scattered. Stragglers scratched at their crisscross burns and whispered.

"At least with Ferula Crowspit suspected, we can stop the trials. It's all gotten a bit . . . nasty, hasn't it?"

"They arrested my neighbor!"

"They took away my cat!"

"They haven't released anyone."

"Oh, that Prince Cyrus is a blundering buffoon!"

"Hush! Don't you know 'speaking ill of the royal family' is now first on the list of witchlike behaviors? It's automatic grounds for a trial."

Willa was thoughtful as she walked, eyes skittering to her shadow every now and then. Something had to be done; this time she couldn't run away from her problems.

Gaspard was looking for a cure, and the royal guards were searching high and low for Ferula, but that wasn't enough. Willa needed to help too. Gish was her friend.

She turned to Marceline. "What do you do when you need to find a witch who doesn't wish to be found?" she asked.

Marceline screwed up her face in thought. "You see a witch expert?" she suggested.

Willa nodded her head. "Just what I thought."

Gaspard's desk was piled high with books. There was a common theme: *Ibbity Jiggity Joop: A Comprehensive Dictionary of the Most Dangerous Language in Existence. Unpleasant and Traitorous: The Horrifying History of the Irontongue Coven. Irontongues: Why Are They So Awful?* Were there any nice books about Irontongues?

Willa's extra sleeves flapped as she hurried into the classroom. Her tutor was hunched over an open book at his desk.

Cold tea, crinkled pajamas, purple smudges under his eyes: he had not made it down for breakfast this morning.

"Have you been here all night?" Willa sat in her usual chair.

Gaspard scrubbed a hand over his face. "I think," he said before he broke off to yawn, "so. Honestly, it's hard to keep track of time. The prince has me looking for a cure, but . . ." He shook his head. "Let's not talk about such maudlin things. Not when we have your successes to celebrate." He pushed back from his desk and grinned. "You cast your first proper spell! Silverclaw, no less—that one-on-one lesson with Eladar worked a treat. How did it feel?"

Willa chewed on her thoughts a moment. "It felt like trying to hold back a tidal wave with a sieve," she answered. "Does spell casting always feel so uncomfortable?" She thought of all the times her magic had flowed free and wild, even without her realizing it—turning her sprouts into chocolate cake had felt *good*. Until her parents had scolded her for being a trouble-maker, of course. But even though she knew what was right, her magic fought tooth and nail against it. Sometimes Willa thought she was too much like a cat. There was no telling a cat what to do, and Willa's magic was the same.

"The discomfort will pass," said Gaspard with a flap-flap of his hand. "Takes time to adjust."

He walked his swivel chair over to Willa, resting his teacup on his knee. His smile was kind, but up close the purple bruises were deep and puffy. "You remember what happens when you *don't* control yourself, right?"

Willa nodded. *Vast wastelands of evil were formed after you exploded.*

"But if Ferula is using new spells and—"

"Oh dear, no!" Gaspard shook his head. "They aren't *new* spells. She's still using Irontongue magic, just with a little twist. No one can invent entirely new spells."

"But—"

"There are rules governing magic for a reason, Willa." He gave Willa's knee a pat. "It's always better to follow the rules. Unlike Ferula, who broke the truce *and* attacked Ordinary Folk. I did try my best to warn you that Irontongue is horri—*bah!*" He smacked his lips. "I mean they are truly—*gah!* Oh, this silly contract! All I'm trying to say is Irontongue is—*hmm-mm-hm! Mmm!* Oh dear!"

Willa shrugged. "It's not—"

"I only wish I could have done more, but this blasted contract," he rushed to add. He worried his fingers through his hair. "At least now you can see—"

"Actually," said Willa. She rolled back her shoulders and opened her workbook—after all, she had a plan. "I'd like to know more about Irontongue."

"More?" Gaspard knocked over his tea in shock, spilling it all over his trousers. "Blast! Even after—Well! That's certainly *interesting.*" His smile was strained.

"For instance," continued Willa, unperturbed. "Favorite flavor of cake, favorite type of spider, do they prefer summer or winter, where would they hide if they were playing hide-and-seek or, say, running from the law?" She cleared her throat. "Favorite color, hobbies, and so on."

Gaspard blinked several times, his smile frozen on his face.

"Eh," he said, then blinked some more. "You *have* read *The ABC of Witches!* entry for *W* by now, haven't you?"

Willa shook her head.

"I do wish you'd read it. It's, eh, very enlightening."

Willa nodded. "Favorite flavor of cake?" she prompted him. He was the witch expert, after all, and Willa needed expert answers.

With a strained smile, Gaspard suggested that an Iron-tongue's favorite flavor of cake was probably mud (actual mud, not chocolate) and that their favorite type of spider would be "hairy" and "venomous," and that they would absolutely prefer winter over summer and their favorite color was either black or green. "The sickly, vomity kind of green," he added.

"And where would they hide?" asked Willa, pen poised over her notebook, her face the picture of innocence. "If I joined Irontongue and was invited to play hide-and-seek, where would I look first?"

"Well, they live in caves and holes—anywhere that's dark, damp, and dingy. So I'd look in places like that. In dungeons, cupboards, pits, underground tunnels, that sort of thing."

Willa nodded, taking notes. "And if you had to convince an Irontongue witch to do something," she asked, "something they really, really didn't want to do — such as never spitting again or smiling at a Silverclaw witch or undoing a spell they cast or saying please and thank you — how would you go about it?"

"These are oddly specific questions."

Willa held Gaspard's gaze. "I'm just curious," she said. "In case I choose Irontongue."

He stroked his chin. "Well, Irontongue witches are naturally selfish. And corrupt. So you'd have to offer them something in exchange. A bribe of sorts."

Give them what they want, thought Willa. Just like offering socks to *The Long and Thoroughly Ordinary Tales of Pearl B. Purcep, an Explorer of Little Note.*

Willa looked down at her page of scribbled notes. "But what does an Irontongue witch want more than anything?"

Gaspard frowned and bit his lips and tilted his head side to side as he juggled answers in his head. He walked back his chair, then spun it a few times as if trying to dislodge an idea.

It was five minutes before he answered.

"Power." He nodded. "Yes, that's it. Power."

Willa startled as though struck with a *Shock-me!* curse.

"Anything that will help them get ahead in the war," continued Gaspard, unaware of Willa's internal crisis. Because all at once she knew how to return the stolen voices.

Me.

I have to give her me.

CHAPTER FIFTEEN

S HE'S BALD! AND GREEN! And a witch!" screeched
the prince. "How is she still *missing?*"

The Royal Guard had begun tiptoeing around the castle,
scattering like cockroaches at any sign of the prince. One poor
guard, a lanky girl with big red freckles, hadn't been quick
enough.

"W-w-we've looked e-e-everywhere, Your Highness."

"Clearly," said the prince, every syllable dragged through
clenched teeth as he bore down on the guard, "you haven't. Keep
searching. I want that witch weeping in the dungeon by noon!"

The guard nodded and ran.

Willa followed the prince into the breakfast room, where
the air buzzed with gossip.

"I heard the cats ate her!"

"I heard she blew herself up practicing unpleasant-level
spells!"

"I heard she's roaming the southlands, eating children!"

"I heard the ants gossiping about the spiders," tittered Eladar as he swept into the room and he plonked himself at the
head of the table before the prince could get there. "I do not
care for their opinions on hairy legs." He burped, ignoring the
prince's indignant splutters.

The clerk cleared her throat and leaned forward. "No one has seen hide nor tail of her! Which form do I fill in? Notice of Suspected Witchnapping or Notice of Suspected Magical Mishap, Subsection F: Self-Combustion?"

"No one cares about your silly forms, Florestine," huffed the prince. He sat, nose in the air, halfway down the table. "I just want that witch found. How dare she terrorize *my* citizens!"

Willa frowned at the spot where Gish normally stood, behind the clerk's chair, making silly faces and grinning. But it was empty.

She slumped in her usual chair at the far end of the table, surprised when Marceline sat primly in the adjacent seat — usually she sat all the way up the other end.

Marceline smiled; Willa smiled back.

Together they had looked for Ferula in every dank, dark hole in the city. All they'd found were mud and spiders and cobwebs. Three days and not a single clue.

Marceline slid the toast in front of Willa before the prince could snap it up.

"If only we could sneak into her room," whispered Marceline. "I bet there's all sorts of clues there."

But Ferula's bedroom door had been rigged with magical mousetraps (some of which turned your clothes into bubble gum and flung you to the ceiling, as two unfortunate guards had discovered).

But if they *could* find a way in and there *were* clues, then . . . Willa pushed her plate away; she had suddenly lost her appetite.

How bittersweet, to have the means to save a friend but only by leaving his side forever. It seemed Willa Birdwhistle was destined to be lonely all her life.

Willa turned to Gaspard, on her other side, who was half-asleep and unaware he was buttering his tie and not his toast. She wanted to quiz him, but he wore his tiredness like a mountain on his back—he wasn't even smiling.

A sudden blast of trumpets startled the clerk; her knife and fork flew out of her hands. "The king? The king is *here?*"

A dull-looking man poked his head in the doorway. Was it King Teebald? Willa thought she'd have a better chance at recognizing him if he was hiding behind a potted plant. "Ran out of crumpets and I thought — *eep!*" He spied Eladar at the head of the table and jumped back.

"Sire! How delightful of you to grace us with your presence!" cried the royal entourage, pawing at him, dragging him into the room.

The king yelped and stumbled back until he was flush with the wall. "I'm not hungry. False alarm! I'd best be—eep!" He noticed Willa. "Two witches! Oh dear!" Sweat gathered at his temples. "I'll just—" He turned and made a run for the door.

Pop!

Everyone froze.

A glittering rope wrapped around the king's ankles, pinkish-purple instead of the usual sickly yellowy green. With eyes that boggled, the king watched it snake up to his chin before it vanished. Everyone held their breath; the king whimpered. But when he opened his mouth, it wasn't to cough up a voice bubble.

"I hate broccoli!" he shouted at the top of his lungs. "I scoop it off my plate and hide it in the potted plants!" He covered his mouth, but the words kept spilling out. "I'm terrified of witches! I stole one of the clerk's feather pens! I pick my nose and eat it!"

"Surely broccoli tastes better than snot?" whispered a lord.

"Prince Cyrus is scared of horses!" shouted the king.

"Do something!" hissed the prince. He glared at Eladar. "Make him stop! These are lies! All lies!"

But Eladar was too busy laughing to help.

Gaspard elbowed Willa. "Perhaps you ought to . . ." He nodded at the king. *"Zip-lip!* will do the job."

Thoughts of a city wrapped entirely in yarn flashed through Willa's mind. But she squished it down. *I can do this.*

She said, "Zibity-jig bobibit!" With a thumping heart, she licked her lips once in a clockwise direction, then three times counterclockwise. She fizzled all over.

The king howled in fright as the lemon-yellow word lightning of the *Zip-lip!* curse flew from Willa's mouth. His lips were instantly turned into a small zip that didn't quite do all the way up.

"I . . . bath . . . smell . . . never . . ." muttered the king.

"Not bad," said Gaspard. "Power levels still a bit wonky, though, eh?"

Willa tried to open her mouth but she couldn't. She was

suddenly on *fire*. It burned from the tips of her toes to the ends of her hair. What was happening? The air in her lungs evaporated—*poof!*—replaced by smoke and ash.

"Willa?" Gaspard grabbed her wrist. "Oh dear, you're burning up! Are you all right?"

Marceline handed her water, which Willa greedily gulped down.

As suddenly as it had arrived, the burning sensation passed. Willa sucked in air. She could move again, breathe, speak. "I'm . . ." she started, but her words had burned away.

Was that what it felt like . . . to explode?

"Ignore her!" shouted the prince. "She's attention-seeking again. Someone tell me what just happened." No one in the room dared move. "Why did my father do . . . *that?*"

"Butter . . . rub . . . feet . . . skate," said the king.

"It's a different spell from last time," said Gaspard. He addressed the prince but kept a concerned eye on Willa. She felt . . . fine. Had she imagined it? "Perhaps a version of the *Secret-spilling!* curse," he continued. "Not sure how it's been modified, but the rope thingy was pinkish-purple, so something's not right."

"A *different* spell?" screeched the prince. "We haven't fixed the last one yet! I want a full investigation." He gestured for two guards to take the still-mumbling king away. "And I want you all to know what my father said about me was a lie. I am not afraid of anything."

"Willa?" Marceline handed her another glass of water. Concern made her voice soft. "Are you okay?"

"I'm fine," said Willa. She frowned at her hands. "I'm fine."

Three more secret-spilling mousetraps were triggered before the breakfast dishes had been cleared away. A guard suddenly shouted about stealing his neighbor's apples, a carpenter blurted out his love for Mary-Ellen, and the head cook revealed she picked the king's broccoli out of the potted plants and reused it in soup.

How was Ferula setting up new traps, yet no one had seen her?

Gaspard bustled Willa out of the breakfast room and announced it was National Taking It Easy Day. "A day for witches to relax and absolutely definitely *not* explode," he explained.

"But I'm fine," argued Willa. She'd crawled through sewers searching for Ferula — no doubt she'd picked up a bug. A very strange bug.

Gaspard held his palm to her forehead. "Headaches? Stomachaches? Shortness of breath? A feeling of impending doom?"

"Mr. Renard!"

"It's just that it's not entirely . . . *traditional* for an untamed witch to feel like she's on fire after casting a spell," he said. "Eat cake, Willa. Have a nap. Read a book. Relax." He waved goodbye and hurried away, muttering about "tricky spells" and "unreasonable princes."

"*You* need a National Taking It Easy Day," Willa grumbled at his retreating back. But at least she now had time to visit Gish.

The first thing Willa saw in the hospital wing was the king tucked up in bed surrounded by guards wearing earmuffs.

"I'm terrified of bees!" he cried. The *Zip-lip!* curse had worn off, but not his need to spill secrets. "Eep!" He drew the sheets over his head at the sight of Willa.

Willa hurried past and found Gish sitting up in bed picking listlessly at the plate of food in his lap. Talon was asleep at his feet, and seven more cats were perched outside the window, blinking their sleepy eyes. The prince had decreed the castle a "feline-free zone," but Willa's cats clearly had their own ideas.

"How are you?" She placed a large slice of chocolate cake and her reading book on the bedside table. They sat next to the glass jar holding Gish's voice; the golden words inside swirled sluggishly as if half-asleep.

Gish reached for a pen and pad of paper.

Bored, he wrote. *But better now that you're here. Is that cake?*

She pulled the curtain around his bed in an attempt to block out the king's rambling, and together they ate the cake while Willa read aloud from *The ABC of Witches!* She was going to make the most of whatever time they had left together. Before she joined Irontongue and had to live in a cave and eat worms and fight in a war.

"*T* is for *transport!*'" read Willa. "'Did you know that witches can fly short distances and always land on their feet, like cats? Takes practice but is a handy skill to master. For longer distances, Silverclaw witches prefer riding specially trained wolves, and for entertainment Irontongue witches enjoy racing dragons (even though it quite often ends in death).'"

You can fly? wrote Gish.

"If I practice, I guess I can," she said with a shiver of excitement. Flying? That was a silver lining to being a witch, for sure. "Don't tell Marceline it's possible to ride a dragon," she added. Gish laughed—no sound, of course, but his shoulders shook like jelly. The sight warmed Willa's heart.

She kept reading: *U* was for *undergarments* and *V* was for *voice*. And it turned out that *W* was for *war*.

Did you know that once upon a time there was no such thing as a Silverclaw or an Irontongue? Witches were witches and Ordinary Folk were Ordinary Folk and they all lived together in one (not-so) happy kingdom. You see, King Moloch (the Forever King!) had discovered a way to inhibit magical output, and anyone proven to be a witch was punished severely.

The flogging and rough music got to be a bit much for one witch. In retaliation, she kidnapped an Ordinary man and cut him into pieces. She joined him back together again all mixed up with bits of crocodile and raven: the very first jumble!

Other witches were horrified. "You can't do that!" they cried. "You've gone too far!"

But some witches were pleased. "Ordinary Folk are lower than worms!" they said. "We should squash them under our thumbs and rule this land!"

By this time, Queen Arabella II ruled the throne, and the mysterious thingamajig that restrained magic had up and vanished (no one knows where it went or even what it was). That's when the fighting began. The war separated the witches into two covens—those with malicious intent were called the Irontongues, and those who wanted peace and harmony were called the Silverclaws. And the fighting has never stopped . . .

Gaspard was right, thought Willa, shaking her head. *That entry is enlightening.* She hardly needed more proof that Irontongue witches were bad news, but here it was in black and white. No wonder Gaspard couldn't talk about the war without the contract zipping his lips.

And this was the clan she would be joining . . .

She swallowed over the lump in her throat and looked down. There were now *two* books in her lap: *The ABC of Witches!* And *You're a Horrible No-Good Witch* by Eve Rybody.

"That's not nice." She frowned. The new book was thick—you wouldn't want to drop it on your toe—and bound in sludge-green leather. The cover depicted Willa picking her nose and eating it. "That's not nice at all!"

She opened the book to a random page. There was only one line: It's true. You're horrible.

"How rude!"

The book leapt out of her hands and landed upright on the bedside table. Gish scooped up his voice jar before the book could knock it off.

"How did—"

The book spun a full circle. Suddenly it was no longer sludge-green, nor was it called *You're a Horrible No-Good Witch* by Eve Rybody. The title now read in large block letters: *The Long and Thoroughly Ordinary Tales of Pearl B. Purcep, an Explorer of Little Note.*

"You!" Willa leapt to her feet, spilling *The ABC of Witches!* to the floor.

The book balanced on one of its corners and began to pirouette. Around and around it spun before its pages flung open and out shot balls of paper, firing at Willa and Gish.

"Stop it!" But the book did not let up.

Willa and Gish crawled under the bed with Talon. The cats on the windowsill swished their tails.

"I guess it's still mad at me for trying to trap it," said Willa. Talon winked at her.

"I'm sorry!" she called out. "I only wanted to know more about Rab Culpepper."

All at once the snowstorm stopped. Willa peeked out from under the bed: the floor was littered with paper balls.

She looked at Gish, but all he could do was shrug.

Carefully, Willa slid out from her hiding place.

The cursed book had vanished. Gish stayed under the bed,

only his head peeking out. Willa looked down at the papers scattered at her feet. She couldn't help but wonder . . .

She crouched and picked up one, carefully prying it open. There was only one line written in the very center of the page: Not this one.

Willa gritted her teeth and reached for another page.

Not this one either, it said.

With a sigh, Willa set about opening every last ball of scrunched-up paper.

Nope.

Not this one.

Not even close.

Actually . . .

A little closer this time.

Whoops! Cold again.

Very cold.

Freezing.

Brrrr!

Not quite as freezing.

A little warmer.

Warmer.

Getting toasty.

So hot!

Boiling!

Aren't your fingers burning?

Willa opened the last paper. Her fingers trembled with anticipation.

But the paper read: Hahaha! Got you! Cold again! Freezing! Brrrr! (Tricked you, didn't I? You really are a terrible witch!)

She screwed up the paper and tossed it aside in anger. The book reappeared above her, balanced on the curtain rail. "Really, you're quite awful," Willa snapped as it danced up and down the rail in glee. "I don't know why you—"

Pop!

The book had danced all the way into a mousetrap. A pinkish-purple glittering rope wrapped three times around the cover before vanishing. The book teetered side to side and then spat out one more piece of paper; it landed in Willa's waiting hands.

This scrunched-up ball of paper was smaller than the rest, creamier in color, stained with large tea rings, and filled with scratchy handwriting she had encountered once before.

no other explanation. Not only does he think he's exempt from choosing a coven, but now he also says there are three, not two, forms of magic. Three! Silverclaw, Irontongue, and another, which he says is a secret. "And where did you learn such a thing?" says I. "In the library, of course," says he. "Just ask the ghosts. The ghosts know everything." The ghosts know? Hogwash! I have no choice but to inform the king that

"The ghosts?" said Willa. Gish crawled out from under the bed and read over her shoulder. "The same ghosts I knotted up in ribbons?"

Gish quickly scribbled something down. *Has to be true because the book was hit with the secret-spilling curse.*

Willa read the diary entry again, frowning. *Three* forms of magic? Not just modified coven spells, but an entirely new magical system that had nothing to do with either coven? Was it possible? Willa sure hoped so.

When she looked up, the book had vanished. "I guess we should go ask the ghosts if—"

The loudest *pop!* yet rocked the entire hospital wing.

The king cried out in terror. "I only change my underwear once a week!"

Screams erupted outside the hospital—something terrible was happening in the market square.

Gish and Willa ran to the windows and looked out.

Hundreds of pinkish-purple glittering ropes, all woven together to make a giant blanket, had settled over the square. The blanket shimmered for a moment before it vanished. All at once, people were bent over double, coughing and spluttering.

"This can't be good," said Willa.

She rushed out of the hospital and through the castle, Gish chasing her heels.

By the time they reached the market square, folk had begun to shout their secrets.

"I've got stinky feet!" shouted one gentleman. "I wear three pairs of socks to hide it."

"I stole eggs from my neighbor's chickens and blamed it on the dog!" shouted a young woman.

The woman beside her turned to face her with a look of horror: "I knew it! My husband sold that dog because he wouldn't stop eating our eggs. My daughter cried for weeks!"

On and on people shouted, spilling their secrets like milk.

"I stole fish eyes from the fishmonger and put them in my little sister's bed!"

"I threw eggs at Mr. Nibler's house and blamed it on witches!"

"Listen to *me!*" shouted the prince from the Theater of Trials. "Every time you ignore me, I cry myself to sleep." He clapped a hand over his mouth. "No I don't!" he said, quickly followed by "Yes I do!"

Marceline appeared in front of them, clutching her stomach as if about to be sick.

"Marceline?" Willa reached for her.

"I'm lonely and I want to be your friend," blurted the princess. Her skin turned a sickly shade of green.

Suddenly she keeled over. Gish and Willa watched in horror as everyone else in the market square turned green and keeled over too.

"Gah!" they cried. "Ah!" they groaned. "Wah!" they wailed, throwing their heads back. Plumes of green smoke poured from their open mouths and gathered high above the city like an angry rain cloud. On and on the moaning went, growing louder and louder and louder. The moaning reached a deafening crescendo before all at once it stopped.

"What in the Wild just happened?" asked the baker, hiccupping.

The green cloud above the city rumbled. It squirmed and shivered and rolled. It was about to burst.

"I do hope it's not frogs again," said Willa.

It wasn't frogs.

It was hail.

But not ordinary hail: fish eyes.

Glassy, beady, gooey fish eyes rained all over the citizens of Bad Faith and bounced through the streets.

Willa grabbed Gish and Marceline and ran to the nearest shop for shelter. The cloud rumbled again, louder and longer and—

This time it was broccoli.

The green florets pelted the streets, ricocheting off the heads of Ordinary Folk trying to escape the downpour. Broccoli and fish eyes, all their secrets raining down on the city of Bad Faith.

Because that's what it was—a storm made entirely of secrets.

From under the cloth merchant's awning, Willa, Gish, and Marceline could only watch and wait. A single fish eye rolled along the ground until it bumped against Willa's shoe.

"This is not good," said Willa as the cloud rumbled again. This time it poured stinky socks. "This is not good at all."

CHAPTER SIXTEEN

IT RAINED SNOT, BROCCOLI, EYEBALLS, and assorted gunk for a week.

"Best guess? It's a combination of *Spill-your-guts!* and *Storm's-a-rising!*" said Gaspard from beneath an umbrella. He and Willa stood at the castle entrance, watching the downpour. It was currently hailing soft-boiled rotten eggs.

"Ferula used a giant mousetrap," he added. "Very tricky spell work—brilliant, really." He shook his leg. "The fishmonger claims he saw a cloaked figure lurking in the square before the mousetrap burst. He says the figure in black released the spell and *then* stole his precious pet fish." Another egg landed—*splat!*—on the toe of Gaspard's shoe. "Er. Perhaps we should head inside."

Willa nodded and retreated into the castle with her tutor. But she wondered: Where was Ferula hiding? What spell would be next? Why was she doing this?

Willa had searched every dank, dark hole in the city. She'd tried talking to the library ghosts—but after waiting in section G for hours, none had appeared. She had tried *everything*.

Willa had so many questions but no answers.

The healer poked a silver, pointy thingamajig in Willa's ear. "And you say it feels like you're boiling from the inside out?"

Willa nodded and squirmed as the silver pointy thingamajig was suddenly shoved up her nose.

Gaspard had insisted on a visit to the hospital after a simple *Stitch-in-time!* curse had caused another overwhelming rush of fire through Willa's blood. "But I'm sure there's nothing to worry about," he'd said worriedly.

Willa had ended up in Healer Berwig's office, perched on a metal stool; every bed in the hospital was full.

Broccoli-soup rain lashed the windows, casting an eerie green glow throughout the room. The shelves were crowded with things that ought to have been in the supply room: bubbling potions and jars filled with teeth and fish scales and crickets and a familiar hairy spider.

"I'm not really going to . . . *explode,* am I?" asked Willa. She swung her legs nervously. "I'm not thirteen yet!"

The healer held a magnifying glass up to Willa's eye. "Seems unlikely."

Willa breathed a sigh of relief.

The healer drew back. The magnifying glass clanged as she dropped it on her tray of instruments. "Your Mr. Tutor says you can cast proper spells now."

"Sort of." If only she could get the power levels right.

The healer gave Willa a shrewd look. "How do you find taming your magic?"

"Strange," Willa admitted. "Uncomfortable. My mother

always said there was an imp in me that made me do naughty things—I didn't know it was magic. So it's hard to keep it locked away. It wants to misbehave."

The healer frowned but didn't say anything. She poked and prodded Willa for a while longer. "A perfect specimen of health," she declared as she dropped the last shiny, pointy, jabby thing-amajig on the tray. "Avoid spicy foods and hot baths. Take this cooling potion if you experience another episode. Three drops under the tongue." She thrust a squat bottle of green liquid into Willa's hands.

Willa hopped down from the stool. Through the open office door she spied Marceline waving madly at her from the hospital entrance. The princess had buried herself in research for the last three days. Perhaps she had found something.

Willa slipped the potion into one of her many pockets. "Thank you," she said, and turned to leave. But when she reached the door, the healer's voice stopped her in her tracks.

"You don't have an imp in you."

Slowly, Willa turned back. "Pardon?"

The healer fiddled with the instruments on the tray: *ping, clang, pong!* "Magic," she huffed. "It's not some naughty imp looking for trouble."

Willa frowned. "But I was always doing the wrong thing. I was *always* in trouble. My parents said—"

The healer snorted. "If a swan can't quack like a duck, is it the swan's fault?"

Willa opened her mouth but nothing came out. It was as if every thought in her head had been flipped upside down.

"Think about it," said the healer with a smirk. She shooed Willa out the door. "Now scram. I'm busy. See what your friend wants before *she* explodes." She slammed the door in Willa's face.

Willa was frozen to the spot. *If a swan can't quack like a duck, is it the swan's fault?* Swans didn't quack; they honked. Willa and her mother had fed the swans that lived on the River Disappointment once. A swan had snapped the bread out of her mother's hands while another had snapped the hat off her head. A third had splashed them with water. Mother had been furious.

"Finally!" Marceline grabbed Willa by a spare sleeve and dragged her from the hospital. "I've been waiting *ages*. I've got something to show you."

Marceline tugged them into an alcove and thrust a piece of parchment at Willa's chest.

Willa grabbed it. "What is it?"

"I was sitting at my desk in the library thinking, 'Wouldn't it be fabulous if there was a spell that could disarm mouse-traps?' And then Huggin knocked over a pile of books and this just fell out." She tapped her finger against the page: *"Pop-goes-the-mousetrap!"*

It *was* a spell. Yellowing parchment with handwriting that was somehow bursting with laughter — looping and messy and wild: Concerned about tricky mousetraps lying in wait to curse you? Never fear! The perfect spell to burst those nasty booby traps is here!

Surprise hit Willa like a bucket of ice water. This was exactly what they needed to break into Ferula's room! But it wasn't a Silverclaw or an Irontongue spell—neither clan had anything that could safely burst a mousetrap. So how was it possible? All spells came from *The Original Book of Spells,* as *The ABC of Witches!* had explained.

 is for *Original Witch.* Did you know that the Original Witch was the first ever Drearian born with magic and the only witch who could create spells? It was because of her very special book—*The Original Book of Spells.* As soon as she wrote in it, the spell would come to life. How fabulous!

Each new witch born in the Isle of Dreary learned their craft from the Original Witch. But after the war broke out, witches on both sides wanted the magical book for themselves—whoever had the power to invent spells could win the war. They fought, ripping the book in half. Oops! Suddenly, no more spells could be invented. And to make matters worse, each clan was limited to only casting spells from whichever half of the book had ended up in their hands.

Willa gripped the parchment until it crinkled. Was this a

modified spell, like the ones Ferula had been using? Or was it a *new* spell? Willa's heart thundered. Because if there really *was* more than Silverclaw and Irontongue, then . . .

Just as quickly as Willa's hope rose, it plummeted back to earth. Because it didn't matter: Willa had to join Irontongue. For Gish. After all, there was no way Ferula would cast the counter curse to the voice-stealing spell *without* enticement.

"We can finally explore Ferula's room for clues," said Marceline. She bounced on her toes. "So what are we waiting for?"

Willa forced herself to smile. "We're waiting for one more person," she said. "Come on."

Willa gripped the parchment tight as she tiptoed down the hallway, listening to the *thump, thump, thump* of her heart and the *tap, tap, tap* of Marceline's and Gish's footsteps following close. Gish had tucked his glass jar in the crook of his elbow — he'd refused to sneak out without it. Willa was just glad he was here. Friends made dangerous missions a little less frightening.

She was going to miss him; she was going to miss both of them.

"That one," whispered Marceline, pointing to a door at the end of the corridor. Talon was already sitting in front of the door, cleaning his ears.

"Talon! Get back! It's not safe!" hissed Willa, but the cat ignored her — he never did as he was told.

With a sigh, Willa crept as close as she dared before stopping to read over the spell's instructions again. It really was unlike any spell she had ever come across.

To cast the Pop-goes-the-mousetrap! spell, you must:

1. Wriggle like a monkey with a bee sting on its bottom.

2. Shout five words that rhyme with *gloop* followed by the words *Winklepicker diggle popsnoodle spaghetti fluggetty plink* (use a squeaky voice if you suspect there is more than one mousetrap nearby).

3. Think very hard about a hat made of cheese.

4. Point at the area where the mousetrap is hidden and wave your finger like you're scolding a naughty child.

5. And *poof!* just wait and see what happens!

Willa folded up the parchment and slid it into one of her pockets. *Thumpthumpthump* went her heart. "Here goes nothing."

Willa followed each step carefully, then held her breath, waiting. Instead of fizzing or zizzing, she shivered. It was a cool and pleasant feeling, like the first lick of an ice pop on a hot day. The magic seemed to glide through her—it had never felt so easy! There was no puffy cloud and no word lightning. There wasn't even a glittering rope. There was, however, a cat.

Talon flicked his tail at the glittery, silvery, translucent cat that appeared in the middle of the corridor. The cat leapt into the air, claws out. It swiped three times, and each time there was a gentle *fthzzz* as a hidden mousetrap was popped. The cat landed on the floor and vanished in the blink of an eye.

Talon's whiskers twitched.

"I think it worked," said Willa, stunned. Casting the spell had been a piece of cake. And she didn't even feel the slightest spark of heat after it.

She crept toward the door, but no mousetraps went off. She grinned. "It worked!"

Talon rubbed against Willa's shins as she rattled the handle; it wouldn't budge. She peered through the lock. "Cheese and rice! It's locked on the inside." She could see the key stuck in the other side. "And I haven't learned a spell for unlocking doors yet."

But if they could somehow push the key out of the lock, then Gish could open the door with his . . . Willa frowned at the belt loops on Gish's trousers. Each one was empty. *Shouldn't there be a large silver ring loaded with keys dangling from one of those loops?*

"The clerk gave him an Unavoidable Suspension of Duties Due to Magical Misfortune notice," explained Marceline, guessing the direction of Willa's thoughts. "And took his keys."

Gish's cheeks flushed.

"So we can't even get inside?" said Willa. "After all this trouble?"

"Luckily, I have an idea," said Marceline. She picked Huggin out of her pocket and whispered in his ear. She placed the mouse on the floor, where the small creature immediately squeezed through the gap under the door.

Marceline removed a pin from her messy bun and poked it through the lock. Willa heard a gentle *ping* as the key hit the stone floor on the other side. Soon Huggin squeezed back under the door with his tail hooked around a brass key.

"That's quite a trick for a sensible young librarian to know," said Willa.

Marceline scooped up the mouse and inserted the key into the lock; it clicked, and she turned to Willa with a smug grin. "I read about it in a book," she said.

Ferula's room was small and dark. There was an unlit candle, a straw mattress, a wall tapestry, a basin of water, and a perch for a crow. But there was no crow. And no Ferula.

Willa took a step inside and immediately heard a *pop!*

Oh.

Red ropes shot through the room like electrical whips: *Zing! Zap! Zip!*

When they vanished, a shrill voice cried out: "Get out! Trespassers! Filthy, fiendish, foul-hearted snoops! Get out, get out, GET OUT!"

"It's another mousetrap!" said Willa, but the screeching disembodied voice drowned her out.

Willa had an idea. She shouted, "Zibity-jig bobibit!" and licked her lips once in a clockwise direction, then three times counterclockwise. She clenched her jaw, struggling to ease the magic from the Rapscallion's Cage. *I knew you wouldn't behave for long,* thought Willa as the magic refused to glide easily this time. *Why must you be so contrary?*

Word lightning shot from her fingers and bounced around the room. Huggin dove into Marceline's nest of hair. But when the spell cleared, the voice was no longer screeching. "Mmm mmm mmmmm!" complained the disembodied voice. The *Zip-lip!* spell had worked! "Mmmmm mmmm mm mmm!"

Gish gave Willa a thumbs-up. Her cheeks flushed with warmth, pleased to be noticed. But the flush didn't stop there. Suddenly heat seeped through every part of her — *Oh no!* It was happening again. Willa pulled the healer's potion from her pocket. With shaking hands she placed three drops under her tongue. An icy sensation immediately swept through her and the fire drew back to a gentle, tingling warmth. She was breathing hard.

Gish tugged on her sleeve. *You okay?* he mouthed.

Willa nodded. But her hand still trembled as she tucked the potion back in her pocket. What was wrong with her? And why hadn't it happened when she'd cast the *Pop-goes-the-mousetrap!* curse?

"Look!" Marceline pointed to where something small and white lay on the floor in front of the wall tapestry: Ferula's bone bracelet.

Willa lifted the bracelet and inspected it. Bones and teeth. She shuddered.

"The bone bracelet is a symbol of the Irontongue witch's powers—the most powerful will have shards of dragon claws, and the least will have rats' teeth and chicken bones," explained Marceline. "An Irontongue witch would *never* go anywhere without their bone bracelet and would bite the hand off anyone who tried to take it from them."

Willa remembered how proud Ferula had been of the ghastly thing. Marceline was right—this was too important to Ferula for her to discard it like this.

She slipped the bracelet into her pocket and looked at the wall hanging. It was a giant White Devil dragon atop a smoking volcano. *I wonder . . .* thought Willa. Her fingers trembled as she reached for the tapestry, pulling it back to reveal . . .

"A secret door?" Marceline smacked her forehead with the palm of her hand. "If there's a secret door leading to a secret passage in my castle and no one told me about it, I'm going to have stern words with Father."

As Willa tugged it open, the door groaned like creaky old bones. Behind it was a gloomy passage ("I knew it!" cried Marceline). Candles suddenly lit up, nestled in sconces along the curved passage walls, but the shadows remained thick and impenetrable.

Willa took a steadying breath and stepped into the passageway. Talon trotted out in front; Gish and Marceline followed behind Willa. The ground sloped and spiraled down and down and down. The air was thick, like a choking fog.

The fire had fully subsided from her veins, but the worry had not. The healer had assured her she wouldn't explode, but worry was like a weed—it grew and grew and grew. She kept walking.

After a long while the passage leveled, but it did not end. It weaved for what felt like miles, twisting and turning. The air became so thick it was like breathing mush.

They finally came to a blackened old door. Slits of light shone through the cracked wood like tiny dancing fairies. Talon sat, waiting.

"Where do you think this leads?" whispered Willa.

Gish tugged his earlobe and shrugged.

"Only one way to find out," said Marceline.

Willa lifted the heavy bolt and pushed open the door.

Behind it was a narrow stone room. There were cages on chains hanging from the ceiling and cauldrons filled with viscous liquids and long wooden tables stained black with blood. There were saws and buckets and glass jars filled with critters and books and candles and a heavy cloud of sickly-sweet-smelling potions.

"This is where Ferula created the jumbles," said Willa. Her heart pounded in her ears: *thumpthumpthump*. "Look!"

A black bird was perched in a hanging cage. Instead of wings it had rat feet and instead of a beak it had a crocodile snout. The snout opened and the creature let out a mournful "Craark!"

It was Ferula's crow.

Willa's heart ached at the cruelty. Her own familiar! Turned into a monster!

"Come on." Marceline tugged Willa's sleeve. "Let's keep looking."

Candlelight danced along the tabletops and walls as the three children explored the room. None of the books were about Rab Culpepper. They had waxy bloodred covers, crinkled yellowed pages, and terrifying embossed symbols under titles such as: *A Compendium of Evil* and *Malignant Magic* and *The Death of the Ordinary*. Willa shivered just to look at them.

She found handwritten notes, too, scratchy diagrams and wild, looping words that made no sense: *Transposing the valorgium-essent with a modified corpanimo (centrinix?) is equal to haureus-gangus (with a spinex variant?). Test for danimotrum poris effects.* One diagram was of a man's head and the head of a wolf. Between them was a large bubble with arrows pointing from one to the other.

Willa shoved it all into her pockets (thankful she had so many). She would show Gaspard—perhaps he would understand it; perhaps it would help return the voices.

Suddenly Willa heard a noise. A *scratch-scratch, scratch-scratch* that sent chills up her spine. Gish was beside her, so it wasn't him. "Is that you?" she asked Marceline, but the princess was behind her, sniffing a bubbling cauldron of purple syrupy liquid. She shook her head.

Talon trotted toward a cluster of shadows in the far corner.

The black-and-white cat merged with the darkness and didn't come out again. With a thumping heart, Willa decided to follow him. Gish and Marceline were close on her heels.

In the shadows, Willa found a hallway. It seemed to continue forever, but she halted when she noticed a cage off to one side. At first Willa thought it was empty, but a flicker of movement caught her eye.

"Hello? Is someone there?" Willa's voice trembled.

Scratch-scratch, scratch-scratch, scratch-scratch . . .

Something in the cage was coming toward them. She clung to her friends.

Scratch-scratch, scratch-scratch, scratch-scratch . . .

Out of the shadows appeared a jumble. The most jumbled jumble Willa had seen yet. Crocodile scales over chicken legs, a torso that was half wolf, half bear, one arm belonging to a pig and the other belonging to a rabbit, leathery dragon wings, and a line of spikes down the spine that weren't spikes but little black snakes that hissed.

And the head.

The head was Ferula's.

CHAPTER SEVENTEEN

"Hello, DEARIE," croaked the Ferula jumble. She hobbled up to the cage bars. "How lovely of you to visit me."

Willa stumbled back. "What happened?"

"I underestimated an enemy," said Ferula. The snakes along her spine hissed. "It won't happen again. And I'll have my revenge. If only I was free . . ." She heaved a sigh, long and pitiful. "There's a key hanging on the wall behind you, but alas! I can't reach it. Woe is me!"

Ferula was right: a chunky brass key dangled from a hook nailed to the wall. Talon was sitting underneath it.

Willa glanced at Marceline. The princess shrugged. She looked at Gish: his knuckles whitened as he flexed his grip around his glass jar. Then he nodded.

"Undo the voice-stealing spell," she said to Ferula. She took a deep breath. "And we'll set you free."

The witch cackled. "Now, why would I do that?"

"Because we won't set you free otherwise," huffed Marceline.

"That's not what I meant, *Princess*." Ferula's beady black eyes burned into Willa. They seemed to say: *Why would I undo the spell without getting what I want first?* And Willa knew what the witch wanted.

She closed her eyes. *Just breathe.*

"If you undo the spell . . ." she said. The words felt like scorpions in her mouth. But she had to get them out. It was for Gish. "If you undo the spell, I'll set you free and . . ." She opened her eyes. Ferula watched her eagerly, licking her lips. "And . . . I'll join Irontongue," she finished in a rush.

Gish's hand snapped around her wrist: *No!*

"You'll do no such thing!" Marceline scolded. "We'll help Gish another way."

Gish nodded furiously.

"But—"

Ferula's cackle startled them. "As much as I'd love to make such a bargain with you"—her lips twisted into a condescending sneer—"you're *still* misunderstanding me. Why would I undo the voice-stealing spell . . . when I didn't cast it in the first place?"

A shock of laughter escaped Willa's lips. "Of course you did!" She stared down the jumble, hands on hips. "You're the rogue witch. You can cast mousetraps and you know about Rab Culpepper and you're an Irontongue and you're . . . evil."

"Is that so?" said Ferula. "Are you sure?"

"Yes."

"How sure?"

"Very."

"Enough to stake your friend's voice on it?"

Willa swallowed. Doubt clawed at her. She shook it away— this was a trick. It *had* to be.

"Answer me this, dearie." Ferula's smile turned knowing. "Why would I transform myself into a jumble?"

"You . . . you didn't, I suppose," she admitted. "But perhaps someone else did, to stop you being awful and casting all those spells."

"And didn't tell a soul about me?" said Ferula sweetly. "Just turned me into a monster, locked me up, and never said a word?"

Now that Ferula said it like that, Willa wasn't quite so sure. "But if it wasn't you . . ."

"I was set up!" spat Ferula. "The spells, the jumbles, everything! You think *I'd* create such flimsy jumbles? I'm insulted! I didn't even know there was a secret door in my room until *someone* left me a note telling me where to look. But if you let me go, I'll tell you who tricked me and turned me into a jumble. I'll tell you who the *real* rogue witch is."

Willa shook her head. If Ferula wasn't the rogue witch, then . . .

Her hand shot to her pocket, the one that crinkled when she touched it because there was parchment folded up inside. A spell that might not be Silverclaw or Irontongue. Could she be free to choose something different after all?

"Tell us what you know first," said Marceline. "Then we'll let you go."

The Ferula jumble smirked. "And why would I do such a thing? If I tell you what I know — and oh, do I know a great many *interesting* things! — what's stopping you from double-crossing me? You'll have what you need, so you'll fetch the guards and I'll be locked up in the castle dungeons. Why would I swap one cage for another?" She gripped a bar with her little rabbit's paw. "Free me. *Then* I'll tell you what I know."

Willa turned away and huddled with her friends. "What do we do?"

"She'll double-cross us for sure," whispered Marceline. "We can't trust her."

Gish nodded.

Willa glanced over her shoulder. Ferula looked away, pretending she hadn't been listening. Willa lowered her voice as she turned back. "But if I don't do as she says? She might curse us."

"Why hasn't she magicked herself out already?" asked Marceline.

That, thought Willa, was an excellent question.

She turned back. "How come you haven't unlocked the cage with magic? There has to be a spell that unlocks doors."

Ferula narrowed her eyes. "There is," she snapped. "But we didn't get that half of the book when it ripped. Only Silver*snores—ptooey!*—have an unlocking spell. Besides, there's a *Mirror-mirror!* curse on these bars. If I dared cast a Silver*bore* curse, it'd only be thrown back in my face."

Willa sighed. There was no other choice—she *had* to set Ferula free to uncover the truth.

She fetched the key.

"Wait!" Marceline grabbed Willa's arm. The princess gave

her a steadying look before she turned to face Ferula. "First give us a clue. So we know you're not going to double-cross us. We won't set you free otherwise."

Ferula smacked her gums. Her glare had the sting of a fire-breathing bee. "Silverclaw," she huffed. "That's your clue. It's the only one you'll get."

Willa deflated. Of *course* the Irontongue witch would blame the other coven. But Silverclaw witches didn't make jumbles, and both modified spells were based on Irontongue magic. It was *possible* to cast another coven's magic, as Gaspard had explained in his first magic lesson, but unlikely given the severe consequences.

"That shouldn't count, because you're lying," said Willa, though the clue did give her an itchy feeling in the back of her head. "But there's no other option."

With fear in her heart, Willa stepped forward. Every part of her rebelled against what she was doing. Trembling, she forced her hands to insert the key into the rusty keyhole. As soon as she heard the click of the lock opening, she hurried backwards. The key dropped from her hands, clanging on the stone floor.

The cage door slowly swung open.

The Ferula jumble stepped into the opening, eyes never leaving Willa.

Willa backed away until she hit the cold stone wall; Marceline gripped one arm and Gish the other. "Tell us who did this to you," she said. Her voice quivered. "Tell us who the rogue witch is."

"I told you," said Ferula. She stepped out of the cage. "This is about Silverclaw and Irontongue."

"I know about the war. I read about it."

"Then you should be careful what you read."

"Just say a name," said Willa. "Who is the rogue witch?"

"*Tsk, tsk, tsk!*" Ferula chuckled. "Look how terrified you are of me! I'm the nicest one in here, you know." She flicked her gaze toward the shadows and smirked. Willa turned too, but she couldn't see where the hallway led—it was too dark. Were there other cages? Other jumbles? She gulped.

"You made a promise," said Willa.

"So I did." Ferula inched forward. From deep in the shadows came a long, low growl. Willa felt it in her bones. "But I fear you have more pressing concerns," continued the witch. "Groompity bilbuggy quggity!" she cried suddenly. She waggled her tongue in and out, and shocks of blue lighting flew from her lips and down the dark hallway. There was a loud crack and a clattering *bang!*

Willa's eyes widened. *Run!* cried her feet. *Please run!*

Ferula threw back her head and laughed. "Irontongue might not have an unlocking spell, but who needs one? It's such delicious fun to blast things open!"

"What did you do?" said Marceline.

"Nothing personal, my dears." Ferula hobbled away from them. "But I have important revenge to attend to. I can't waste my time with—"

A sharp *pop!* pierced the air.

Ferula's eyes grew wide as the sickly yellowy green rope wrapped around her legs, winding all the way up to her head.

"Blast!" She gagged and out popped a shimmery voice bubble. It zipped toward the workroom and Ferula took off after it, as fast as her chicken-crocodile legs could carry her.

"Wait!" cried Willa. The jumble was out of sight before Willa could even think to cast *Freeze-frame!*

Willa made to give chase but Marceline tugged her back. "Cast *Pop-goes-the-mousetrap!* first. We don't know how many are in the room. We were lucky to miss them the first time."

Willa nodded and cast the spell easily. Another silvery, translucent cat appeared, popped five bubbles, and then vanished.

"Come on!" she cried.

They ran into the main room, Talon zooming ahead of them. Ferula had swept aside a bookcase to reveal another hidden door. Her spine of wriggling black snakes disappeared through the opening before Willa could even call her name.

They charged after the devious witch and found themselves in another tunnel, this one with a steep staircase leading up and up and up. Blazing candles were pinned to the wall, lighting the way. High above them Ferula was already at the top of the stairs, disappearing through another door.

"Catch her!" shouted Willa.

They puffed their way up the staircase and through the door at the very top. Willa shielded her eyes from the blast of sunshine that greeted them. Her vision danced until several things came into focus.

They were outside a building carved from granite, a building of many spires like melted slate-gray wax, and many round windows. It was the Academy of Ordinary Studies.

The door they had escaped through was hidden by a creeping vine at the base of the building. It led to a courtyard filled with shrubs trimmed into shapes of Prince Cyrus engaged in various acts of valor. There were also fifty or more cats perched on the courtyard walls, flopped on flower beds, or lounging in pools of sunlight on the cobblestone paths. They purred with contentment and watched the students and professors of the academy run for their lives.

They were running because of Ferula. She was tearing through the courtyard, chasing her golden voice-bubble in circles.

"Another jumble!" they cried. "Save us!"

Willa began to cast *Freeze-frame!* but the earth beneath her feet suddenly trembled. It was followed by a bone-rattling roar. Was it an earthquake? The ground shook and Willa stumbled. Marceline and Gish wore identical looks of fear as they struggled to keep their balance. They backed away as the cobblestones began to crack.

The ground tore apart, and out shot a jumble. It flew into the air, its leathery wings sending gusts of wind so strong the leaves were ripped from the trees and Willa fell to the ground. She looked up as the monster eclipsed the sun, letting rip an earsplitting roar.

This was the creature Ferula's spell had set free.

It was mostly dragon. A fully grown White Devil, the largest and nastiest of all dragons, only found deep in the Hellion Caves of the Waste Mountains in northern Miremog. It breathed ice, not fire, and had two heads and a very bad temper.

But it wasn't all White Devil. Its forked tail was covered in poison-tipped porcupine spikes. It had six legs—the back four were wolf legs and the front two were red-bellied snakes. At the top of its twin giraffe necks sat two heads: one an eagle and the other Frank the Finger Eater.

Willa could hardly breathe.

"I have decided that coming face-to-face with a dragon," said Marceline, as she slowly backed away, "is too much adventure, even for me." She screamed as the dragon jumble dived toward them, shooting ice daggers from its mouths. Willa leapt out of the way as the icicles punctured the ground around her. She crawled behind a flowerpot; Marceline and Gish took cover behind a tree. The cats paid no attention, continuing to sun themselves and clean their whiskers.

The Ordinary Folk screamed. "We're all going to die!" They ran; they hid; they screamed harder.

Think, Willa! Which spell?

As the dragon jumble swept overhead with a roar, Willa jumped out from behind her flowerpot and began to dance like a lopsided frog.

Midnight-blue clouds burst from her fingertips and swirled upward, gathering around the dragon jumble's mouth as the *Ice-melt!* spell took effect. The creature swooped again, but this time instead of knife-sharp shards it breathed only drips of pleasantly warm water — the ice had melted.

"Ha! Take that, dragon jumble!" cried Willa, and then gasped. The fire! It burned in her belly, radiating out and filling every inch of her. It was happening again! She reached for the potion in her pocket, but the jumble swooped, swinging its tail covered in poisonous spikes. Willa dived out of the way and the tail crashed into the side of the academy. Bricks and dust flew everywhere as the whole west wall collapsed.

Willa's blood boiled and her skin sizzled with the invisible fire. She gritted her teeth and stood. As the dragon jumble prepared to swoop again, she cast another spell. "Gebbity tabbity-joop!" she shouted, then wiggled her tongue in a figure eight.

Lightning shot from her mouth, red bolts that morphed into ropes. The ropes sailed through the air and wrapped around the dragon jumble's body, pinning both wings to its sides. It screeched as it fell, crash-landing in the fountain. Water gushed everywhere, and a statue of King Teebald fainted. Willa cast the spell again, wrapping up the dragon from its necks to its tail. She stumbled as another wave of fire roared through her.

"That was *brilliant!*" said Marceline, running to Willa's side.

Willa's hands trembled as she reached into her pocket for the cooling potion. Black spots danced in front of her eyes. Her fingers were clumsy — she couldn't grip the bottle.

"But where's Ferula? Where did she go?" Marceline's voice was odd: slow and deep and echoing. Willa looked up — the librarian was fuzzy around the edges and Gish was a blur. So was the dragon jumble, huffing to itself in the courtyard as a few brave Ordinary Folk crawled out of their hiding places to examine it. The whole world had gone fuzzy. And inside, Willa was burning.

"Willa?" A blurry Marceline peered curiously at her. "Are you okay?"

Before she could answer, screams broke out across the courtyard.

One of the jumble's heads had broken free of the ropes. The long neck reared in the air and swung toward them; Frank the Finger Eater was headed straight for Willa, jaws wide and salivating.

She was too slow; she couldn't move. All she saw were teeth, teeth, teeth—*snap, snap, snap!*

A body crashed into hers from the side. She flew and hit the ground, hard. Glass shattered. Her vision shimmered, a fiery glow. She glimpsed Gish sprawled on the ground next to her. A flash of gold.

She tried to sit up, but the fire in her grew. It was molten lava. It was building, bubbling, boiling, bursting to . . . to explode.

"Oh dear," said Willa.

And the world went dark.

CHAPTER EIGHTEEN

WILLA WOKE with a yawning black hole where her memory should have been. She glanced around in confusion. She was in her room, sheets tucked up to her chin. Talon was curled asleep on her feet, while next to the bed, in a comfortable chair, Marceline read from *The ABC of Witches!* Gish was perched on a weeping table, his legs swinging.

How did I get here?

She stretched her mind, searching, searching, searching, then . . .

Ferula. The jumble. The fire. It all came flooding back.

She sprang up in bed. "Is everyone okay? Sorry, Talon." She had startled the cat; he stretched and gave her the stink-eye. "I didn't explode? Oh, don't look at me like that, Talon."

"Everyone is perfectly fine." Marceline put her book aside. "How are *you*, more to the point?"

Willa felt fine. Which was . . . strange. "I've still got all my fingers and toes," said Willa with a wry smile.

Gish hopped off the table and shuffled closer to Willa's bed. Something about his appearance was odd, but Willa couldn't put her finger on *what*. She sifted through her memories. A body crashing into hers. Hitting the ground. Glass shattering. Vision shimmering. Gish lying next to her. A flash of gold. Darkness.

Glass shattering?

A flash of gold?

Willa gasped, eyes drawn to Gish's empty hands. He didn't go anywhere without his voice bubble . . .

Oh no. "The jar broke. Your voice is gone, isn't it?" Her voice shook.

Gish nodded, scruffy hair falling into his eyes.

Willa's heart shattered. She'd tried to do the right thing and it had ended in trouble *again.* She slumped like a puppet with its strings cut.

Gish grabbed a pen and paper and scribbled furiously. *Not your fault,* he wrote.

"But I—"

He shook his head firmly.

"Why is it *your* fault?" Marceline folded her arms in disapproval. "Honestly, first you try to hand yourself over to Ferula and now you want to take the blame for an accident. If it's anyone's fault, it's the rogue witch who stole his voice in the first place!"

Gish nodded. *You tried to help me,* he wrote. *You're my friend.*

Tears welled in Willa's eyes.

It was just . . . she was used to feeling guilty. Guilt clung to her and wouldn't let go, like bubble gum stuck in her hair. When things went wrong, the blame *always* landed in her lap. If the spiders started dancing because she was lonely, if it rained inside the house because she was sad, if her schoolwork burned because she didn't understand it, it was always her fault.

But . . .

If a swan can't quack like a duck, is it the swan's fault?

Willa sat up straight.

All the thoughts that had been turned upside down were suddenly the right way up again. Only now they looked different. She knew what the healer's riddle meant: her parents had tried to squeeze her into a shape that had never fit her, even when she'd pretended.

And it wasn't her fault.

Just like it wasn't her fault neither coven would fit her.

Her hand went to her pocket—the crinkle of parchment was reassuring.

If she didn't have to choose Irontongue or Silverclaw, perhaps she could just . . . *be.* Just be Willa Birdwhistle. Friend of Gish and Marceline. Queen of cats. A swan, not a duck. Someone good. A witch of her own choosing.

"Oh, Gish!" Willa threw her arms around his neck. She hugged him tightly. *How lovely to have friends,* she thought. "You too," she told Marceline, and threw her arms around the princess.

"Oof!" said Marceline in surprise. But after a moment she hugged back just as fiercely.

"Together, we'll find the rogue witch," said Willa as she pulled away. She squeezed Gish's hand. "Then we'll find out more about these new spells so I don't have to leave and join a coven. So I can stay here with both of you." She jumped out of bed.

As Willa got dressed, Marceline paced.

"Here's what we know," said the princess. "The rogue witch first struck not long after Willa moved into the castle and the magical truce started. They use impossible spells that are a combination of two smooshed together, an idea first proposed by Rab Culpepper—"

"Ferula stole the book on Rab Culpepper from the library," interjected Willa.

"And the spells are all Irontongue-based," continued Marceline, "as well as the jumbles. The rogue witch can cast mousetraps—"

"Like Ferula," said Willa.

"—a rare skill that Ferula also has," finished Marceline.

Gish tugged on Willa's arm and wrote on his little pad of paper: *Are we sure it isn't Ferula?*

Marceline snorted. "Well, my brother thinks it is. While you were sleeping, Willa, we told him everything that happened, but he insisted it was a trick Ferula was playing. We tried to show him the hidden workshop, but the door had vanished. He's convinced she's the rogue witch and won't change his mind."

"But why would she turn herself into a jumble?" asked Willa. "And how did she create the second lot of mousetraps, the ones with the secret-spilling curse, while she was locked up in that cage?"

"Exactly," said Marceline.

But why did she steal the book on Rab Culpepper? wrote Gish. Willa frowned. That she did not know.

Her head ached from carrying the weight of too many unanswered questions. Most of them were about Rab Culpepper; so much of this mystery was tied up in him.

"I wish we knew more about Rab," said Willa. "I think he's the key."

Gish lit up like a firework. He scribbled a single word, then thrust the paper at Willa: *Ghosts!*

"What use are ghosts?" asked Marceline.

But Willa understood. That horrible, no-good book had said the library ghosts knew about Rab Culpepper. "But I tried already," she explained. "They hid from me. I think they're scared."

"Oh, that's easily fixed," said Marceline. Her eyes shone with mirth.

But she didn't have time to explain, as the bedroom door opened and footsteps approached. Willa quickly climbed back into bed—she was sure they would expect her to be taking it easy. Planning to uncover the real rogue witch was *not* taking it easy.

Just as Willa had pulled the bedsheets up to her chin, Gaspard and the clerk appeared from under a weeping table.

"Well, isn't this a pickle we find ourselves in," said Gaspard. He wore sleeplessness in the bruises under his eyes and the crinkles in his suit. He smiled at Willa.

"It's more than a pickle," huffed the clerk. She stayed as far away from Willa as possible. "It's a whole sandwich!"

Gaspard perched on the edge of Willa's bed. "Feeling better?"

Willa nodded. "Much better, thank you. I'm sure I could even get out of bed and—"

Gaspard shook his head sadly. "It's not good news, Willa. The healer took another look at you while you were sleeping and . . . oh dear. I'm afraid it's a bad case of Unanticipated Explosion Syndrome."

Willa blinked rapidly. "Unanticipated *what?*"

"It means your magic is *so* wild it's resisting being tamed and . . . You're going to have to take the initiation early, Willa."

Coldness hit her core. *Early?* But she didn't . . . She couldn't . . . She had just . . .

"Early?" Marceline gasped the word.

"If she doesn't, she'll explode at any second," said the clerk. She glared at Willa as if she might dare explode on purpose.

But Willa couldn't even think straight. "Explode?" The word made her tongue feel numb. "But I'm not thirteen. I'm . . ."

"The initiation is a spell that creates a real magical cage inside you that permanently keeps your magic in check," explained Gaspard. "Witches mostly learn to control their magic on their own, and the initiation is really only symbolic, a way to show allegiance to your coven. But of course every now and then along comes a witch whose magic is much too powerful, and the only way to safely tame them before they explode early is the initiation."

Willa's heart raced and with it all her thoughts, zooming by quicker than she could grab hold of them, like trying to catch confetti in a tornado. "But I can't choose early! I still need to find out more about the third kind of magic and—"

"*Third* kind?" The clerk snorted, sharing a look with Gaspard. His smile had devolved into a grimace. "Where would you get a fanciful notion such as that? Who ever heard of a third kind of magic?"

Willa sat up. "But Rab Culpepper—"

"Ha!" snapped the clerk. "Who'd listen to anything that troublemaker said?"

"But—"

"Willa, I don't know what you think you know about Rab," said Gaspard. He kept his voice kind as he leaned in. "But the truth is—and this is something of a secret, Willa—Rab Culpepper exploded early because he was trying to invent new spells. At first he was just trying to modify existing ones, like what Ferula has been doing. But when he attempted to create entirely new spells . . . Even if you weren't going to explode early, there is no third kind of magic, Willa. Ferula's spells might be unusual, but they're still Irontongue. *She* is Irontongue. I'm sorry. You still have to choose a coven."

Willa's mind swirled in turmoil. This was too fast. Too hard. She was a swan! She didn't want to quack! "Can I at least have a few days to think about it?"

Gaspard shook his head. "The covens have already been called. They're on their way. Surely you know which coven is better by now?" He smiled at her hopefully.

But Willa couldn't return his smile. Her chance at living the life of *her* choice—with friends and cats and *no* war—was slipping through her fingers.

"Well, whichever coven you do choose can take you with them *immediately*," snapped the clerk. "You and your blasted cats. They ate all my Notice to Declare the Castle a Feline-Free Zone posters! They simply will not do as they're told!" She scowled at Talon. Talon scowled back. "In the meantime," she huffed, "there is to be no magic *at all*. Is that clear? You'll blow the whole city to smithereens if you try." She turned on her heel and left.

Gaspard patted Willa's head jovially. "There, there!" he said, and stood. "It's not such a hard choice, is it?"

Willa watched her tutor leave, taking all her hopes for happiness with him.

"What are you going to do?" asked Marceline. Gish's eyes were wide with worry.

On the day her parents had been turned into clouds, Willa had cried. Heaving sobs that left her ribs aching, left her feeling lost, afraid, and heart-sore. But as the sun had set, she'd wiped the tear tracks from her cheeks and rolled back her shoulders.

No more, she had said, and built herself a little Rapscallion's Cage deep in her heart. She'd poured all her grief into that cage and locked it. *Get in there and stay there,* she'd told it. Because her grief had been wild and untamed and it would have exploded too.

But hadn't she lost the shape of herself when she'd carved

away her grief and her memories and all her raw edges? Hadn't she forced herself to quack too?

What if, this time, she took her hurt and her disappointment and her fear and her worries and let them grow wild? Let everything she felt fill the entire space of her, to see where she began and ended, to see what shape was possible? How could she know who she was—and what she was capable of—if she kept such large parts of herself hidden? Wasn't that what her parents had done? Tried to shape her into someone she wasn't by forcing her to hide the parts of herself they didn't understand? Even the bruises on her heart were a part of who she was.

No, this time she would not retreat to silently lick her wounds and pretend everything was fine.

Willa threw back the covers and climbed out of bed. She smoothed down her sweater—four sleeves and twenty-seven pockets. "We don't have long. But I'm going to uncover who the real rogue witch is," she said. Her chin was raised. "And I'm going to get Gish back his voice."

The shadows in section G gobbled up the flickering candlelight like pudding.

"Is this really necessary?" Willa frowned at the thick rope looped around her waist, which pinned her arms to her sides.

"Shush!" said Marceline. She led the way, holding the candle out in front. "You're bait. Bait doesn't talk."

Willa rolled her eyes.

The way to get the ghosts to come out again, according to Marceline, was to give them what they wanted. Which was to eat the one who'd scared them.

"This is a terrible plan," grumbled Willa.

Gish gave her a friendly pat on the shoulder. At least he'd tied the rope loosely.

They walked in silence for some time, the only sounds the cautious *tap, tap, tap* of their shoes and the hitch in their breath at every flickering shadow.

"Remember: no magic," whispered Marceline as they neared the end of the aisle. "I'd rather you didn't explode. I quite like you." Willa flushed with an embarrassed sort of pleasure, but then Marceline started to yell: "Hello, ghosts? I've brought you dinner! She's a bit scrawny but she'll taste delicious."

If Willa hadn't been at risk of exploding, she would have transfigured the librarian's hair into worms.

"Are you there?" shouted Marceline. "I've brought you the witch who turned you into ribbons so you can—"

"Woo!"

The three friends froze as one.

Willa gulped as the old man wrapped in chains appeared out of the shadows. He limped toward them, jangling and clinking.

"Woo!" said the old man, rattling his chains. "WOO!"

For a horrible moment Willa wondered what it would be like to be eaten by a fictional ghost. Hopefully, she wouldn't find out.

"Now!" cried Marceline.

Gish whipped out a lasso from behind his back and tossed it at the ghost. It was *supposed* to wrap around him, holding him in place. However, the rope sailed *through* the apparition and landed with a plop on the floor.

"Ah," said Marceline. "I didn't think of that."

"I told you this was a terrible plan!" cried Willa.

The old man frowned at the lasso at his feet. "Woo?" he said.

"Look, we're very sorry," explained Willa. "It's just that we have some important questions to ask and you were hiding from me. We didn't think there was another way to ask you. We were going to set you free after. Promise!"

Marceline nodded. "So don't eat us, please."

The old man narrowed his eyes. His chains jingled.

Gish nudged Willa in the back: *Go on!*

"Right! Um, so if you're not going to eat us, at least for a moment, could you please tell us if you knew Rab Culpepper?"

"Woo?"

"A boy. Very wild. About seventy years ago."

"Woo," said the old man. He rattled his chains.

"Honestly," said Marceline. "Just nod or something. Did you know Rab Culpepper?"

The ghost tilted his head. He seemed to be thinking: *Why am I talking to these three children when I could be eating them?* He grinned as he reached a conclusion. He only had one rotted front tooth. "Woo."

"I think our luck just ran out," said Willa.

The ghost rattled his chains and lunged at them. "Woo!"

Suddenly a willowy woman blinked into existence next to the old man. "Oh, do pop off, you silly bore," she said. She gripped him by his chains and tossed him into oblivion.

"Woooooo!"

The woman dusted off her hands—her *see-through* hands—and turned to the three children. "I'm sorry about him. He has no manners."

Willa gaped at the woman. The *ghost*. Her long gray hair was piled like a four-tier cake on top of her head. She wore a sparkly jacket, a lacy shirt, wide-leg plaid pants, and a spotted neckerchief; her feet were bare.

Marceline almost dropped the candle. "Queen Arabella the Second?" she gasped.

The woman smiled. "A version of her, at least. I was in a biography and now I'm stuck here." She shrugged. "It's not so bad. I've had time to reorganize all of section G, from top to bottom. I can't tell you how many books were lurking in the wrong spot. And I get a lot of visitors. Did you bring tea? Scones? Jam? I like jam."

"Visitors?" said Willa, struggling out of the ropes with Gish's help.

"Well, there was the bald witch with the fabulously large warts who was looking for *Five Thousand and One Delicious Ways to Cook with Worms*."

"Worms?" said Willa. She froze. It couldn't be.

We let the last visitor leave with her prize because we liked her bird; she'll be cooking up all kinds of trouble by now . . . Willa groaned. Of course! Ferula *had* been here, but the "prize" she'd taken wasn't Rab's book. So where was it?

"Then there was the prince," continued the ghost queen. "Rude boy. Can't believe we're related."

"Prince Cyrus?" said Marceline.

"That's the fellow. Very pointy. Said he was looking for books on how to suppress magic. When I told him he wouldn't find such a thing, he called me a very rude name and left in a huff."

Willa shared a nervous look with her friends.

"Then there was that strange figure in the black cloak," continued the ghost queen. "They were looking for a book too. With a title like *The something something of Rob Dullpepper something Explosive something*. Very cross to find the book missing, I can tell you."

Ka-boom, ka-boom, ka-BOOM went Willa's heart.

"What did they look like?" she asked.

The ghost queen shook her head. "I'm afraid I didn't see. The cloak covered their face."

Willa slumped in disappointment. If the cloaked figure was the rogue witch and the book had been missing already, where was it? "Did *you* know Rob Dullpepper—I mean, Rab Culpepper?" she asked.

The queen tapped her chin with her finger. "Hmm. Doesn't

sound familiar. Is that the name of the bald witch with the fabulous warts?"

Willa shook her head. "A boy. Well, a witch. This would have been seventy years ago."

"Oh no," said the queen, shaking her head. The tower of gray hair wobbled like jelly in an earthquake. "I wasn't here seventy years ago. None of us were. The *Get-real!* spell hit perhaps four years ago? I'm a spring chicken!"

"None of you? Don't tell me *The Long and Thoroughly Ordinary Tales of Pearl B. Purcep, an Explorer of Little Note* tricked me again. The diary said the ghosts in the library knew." Willa stomped her foot.

"Ah," said the queen with a knowing smile. "That explains it, then."

"Explains what?"

The queen chuckled. "I'm not a ghost. I'm a ghost *from a book* come to life. You'll want to talk to the *real* ghost."

Willa's jaw dropped. "Real ghost? But there's no such thing."

The queen snorted. "Says you! I come from the last chapter in the queen's biography, the chapter all about the *real* ghost of Queen Arabella the Second. She haunts the library, didn't you know?"

Willa looked at Marceline, who shrugged. "Don't look at me; *I've* never met her."

"You wouldn't have," explained the fake ghost queen. "She's very shy. Not even *I've* met her. But it will be her you need to talk to."

Willa turned to her friends. "We don't have time to hunt for a *real* ghost," she said. "We need to find out who the person in the black cloak was. But how?"

Marceline pushed her glasses up her nose. "We could search the library, see if there aren't any more of Rab's secret spells lying around. There might be something to summon a witch."

Gish wrote: *Chase down that awful cursed book again?*

Willa shuddered at the thought.

"We could set a trap?" she suggested.

"Or you could ask me," said the queen.

"But you said you didn't know," said Willa.

"I don't know who was wearing the cloak," she agreed. "But I *did* see something."

Marceline tapped her foot. "Well?"

"The mysterious person in black performed a spell. A book-summoning spell. It didn't work, but it was interesting nonetheless."

"Why would it be interesting to know they cast a spell that didn't work?" said Willa.

"Because of the spell," said the queen. "It was a Silverclaw spell."

CHAPTER NINETEEN

"THERE'S ONLY ONE Silverclaw witch in the castle," said Marceline. She clung to Gish and Willa, jumping up and down in excitement. "We know who the rogue witch is!"

"But *Eladar?*" Willa frowned. Surely Eladar would sooner wear mouse earrings than create a mouse*trap.* "Why would he deliberately attack the city?" And why would he cast Irontongue spells knowing the risk to his health?

"Think about it," said Marceline. "If you were convinced Ferula was deliberately hurting your friends, wouldn't you be more likely to choose Silverclaw?"

Oh.

The truth stung like a slap. "You mean, all these horrible spells are to convince me to choose Silverclaw?" The stolen voices, the secrets, the jumbles, all of it?

Not your fault, mouthed Gish.

Willa took a deep breath. *Swans don't quack, swans don't quack, swans don't quack . . .*

"And we've uncovered his plan." Marceline squeezed Willa's hand. "So we're going to stop him."

Willa nodded. Though he'd worked hard to make Ferula appear callous and cruel, it seemed Eladar was the real enemy. And though his choices weren't Willa's fault, it was within her power to fix the damage. She took another deep breath. It was hard to see the silver lining when she was still left with an impossible choice—if not Silverclaw then . . . Irontongue? Ferula might not be evil but . . . She shook her head. *Focus, Willa!* How would they convince Eladar to undo the spells? Perhaps if she offered to—

Willa felt a tugging on her sleeve. She turned to find Gish waving a note under her nose.

Don't even think about offering to join Silverclaw in exchange for my voice. I won't allow it.

"But—"

He waggled a finger in warning.

"Excuse me!" The fake ghost-queen raised her hand. "Hello, yes! Do you still need to talk to the *real* ghost of Queen Arabella the Second?"

Willa opened her mouth to say no, but the word lodged in her throat. Now that they knew who the rogue witch was, they didn't need to speak with the reclusive ghost. She could possibly tell them more about Rab, but his magic was a dead end, and anyway there wasn't time.

"It's just that there might be clues in my biography," continued the queen, not waiting for an answer. "And it's a cracking read. It was written by Theodore Yockins. Let's see, where is that book." She knelt and inspected the shelf. "Yarsley, Yelder . . . Yockins! Here it is, right next to Youngblood."

"Youngblood?" Willa peered over the queen's shoulder. The ghost's transparent fingers hovered over a cracked spine of green leather. *The True (and Explosive!) History of Rab Culpepper* was written in swooping silver script, along with the author's name: *Amaryllis Youngblood.* "That's the book on Rab Culpepper!" she gasped.

She darted out a hand, but all she touched was air. Within the blink of an eye, the book had moved up one shelf. "Oh, do behave, you silly book!" snapped Willa. She reached out again but once more grasped at nothing. "I'm going to get very mad and curse you with dog-ears on *all* your pages," she warned.

"Perhaps if I try," suggested the queen. "My ghostly fingers are perfect for capturing troublesome books."

Willa gladly stepped out of the way.

"Was it this one?" asked the queen, pointing at the shelf. "*The Long and Thoroughly Ordinary Tales of Pearl B. Purcep, an Explorer of Little Note*?"

Willa shook her head. "No, it's — What did you say?"

The queen's ghostly finger was indeed gesturing at the spine of a familiar cursed book. It sat innocently on the shelf where *The True (and Explosive!) History of Rab Culpepper* had been just moments ago.

Willa gasped. *That horrible, no-good book!*

"Grab it!" said Willa. "Grab that one!"

But as the ghost queen made to seize the cursed book, it leapt off the shelf and hovered in the middle of the aisle.

"How can a book fly?" asked Marceline.

The book jiggled, then let rip a ginormous burp.

"What awful manners you have," said Willa.

With a golden shimmer, the text on the book's front cover changed: it was now *Be Nice or I Won't Tell You My Secret* by The Best Book Ever Written.

"This is the most fun I've had in ages," said the ghost queen, clapping her hands.

"What secret?" demanded Willa.

The title changed again: *Want to Stop the Rogue Witch?* by A Book That Has All the Answers.

"Can we trust it?" whispered Marceline.

Willa didn't trust it as far as she could throw it (which wasn't far at all, considering she could never get her hands on it). *But* the book had given them two helpful clues so far. *But* it also liked to play tricks and Willa didn't fancy being bombarded with socks again. *But* they were running out of time.

"We have to," she whispered back. "If we want to stop Eladar." Willa turned to the book. She bowed and flourished her arms. "Oh wise and wondrous book, please tell us how to stop the rogue witch."

For a third time, the book's title changed: *Pretty Please?* by Someone with Good Manners.

Willa plastered on a smile. "Pretty please?" she said. She added a curtsy just in case.

The book did a loop-the-loop. When it settled in place again it had another new title: *Follow Me!* by Catch Me if You Can. It burped once more before it shot off, zooming up the aisle.

"Follow that book!" shouted Willa.

"Bring scones and jam next time!" called the queen as the three children sprinted after the cursed book.

They sped through the castle. The book raced ahead, casting tricky curses in its wake: carnivorous confetti, sock snakes, quicksand carpets, and more.

"How does a book cast magic?" said Willa as she sidestepped a puddle of raspberry-jam lava that had appeared in the middle of the hall. There was nothing she could do in retaliation—if she cast a spell, she would explode.

"Ferula's room!" she cried as they rounded a corner and spied the witch's bedroom door hanging open. The book flew inside. "Why is it leading us here?"

Inside the room, the voice-alarm spell had worn off. The book was hovering in the air just outside the hidden passage—the tapestry had been pulled to one side, and the door was already open.

"I thought the secret door had vanished," said Willa.

Gish nodded.

"And anyway, we've been down there," said Marceline, panting. "I hope it's not leading us to more jumbles."

The book blew a raspberry, followed by the rapid cannon fire of balled-up fluffy bed socks.

Willa ducked. "Oh, you're truly awful!" she cried.

With a mischievous twirl, the book flew into the secret passageway.

"Come on!" said Marceline, grabbing both their hands. "It's getting away."

They hurried into the dark passage. Their footsteps echoed as they ran, dodging curses—*Achoo-until-you're-blue!* and *Frog-rain!* Did the book want them to follow or not?

Finally, they burst into the workroom.

"Achoo!" said Marceline. Her face was indeed blue. "Oh, blast it! Sometimes I hate magic."

Gish picked a frog out of his hair and placed it carefully on the nearest bench.

"Where's the book now?" said Willa.

The hidden workroom looked the same as last time, including the poor crow jumble. Books, cages, cauldrons, and notes were scattered everywhere. Willa remembered the papers she'd shoved in her pockets, intending to show Gaspard. Would he finally take her seriously if he saw them?

"We don't have time for your games," called Willa. "Come out and tell us how to stop the rogue witch!"

But the book did not appear.

"I really can't tell if it's—*achoo!*—friend or foe," said Marceline.

Willa sighed. "Both, I think."

There was a click followed by a long, low *creeeeaaaak* as, somewhere, a door swung open.

"There!" Willa pointed to the now-open cupboard door. Except it wasn't a cupboard door; it was a—

"Another secret passage?" gasped Marceline. *"Achoo!"*

Willa peered into the darkness of the mysterious cupboard. "I suppose we take a chance?"

Gish nodded.

"Achoo!" said Marceline.

Willa stepped inside the cupboard; the air was icy and the shadows pressed tight. It was a passageway of sorts. Narrow and dark. Thankfully, it was a short walk until another door opened into a small room.

Books and papers filled the cramped space. There was an armchair and a small cot in one corner, and on the wall a painting of a familiar cottage draped in white roses. Everything was covered in a thick layer of dust and grime *except* for the pile of stolen things in the middle of the room—socks and pens and keys and socks and hats and socks and ties and shoes and socks and socks and socks. "Those brown socks are mine!" said Marceline. *"Ah-CHOO!"* The princess blinked in surprise. "Oh, that was a real sneeze. I think the curse has worn off. *Finally.*"

Gish handed her a hankie.

"This was Rab Culpepper's room," said Willa. The cottage in the painting was the same as in the tapestry outside the library: the home where young Rab had grown up. And the scribbles and diagrams and scrawls littering the floor were all about one thing: how to create new spells.

"You're right." Marceline pointed to a photograph pinned to the wall. A young boy and a woman sat outside the cottage, on a blanket in the grass, three cats curled at their feet. The sunshine made them squint, or perhaps it was the toothy smiles that turned their eyes into lovely crescent moons. The boy looked at the camera, but the woman looked at the boy. He was scruffy-haired, his clothes muddied, scabs on his knees and elbows from too much adventure. He looked wild and happy and alive.

"Is that him?" Willa peered closer. A shiver ran the length of her spine. He looked *so* alive, as if his crescent-moon smile could burst open with laughter at any moment. She shook her head. "Why did he have a secret room hidden in the castle?"

She knelt and sifted through papers scattered across the floor until she found something interesting: a partial diary entry.

Not the diary *The Long and Thoroughly Ordinary Tales of Pearl B. Purcep, an Explorer of Little Note* had given her. This was in a familiar laughing scrawl, the words spiraling toward the center of the page instead of ordered lines. Willa had to twist the page around and around to read it.

Willa's lips parted with a gasp. So Amaryllis Youngblood had been Rab's tutor. He was the author of the diaries Willa had already seen, as well as *The True (and Explosive!) History of Rab Culpepper.* It was a pity he was certain to be long gone —after all, he'd been Rab's tutor seventy years ago!—because Willa had a gazillion questions for him (which she could have asked) (if she'd had time) (which she did not) (sadly). Willa sighed.

"Hey, look!" Marceline tugged Willa's sleeve.

On a little desk tucked into the corner sat the book: *The Long and Thoroughly Ordinary Tales of Pearl B. Purcep, an Explorer of Little Note.*

"There you are!" Willa approached, hands on hips. "You said you knew about Eladar. You *said* you'd tell us how to make him undo the spells. Did you bring us here to help?"

The book did nothing.

"Or did you just want to show off everything you've pinched?" On the desk were more stolen things: socks, books, bow ties, the king's underwear, and even Gaspard's *Switcheroo!* feather pen. "He was looking for that," said Willa.

The book wiggled and shook until a small strip of paper appeared between its bottom pages, like a tongue poking out.

Willa grabbed the strip. It came easily when she tugged. On it read a single word: cold.

"Not this again!" Willa balled up the scrap. "Please just tell us where we should look."

Another slip of paper appeared: still cold, it read.

"I swear, if wild magic doesn't make me explode," muttered Willa, taking a giant step backwards, "dealing with *you* will."

Another slip of paper appeared. Gish tugged it free and showed it to Willa.

Cold-ish.

Willa took a step to her right, closer to the squishy armchair in the corner.

Gish grabbed the next paper. He held it up for Marceline to read: "'I see you're still terrible at this game. You're freezing now.'"

Willa bit down a retort and took two steps back to the left.

"'Ah, a fast learner!'" read Marceline. "'Mildly warm now. But you'd still need a sweater.'"

Willa took a step backwards, over a pile of books. "I *am* wearing a sweater," she grumbled.

"'Then take off your sweater, Willa, because you've hit a sudden snap of warm spring weather!'"

Willa took another step backwards.

"'I hope you brought sunscreen, because it's getting hot in here!'"

Willa stepped back once more, and her calf hit the metal edge of the cot. She turned around. The cot was barely long enough to sleep a child of Willa's height. A thin woolen blanket was scrunched up in the middle, covered in seventy years' worth of dust. Above the cot hung the painting of White-Rose Cottage, low enough that whoever had slept in this bed could lie back and comfortably gaze at it.

"'You must be boiling!'" read Marceline.

Willa lifted up the blanket, but there was nothing underneath. Dust mushroomed in the air, making her sneeze. She knelt and looked under the cot: just dust bunnies, spiders, and a pair of worn boots. "There's nothing here," she said.

"'Yes there is,'" said Marceline.

Willa glared at her, but the librarian waved the note. "I'm only reading what this says."

Gish pulled another thin strip from the pages of the cursed book and handed it to Marceline.

"'You're still boiling, Willa. Hot enough to . . . explode!'"

Willa huffed as she stood. Her eyes landed on the painting again. It hung crooked, tilted to the left. She knelt on the cot and peered closer. On the top of the frame the dust had been disturbed, as if fingers had gripped it.

"'Tick, tick, BOOM!'" read Marceline.

Willa gripped the painting and lifted it off its hook. Behind was a hole, crudely carved out of the stone wall. It was big enough to hide a cake (only one tier) or a bag of oranges or perhaps Talon, if he curled up tightly. But it was empty save for a few scraps of paper.

"What's this?" asked Willa. "It's just . . . paper?"

"'Oh dear,'" read Marceline. "'It seems as though someone beat you to it. There *was* a book there that would have been mighty helpful to you. Pity!'"

Willa grabbed the papers. They were instructions for casting spells written in the familiar laughing scrawl but were clearly rough drafts—words had been crossed out, ideas scribbled in the margins. Willa's heart clenched as she read the spell names: *Nose-knotting! Secret-storm! Skeleton-gelatin!*

"Look!" cried Marceline. "'*Bubble-babble!* The perfect smooshing together of *Cat-got-your-tongue!* and *Keepings-off!* to ensure you never have to listen to that annoying neighbor ever again.' That's your curse, Gish."

Gish pulled the paper from Willa's hands and read, lips twisted in thought.

To cast this spell, you must:

1. Dance (waltz?) in a circle like an elephant with ~~a bad cold~~ an allergy to compliments.

2. Whisper three (four?) numbers that remind you of the ~~color red blue~~ pink rainbow followed by the words Hoinky-doinky blubbery foofwinkle muffin (boffin?) ollypolly slurp. ~~slurp~~
   ~~ollypolly slurp~~ ~~slurp~~

3. Think very hard about a (ginger? calico?) kitten wearing gum boots.

4. Point at the nearest lamp and ~~scold it~~ laugh hysterically at it. ~~scold~~ (laugh)

5. And *poof!* just wait and see what happens!

233

Willa guessed these were the rough drafts of the modified spells—or what was left after someone had stolen the rest. Did that mean *Pop-goes-the-mousetrap!* was also just a modified spell? It did follow the same strange format . . . Willa's heart sank.

Gish flipped the sheet over, but there was no counter-curse on the back. Perhaps it was in the book. The one that was no longer there. But even if they could find a counter-curse, they would need Eladar to cast it.

"If there *was* a book hidden here," said Willa, "a collection of Rab's spells, and someone found it . . ."

"Eladar, you mean," said Marceline.

Willa wondered how Eladar could have stumbled across this hidden room—after all, there were only two doors in and out, one in Ferula's room and one in the Academy of Ordinary Studies.

Frustration bubbled up inside her. "None of this tells us how to convince Eladar to undo his spells," she said. She glared at *The Long and Thoroughly Ordinary Tales of Pearl B. Purcep, an Explorer of Little Note.* "You've wasted our time. What if Eladar—"

"Yes?" said a voice. A singsong voice. A *familiar* voice. "Are you looking for me?"

Slowly, Willa turned.

Standing in the doorway, draped in shadows, was Eladar.

CHAPTER TWENTY

ELADAR SWEPT INTO THE ROOM. "The bees said you would be here," he said, lips dancing around the words. He bopped Willa on the nose.

Willa tensed, waiting for the curses to fly. But Eladar simply smiled at her, head tilted, waiting for a response.

"The bees are very smart," said Willa carefully.

Eladar nodded. "They are indeed wise. And tasty."

Willa shared worried looks with her friends. She could see the tension in their limbs, poised to flee like startled cats.

Eladar took a turn about the room, inspecting every nook and cranny.

He didn't *look* unwell—Gaspard had said casting magic from another coven after your initiation took years off your life span. Eladar hid the effects well. "This room is . . ." He sniffed the *Switcheroo!* feather pen. "It makes me feel . . ." He scrunched up his nose, then began convulsing like a cat hacking up a fur ball. *"Guch!"* When he was done, he turned to Willa with a toothy smile. "Should I eat these?" He pointed to a pair of fluffy gray bed socks.

"If you like," she said slowly.

Eladar spun a full circle before pointing one long, curled nail at Willa. "You are wanted by the pointy boy," he cried.

"The prince?"

"The coven delegates have arrived and are waaaaaiiiiiting. There's no time for hide-and-seek. Though I do love to play." With that, Eladar skipped from the room. "Come, come!" he called over his shoulder. "The bees will be angry if we delay-lay-lay."

There was a collective whoosh of breath once the witch was out of sight.

"He didn't curse us?" Marceline cupped Huggin protectively. Her eyes were wide in disbelief. "He must be confident his plan worked and you're going to choose Silverclaw."

Willa frowned at the empty doorway. "Do we follow him?"

We know his plan, wrote Gish. *We can tell everyone else.*

Willa nodded. It didn't feel right — she had a bitter, wobbly-tummy feeling. But what else could they do? Tick, tick, boom, as *The Long and Thoroughly Ordinary Tales of Pearl B. Purcep, an Explorer of Little Note* had said. Speaking of which . . .

"Horrible, no-good book," muttered Willa — the place where it had been sitting on the desk was empty again. The only thing left was the *Switcheroo!* feather pen.

The three children scurried through the cupboard passage and into the main workshop, where Eladar was smiling vaguely at the crow jumble. "How *interesting,*" he said, and kept walking.

They followed him into the dark passage, keeping a safe distance.

"He doesn't *seem* evil," whispered Marceline. "But I suppose you can never tell."

Much to Willa's shame it had been easy to assume Ferula was the evil one. Willa had taken one look at the Irontongue witch and twisted her into the shape she'd *expected* to see. How wrong she had been. At least now she could tell Gaspard the truth—perhaps he could convince Eladar to do the right thing.

"What are you going to do?" whispered Marceline. "About the choice?"

Willa could hardly stand before the covens and the king and declare she wasn't choosing either Silverclaw or Irontongue. They expected an answer, but all Willa had was a feeling, a feeling that she had only just begun to know her magic so it seemed a pity to lock it away again, to force it into a whisper when it so clearly wanted to be a shout. There had to be something more than Silverclaw, Irontongue, *or explode.* But she needed proof.

"I don't know," she whispered. The sadness was so deep she felt it in her bones.

They followed Eladar through the castle; the witch hummed to himself and laughed at blank walls and blew raspberries at passing guards and told Talon he was "most handsome!" as the one-eyed cat trotted up to meet them. And all the while Willa stewed in her worry.

"There you are, Willa!" cried Gaspard. He came charging down the hall in a flap of robes and flailing arms. Guards followed him. "We've been looking *everywhere* for you. What a disaster of a day! Come, come! Time to let the covens know your choice."

Pop!

A blue rope wrapped around the ankles of one of the guards. He trembled all over before his arms and legs suddenly grew floppy. Within the blink of an eye his body was a bag of skin that sagged to the floor like a deflated balloon.

"Oops!" said Gaspard. "Forgot about that. Um, could two of you carry him to the hospital wing? Thanks ever so much."

Willa's jaw dropped in horror as the melted guard was scooped up with a loud squelch. "What in the Wild was that?"

Gaspard flapped his hand. "Just Ferula being evil again. This time the mousetraps are triggered when you say a particular word, and the result is a rather unpleasant bone-melting curse. Please don't say *K-N-O-W.*"

Willa exchanged looks with Marceline and Gish. There was no way Ferula had cast more mousetraps without her voice. It had to be Eladar.

Eladar squinted at the melted guard. "How *interesting,*" he said.

"Um, Mr. Renard?" Willa eyed Eladar nervously. "Could I talk to you? Alone?"

"Unfortunately not! We haven't time!" Gaspard pushed Willa toward the throne room. "You have a decision to make. We were looking *everywhere* for you. Where were you? Oh, library, I suppose—is that a good book? Sounds adventurous."

What book?

Willa looked down and was astounded to find she was holding *The Long and Thoroughly Ordinary Tales of Pearl B. Purcep, an Explorer of Little Note.* "How did—"

"And of course no one kn—I mean, no one *understands* how His Excellency, Mortus Dragonstink, will react when he discovers the trouble Ferula's been up to," continued Gaspard.

Willa hugged the book close. "Actually, Mr. Renard, I really think Ferula is innocent. The real rogue witch is—"

"Innocent? Golly, no!" Gaspard chuckled. "It might seem strange that Ferula turned herself into a jumble, but it was obviously a ploy to put us off her trail."

"But her voice! It was stolen and—"

"Oh, that was surely all an act! She only made you *think* her voice had been stolen so you'd pity her. She's a tricky one." Gaspard clicked his tongue.

"But—"

"I'm afraid you two will have to stay behind." Gaspard nodded at Gish and Marceline.

"I think not," huffed Marceline. But a wall of guards suddenly slipped between Willa and her friends, blocking their path. All Willa saw was their wide, frightened eyes as she was pushed into the throne room without them. She tried to turn back, but Gaspard urged her on.

The doors closed with a resounding *bang!* Willa's heartbeat stuttered. She hadn't even said goodbye!

"All you have to do is choose a coven and you're free, Willa," whispered Gaspard. He pushed her one final time. Willa stumbled several steps forward before she came to a halt.

She looked up.

Her stomach dropped.

On the west side of the room, Silverclaw witches fluttered in a circle around an imposing woman with wavy white hair and a flower crown. The hair was so long the other witches each carried an armful of it and still the ends trailed on the floor. This had to be Queen Opalina Starbright. Eladar joined his coven, grabbing an armful of the queen's hair to cradle.

On the east side, Irontongue witches stood apart from one another, hissing and muttering and spitting on the floor. Among them was an old man with swirling golden lines painted all over his bald head. He was a shriveled old thing, like a prune left to dry in the sun. His green-gray skin was spotted and wrinkled, and he was hunched like a wind-worn tree. Mortus Dragonstink, guessed Willa: the High Witch of Irontongue.

In between the groups stood the clerk, arms full of forms, and on the throne sat the prince, biting his nails, eyes flicking from one corner of the room to the other. The king was nowhere to be seen.

"Here's the troublemake—ah, I mean, here's the lovely girl witch," said the clerk.

All eyes turned toward Willa. She gulped and stepped back, bumping into Gaspard.

"What are you waiting for?" He nudged her forward. "You've nothing to fear."

Willa opened her mouth and closed it. Every eye in the room watched her carefully. She hugged the book close to her chest. Her magic hissed at her: *Don't lock me away,* it begged. *Please!*

Her parents had called her improper, unruly, too loud, too bold. She had tried to be who they wanted. She had worn every ill-fitting version of herself in pursuit of being Ordinary. She had quacked and quacked and quacked and quacked.

Wasn't this the same thing? Forcing her to choose? To become something every atom of her being rebelled against? Wasn't this just as . . . wrong?

"Quickly, child!" snapped the clerk. "Don't be contrary! Just get it over with."

"I . . ." started Willa, but she had no idea what should come next. "I don't kn—"

"Gah!" gasped Gaspard. "You can't say that word, remember? And not just because of the curse. You *have* to decide, Willa. You *have* to." His eyes burned into her, pleading. "You don't want to explode, do you?"

Willa took a deep breath and tried again. She opened her mouth, but no words came out, nothing but a pathetic croak. Had someone spelled a frog in her mouth?

"This is foolish!" said Mortus Dragonstink, his voice crunchy like static. "It's clear the girl wants to join the mighty Irontongue but is intimidated by the Silverclaw *scum*."

The Silverclaw witches tilted their heads and smiled vaguely at the Irontongues. Opalina stepped forward, the others following like a chain, cradling her mass of hair. With a smile, she picked her nose and flung a booger at the High Witch. *"Thbbbbft!"* She blew a raspberry before turning and wiggling her bottom. "Na-na-na-na-nah!"

Mortus Dragonstink was so angry he hissed lightning sparks. "Why, you insufferable ninnyplunk! I'll curse you bald!"

Oh dear, thought Willa. *This can't be good.*

"Now, now!" said the clerk, her hands placating. "Remember the truce. And if you absolutely *must* fight, please fill in these fifteen separate forms first. Start with Permission to Break a Magical Truce for Petty and/or Nefarious Reasons. I have pens for everyone."

Mortus Dragonstink spat at the Silverclaw queen's feet. The Silverclaw queen walked up to him and burped in his face.

Willa backed away as magic crackled in the air like static before an electrical storm. She kept going until she hit the back wall and slid to the floor, next to a potted plant. She just wanted to hide, to bury her head in the sand forever.

"Er, this hiding place is taken," said the plant.

Willa jolted as she spied beady eyes peering at her between the leaves. The king?

"S-s-sorry," said Willa. "It's just that I don't have anywhere else to go."

"Try the bathtub on the fourth floor."

"Thank you?"

Suddenly *The Long and Thoroughly Ordinary Tales of Pearl B. Purcep, an Explorer of Little Note* jiggled in her arms.

"Not now," she scolded it. "Can't you see I'm in the middle of something?"

Gaspard had moved to stand between the clans, arms outstretched and smiling peaceably. "Let's discuss this rationally," he said. An Irontongue witch spat in his eye.

Willa worried her bottom lip. Could she sneak out while everyone was distracted?

The book butted against Willa's belly like a cat demanding head scratches. She tried to ignore it but it leapt out of her grip and flipped open. In the center was another book. A slim volume with a familiar title: *The ABC of Witches!*

"I've already read this one," hissed Willa, but she grabbed hold of the book anyway. *The Long and Thoroughly Ordinary Tales of Pearl B. Purcep, an Explorer of Little Note* snapped shut. Once again, the title changed: *Are you sure?* it read.

"Of course I'm sure."

A new word popped between the others: *Are you* really *sure?*

"Oh, very well," she said. "What do you want me to read?"

The answer was simple: *W,* said the book.

As the two witch covens argued back and forth, Willa flicked open the book and began to read.

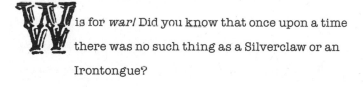 is for *war!* Did you know that once upon a time there was no such thing as a Silverclaw or an Irontongue?

Blah, blah, blah, thought Willa. She skipped ahead.

The flogging and rough music got to be a bit much for one witch. In retaliation, she kidnapped an Ordinary man and cut him into pieces. She joined

him back together again all mixed up with bits of
crocodile and raven: the very first jumble!

Other witches were horrified. "You can't do that!"
they cried. "We should enslave the Ordinary Folk,
not experiment on them!"

"Hang on," said Willa. "This isn't right. The words are different. Did you change it?"

No, said the cursed book. *I changed them* back *to how they were . . .*

"You mean someone changed them *before* I read it the first time? Nonsense!" But Willa read on. The words were almost the same as when she'd first read them, but not quite. Suddenly it didn't sound as if either coven was particularly favorable toward Ordinary Folk . . .

But some witches were pleased. "Ordinary Folk are
lower than worms! We should squash them under
our thumbs and rid the land of them for good!"
That's when the fighting began, between the witches
who wanted to rule the Ordinary Folk and the
witches who wanted to kill them.

"The book is right," said the king.

Willa startled. He was peering through the leaves, reading over her shoulder. "Pardon?"

His eyes darted side to side. "B-b-both clans have been fighting for the right to harm us. When the war's over, we're in trouble. At least while they're fighting each other they've forgotten about us." He slunk down, out of view again.

But who would have changed the book? And *why?*

"There you are!" Gaspard appeared in front of her, smiling and frowning and red-faced and harried. His hair had been cursed into spaghetti. "Why are you hiding all the way over here? Oh, hello, Your Majesty."

"Eep!"

Willa looked around but *The Long and Thoroughly Ordinary Tales of Pearl B. Purcep, an Explorer of Little Note* had vanished. Again.

"Listen, Willa." Gaspard gripped her hand and pulled her to her feet. "They're still arguing, and at any second they're going to break the truce." He ruffled his spaghetti hair. "Well, they already have, I guess. But if you tell them your decision, we can all go home."

Willa frowned. If *The Long and Thoroughly Ordinary Tales of Pearl B. Purcep, an Explorer of Little Note* was telling the truth, then *The ABC of Witches!* had been changed to make Irontongue seem worse than Silverclaw. Was it another of Eladar's tricks?

Gaspard squeezed her shoulder. "If you're having trouble, remember this: my mentor always said, 'You can lead a horse to water, but you can't make an omelet without cracking a few

eggs.' Which, now that I think about it, isn't all that helpful."
Gaspard shook his head fondly. "He was an odd one, Professor
Youngblood."

"Amaryllis Youngblood?"

"Oh, you kn—are aware of him too? Very old and reclusive,
but I was lucky enough to spend a good couple of years with
him, learning about magic."

Willa blinked. "He's alive?"

"Oh yes! Got to be at least a hundred by now. I'd think he
was a witch if I didn't know better!"

Pop!

The plant shook as the king suddenly melted to the floor,
his insides liquified. He didn't even have time to cry out in pain.

"Oops," said Gaspard, cheeks pink with embarrassment.
"I've got to stop doing that. Melting the king is bit of a no-no,
isn't it?" He chewed his bottom lip. "Best not mention it to the
prince for now. We'll distract everyone with your choice, won't
we?" She winced as his grip tightened. "Won't we, Willa?"

Willa's heart began to pound.

Gaspard had given her the book and urged her to read the
entry. *He* had known Amaryllis Youngblood, Rab Culpepper's
teacher. *He* had led her time and time again toward Silverclaw.

He owned the *Switcheroo!* pen that could alter any text to
whichever words you pleased.

The blood drained from Willa's face.

"It was *you*." Her voice was barely a whisper. She tried to back away, but she was already pressed against the wall. "You're the rogue witch."

For a moment her tutor appeared taken aback. His fingers flexed and he blinked. "I don't — I'm not — What are —" But then a grin broke out across his face. "Oh, go on, then!" he said with a laugh. "Smart girl! Indeed it was me. Such a pity there's no time to explain how or why or what for."

Willa was reeling, her head fuzzy with the weight of her realization. "Why not?"

"Because of them." Gaspard gestured to the throne-room door. Suddenly there was a crack as the doors splintered open and several hulking creatures burst through.

Willa sucked in a sharp breath.

Jumble monsters.

CHAPTER TWENTY-ONE

S PLINTERED WOOD CATAPULTED every which way as the giant jumbles burst through the doors. There were dragon-wolf-crocodiles, bear-spider-snakes, lion-lizard-rats, and more. "Dinnertime!" they roared.

The guards screamed and ran, but the witches attacked. They fired off curse after curse: *Dance-till-you-drop! Spaghetti-hair! Daisy-vomit!* For the first time in centuries, the covens fought side by side.

But a strange thing happened: the spells rebounded off the monsters and flung back at the casters. One by one, witches fell, slapped in the face by their own backfiring magic.

"Do you like my new and improved jumbles, Willa?" asked Gaspard, shouting to be heard over the buzz. "They were too easy to defeat last time. So I had a bit of a tinker and I think they're quite lovely, don't you? Bigger, stronger, faster, and with an impenetrable *Mirror-mirror!* shield."

Nothing made sense. *Gaspard* had made all the jumbles? Why? Why had he done any of this? And *how?* He wasn't even a witch. "You're evil," breathed Willa.

"Ha! Not evil. Just very, *very* determined."

Suddenly, half a bookcase came hurtling toward them, heaved from across the room by a giant cockroach with a raven's head and dragon legs. Willa leapt out of the way and fell on her behind with a crash that brought stars dancing behind her eyelids. Marceline was by her side in an instant, dragging her out of further harm's way.

"What's going on?" She helped Willa to stand.

Willa shook the lingering stars from her vision.

Gish flinched as the prince's crown clanged at their feet.

"It's Gaspard," explained Willa. "He's behind it all. He's—" She swung around, but the tutor was no longer where he'd been moments ago. There was only the broken bookshelf and a cloud of dust. "Oh, where is he now? We *have* to stop him."

The throne room was a blur of buzzing spells and roaring jumble monsters. The witches were casting *around* the jumbles now—aiming to knock down walls or send the chandelier crashing, hoping to stop the jumbles in their tracks. The prince was curled under his throne, sobbing. The clerk was trembling behind a curtain, and the king was a pile of melted bone and skin. But Willa couldn't see Gaspard anywhere.

"There he is!" shouted Marceline, pointing to the far back corner. Willa glimpsed the tutor's red suit slipping behind a floor-length tapestry: he was dragging Opalina Starbright with him. Were Opalina and Gaspard in on it together?

"After him!" Willa was already running. She dodged spells and jumbles as she hurried to the far back corner, where she swept aside the tapestry to reveal—

"Another secret passage?" Marceline stomped her foot. "This is ridiculous!"

The three children hurried into the cold, dark passageway. Sconces lit part of the way, enough to see flashes of movement far ahead. They seemed to run forever—the passage weaved up and down and all around.

"Stairs!" said Marceline, pointing.

There was indeed a rickety spiral staircase ahead of them; the passageway came to a dead end, so it was the only way forward.

"Come on!" called Willa. The three children hurried up the spiral stairs, gripping the wonky railing as they climbed. The whole staircase shook with every step.

By the time they reached the top, Willa could hardly breathe. "Only. One. Way. Out," she wheezed, lifting the trapdoor above her. Willa shielded her eyes as she squeezed through the small opening and onto a rooftop, high above the city of Bad Faith. Marceline and Gish followed close behind.

The roof had many spires and sharp slopes. It was high enough that all of Bad Faith was laid before them—and beyond, too: fields and forests and something dark and rocky and haunting in the far distance. The Desolation? Willa shivered and turned away.

"Where are we?" The wind whipped her hair around, extra sleeves flapping. Gish grabbed her arm to steady her as they shuffled along a narrow ridge until they reached a low pitch.

"I think this is the Holy Sanctum of Everyday Wisdom," shouted Marceline.

"Quite right!" said a voice. "Always so smart, our Princess Marceline."

Willa and her friends spun around to find Gaspard perched on a flat ridge above them. Beside him was Opalina Starbright, swaying like a sunflower in a gentle breeze—it was as if she had fallen asleep standing up.

"This is my old friend," explained Gaspard with a flourish at the queen. "I say *friend,* but actually she's my mother. Aren't you, Opalina?"

The witch continued to sway, staring into the distance with unseeing eyes.

"She's a bit quiet right now. A little something I call the *Zone-drone!* curse; her mind is taking a wee snooze. Managed to splice together four spells to make it." There was a nasty twist to his lips as he grinned at Opalina. "How's that for talented, Mother?"

The witch, of course, said nothing.

"Rab Culpepper thought he was smart splicing *two* spells together, but he didn't understand the half of it! I'm better than him. I'm better than all of you!"

Willa's head ached. Every unanswered question was a tiny hammer beating against the inside of her skull. "You're a witch?" She edged in front of her friends.

"The greatest ever witch!" he crowed.

"But how come you're not in a coven?"

Gaspard threw back his head with wild laughter. "Of course you'd ask that. I bet you think it means you don't have to choose a coven. But you do, Willa. You absolutely do. And you *will* choose Silverclaw. Oh dear, would you look at that!" The tutor waved a hand at the city below. "My creations are attacking the city now." A bloodcurdling scream pierced the air. Willa turned and saw the lion-lizard-rat crashing through the market. Ordinary Folk ran for their lives as more jumbles arrived. "*Tsk, tsk, tsk!* There'll be nothing left soon," said Gaspard, grinning. "But if you say you'll join Silverclaw I'll stop them. Mother here can perform the initiation. With me controlling her, of course."

Marceline tugged on Willa's sleeve but Willa dared not look away from Gaspard again. "Why do you want me to join Silverclaw?" she asked.

Gaspard curled his hands into fists. "Because then Mother will finally see what an incredible witch I am, willing to do anything to bring her the most powerful untamed witch yet. I created jumbles and wasted half my life span casting all those blasted spells. And I did it so you'd see the truth about Irontongue. I couldn't say anything outright because I had to sign that silly contract—I just had to nudge you in the right direction."

"But Ferula never did anything wrong! It was you all along."

Gaspard snorted. "She would have misbehaved eventually."

Marceline elbowed Willa again. This time Willa glanced to the side and saw what her friend was pointing to.

Cats.

Lots and lots of cats.

They had gathered on the rooftop and were curled up in the sun, licking their paws and staring off into the distance, unfazed by the battle decimating the city below. What were they doing?

"But Ferula, oh, she was a wily one!" continued Gaspard. "After the jumble attack she confronted me. Said she knew I had magic blood in me—she could smell it—and I was the only one who could be behind it all. I couldn't risk her telling you the truth, so I tricked her into Rab's old workroom and turned her into a jumble. And that worked a treat! Everyone believed it was *her* behind the attack because she'd vanished. And because I only used Rab's spells that combined Irontongue curses. But you *still* wouldn't be persuaded. You asked to learn more about Irontongue magic. So I gave you the secret-spilling curse, a few more adjustments to *The ABC of Witches!*, and then the bone-melting curse. My finest creation to date, if you ask me. Worth all those sleepless nights pretending I was working on a cure when really I was coming up with more spells. I guess I could have used regular old Irontongue spells, but where's the fun in that?"

Willa's mouth hung lax in disbelief. "You did all of that just to make me choose Silverclaw?"

Gaspard nodded enthusiastically. "So imagine my surprise just now when you *still* weren't prepared to choose."

Willa frowned. "Wait, was that a lie too? Do I really need to choose early?"

Gaspard giggled. "I was impatient and you seemed determined to figure things out on your own. I didn't want you coming across anything that would implicate me—like poor Ferula and her chicken legs. So I cursed you when you weren't looking—a harmless *Fire-blood!* curse triggered to fill your veins with boiling heat every time you cast a spell. Ingenious, really. Though I suppose it isn't needed now. Here, I'll take it off you as a show of good faith. To prove how honorable I am." He

253

performed the counter-curse with a flourish; Willa shivered as an icy fizz crawled through her. Suddenly she felt lighter than she had in days.

Until the anger came.

Then she felt a different kind of heat. All those witch trials and lost voices and melted bones and secrets—and all to force Willa to choose Silverclaw? The anger burned fiercely. "But how come you're not part of the Silverclaw coven?" She could barely push the words through her teeth clenched in anger.

The smile slipped from Gaspard's face. His eyes darted to the blissfully unaware Opalina and back again. "I *am* a Silverclaw. I was born to be, but . . ." His grin returned with a sharp, bitter edge. "What I never told you, Willa, is that witches have to face a test *after* their initiation. It's to determine how strong their magical ability is and where they fit in the coven. If you're an Irontongue, it's what determines your tier. In Silverclaw they say we're all equal, but that's not true." His hands were balled into fists again, knuckles white with strain. "After my initiation I took the test. But they said I *failed* it—they said I had so little magical ability I might as well be Ordinary. My own mother kicked me out of the coven. She said I was an embarrassment to her!" He glared at Opalina. "Why don't you ask me how come I'm so powerful now, Mother? How come I can modify spells? How come I'm stronger than any coven witch?"

Willa glanced around her—more cats had joined the others. The roof was littered with them, a whole army of cats.

"It doesn't matter!" cried Gaspard. He tossed up his arms in frustration. "You *will* choose Silverclaw and Opalina will initiate you and take me back. She will have no choice! Because *I* brought you to her, *I* made sure you picked Silverclaw, and *I* am the strongest witch of all!" He thumped a fist against his chest.

Willa shook her head. "No. I won't."

"You think you can stop me?" Gaspard laughed. "You might be powerful, Willa, but you have no idea how to wield that power to its fullest. I will *crush* you in a battle. But obviously I don't want to do that. So let's see if I can find a way to persuade you."

Gaspard twirled his arms, undulated his body, and kicked out his legs. It looked as if a spider had crawled down his trousers and he was trying to shake it out while at the same time mixing a cake. Willa didn't recognize the spell, but she knew something was coming, so she quickly shoved Marceline and Gish out of the way as blue clouds shot from Gaspard's fingertips. In the blink of an eye the clouds turned into rainbow confetti. *Carnivorous* confetti.

"See?" cried Gaspard laughing. "I can cast like a proper Silverclaw witch!"

Willa cowered, hands over her head, as the carnivorous confetti nipped at her until she bled. "Get away! Get back!" she cried, but no matter how hard she flailed her arms, the confetti slipped past, sinking its teeth into her skin.

"Use magic!" hissed Marceline, hiding behind a spire with Gish. "Fight back!"

Gaspard cackled. "Against me? She wouldn't last a minute!"

Willa's anger swelled. He was just like her parents, trying to force her to be something she wasn't. *We'll show him,* hissed her magic.

Fizzing all over, Willa shouted, "Skibity thebbiity libity-jig!" then lapped her tongue as if eating a half-melted ice cream. The magic roared, fighting her efforts to channel it into a babbling brook. *Just enough! Just enough power!* she urged it. But the magic cracked the floodgates and a wave burst through her. Lightning shot from her mouth and turned into screeching bats. The bats flew unsteadily, their right wings smaller than their left.

She curled her hands into fists, fingernails biting into her palms. Gaspard had taken the curse off her, yet her spell casting was as wonky as ever. Why was it so hard? Why was her magic so contrary?

Gaspard dodged the flailing bats with a hoot of laughter. "And *still* she uses Irontongue magic! You really are stubborn, aren't you, Willa Birdwhistle?" He laughed cruelly. "Well, guess what? I can cast Irontongue magic too!"

Gaspard shouted, "Poompity-joop froompity rabbity!" then curled his tongue up to lick the tip of his nose. Purple word lightning shot upward, creating a storm cloud above them. It began to rain frogs. "Poisonous frogs!" cried Gaspard.

They were brightly colored red, green, and purple, and when they hit the ground they leapt about, spitting a sizzling poisonous mucus that burned through trousers and shoes and socks and sweaters. A drop landed on Willa's hand, burning her skin red and raw.

"Ouch!" The pain sucked the breath from her lungs. "You want me to use Silverclaw magic?" she yelled.

Willa danced. She wiggled her thumbs side to side, rolled back her shoulders one after the other, and hopped on her right leg three times. Electric-blue clouds shot from her fingers and turned the frogs into socks — red, green, and purple socks that flung themselves at Gaspard.

From behind the spire, Marceline cheered and Gish clapped. But Willa was breathing hard; her magic roared against the heavily damaged cage, wanting to be free. It felt like holding the reins to a thousand wild horses, all desperate to bolt. No, not horses — cats. Willful, headstrong cats.

Gaspard ducked and weaved to avoid the flying socks — he was dancing side to side so much that Willa didn't realize until too late that he was casting another spell. The clouds burst from his fingers, but they shot past Willa.

"Ha!" she cried. "You missed me."

But then a scream pierced the air and Willa froze. Slowly, she turned; her stomach dropped.

Marceline was floating high up in the air, sailing ever closer to the edge of the building.

"Put her down!" cried Willa.

Gaspard laughed. "Don't want to see your friend go tumbling over the side of the Holy Sanctum of Everyday Wisdom?" He grinned. The disdain in his eyes made Willa shiver. "Then make your choice now, Willa," he said. "And make it right."

CHAPTER TWENTY-TWO

MARCELINE HUNG IN THE AIR as if tethered by an invisible rope. Willa racked her brain for spells to help, but fear left her mind utterly blank. *Think, Willa! Think!*

A sudden gust of wind whipped Marceline sideways, and Huggin slipped from her pocket. A cry caught in Willa's throat as the little mouse plummeted. Gish leapt from his hiding place and threw himself to the tiles, catching the mouse in his cupped hands.

"Nice catch!" Gaspard wiped away tears of laughter. "You kids are a hoot!"

Willa rounded on him. "You bring Marceline down this instant," she snarled.

"Or what?"

"Or *else*."

Gaspard shook his head. "You're a most disobedient student."

"Well, you're a terrible teacher!"

Gaspard lips curved into a cruel smile. "Quite right. So terrible I never taught you to fly."

He grabbed Opalina's hand and shot a wink at Willa. Suddenly he leapt from the roof and *flew*. "Cheerio!" he shouted. Marceline squealed as she was tugged along behind him like a balloon on a string.

Willa and Gish rushed to the edge of the roof. They watched him sail through the air in a ginormous arc, land softly in the market square, and then bounce off again. He bounced and bounced and bounced, leaping over the Inner Circle wall as if riding a giant, invisible pogo stick. Marceline bobbed along behind him, screaming.

"I can't fly!" cried Willa. "How can I chase after him?" Should she find Eladar? No! That would take too long. The jumbles were destroying the city; the other witches had their hands full. *Think, Willa, think!*

Talon appeared beside her, butting his head against her calf.

"I don't have time to cuddle you," she said. Tears of frustration welled in her eyes. The city wobbled as she teetered on the edge of the roof; it was such a long way down. Gish motioned back the way they'd come. But how long would that take?

Defying all expectation *and* the laws of gravity, Talon leapt from the rooftop too. Like Gaspard, he sailed through the air in an arc before safely landing on all four paws outside the butcher's shop. He sat, tail flicking, as if nothing out of the Ordinary had just happened.

Every word Willa might have said crumbled to dust in her mouth. She'd known her cat was magical, but . . .

A ginger tom walked toward Willa, padding along the roof's edge like it was a tightrope before he, too, leapt to the ground. Then a tabby, a calico, and a chunky brown kitten. All of them landed on four paws, graceful like dancers. A white cat sauntered toward her and sat, piercing green eyes boring into hers as it looked up and winked. *Go on,* said the eyes, *give it a go.*

Willa felt a buzzing under her skin, a fizzy, zizzy, orange-soda buzz that was equal parts terror and excitement. She turned to Gish. "Do you trust me?"

Gish tugged his earlobe, eyes brimming with fear, but he nodded. Willa added *because he is brave even when he is not* to her list of reasons to like Gish.

She grabbed his hand. "Hold on!" she cried.

She jumped.

I might have made a mistake, thought Willa as they plummeted.

Her magic beat against the roof of the Rapscallion's Cage. *Let go!* it hissed. *Let go. Let go. Let go!*

Gish gripped her hand like a vise. The wind smacked against her face. Her magic roared: *Let go!*

Cheese and rice! thought Willa.

She let go.

The cage fell apart. The fizzy, zizzy, orange-soda feeling roared through her like a rocket. It reached for the sky, pulling Willa and Gish up and up and up with it. They were no longer falling. They were flying.

Flying.

Willa whooped at the rush of the wind, the city blurring below, the tight squeeze of Gish's hand in hers. Her magic filled every inch of her. And when it reached the edges, it pushed and pushed and pushed until she felt herself expand, like the first gasp of air after holding your breath underwater.

She felt endless.

After a moment, the magic guided her toward the ground. She wasn't as graceful as the cats, stumbling like a baby deer on ice as she landed.

Her heart was racing, trying to take its own flight.

Gish looked at her with wide eyes; he gripped her hand so tightly it hurt.

Willa grinned. "Want to do that again?"

He gulped and nodded.

She leapt off the ground, letting her magic soar high over the Inner Circle wall. Behind her, the army of cats flew. She was *flying*. Flying!

Willa, Gish, and her cats bounced through the city on their own invisible pogo sticks. They chased Marceline's faint screams and the flash of a red suit far ahead.

But as they flew over the Outer Circle, Willa was hit with a *Wacky-wind!* curse. The wild wind tossed her like salad. Her grip on Gish's hand broke; with his mouth open in a silent scream, he fell. Willa whipped around in the air, desperately casting *Float-like-a-feather!* The spell hit Gish square in the chest and he floated gently to the ground. Willa tumbled after him and landed on all fours in the dirt beside the lane. The cats landed around her, flopping on the grass to groom or sun themselves as though they hadn't just flown halfway across the city.

Willa climbed to her feet, dusting herself off.

"Did you enjoy that?"

She looked up.

Gaspard stood in the middle of the lane with Opalina swaying beside him. Marceline had been cut from her invisible tether but was now wrapped up in bright yellow yarn from the mill. Gaspard held her collar as she squirmed in his grip. "I thought I'd bring you closer to home." He nodded at Mr. Nibler's garden on one side and Mrs. Tewksbury's on the other. "For old times' sake. I know it—"

Pop!

A blue rope snaked up Opalina before she melted into a gooey pile.

"Oops," said Gaspard with a giggle. He toed the pile of skin and melted bone. "I forgot about that. Oh well. I'll fix her in a bit."

Willa's skin tingled like a gazillion tiny electrical storms brewing all over her. How could he care so little about others?

"Get back," she warned Gish.

He hid behind the cats.

Willa's magic fizzed so much it roared in her ears. "Hand over Marceline now and undo all the curses," she said.

Gaspard scoffed. "Silly girl. Why do you persist with this nonsense? You have to choose a coven no matter what, so why not Silverclaw? Surely you can see they're superior? Do you honestly think you can beat me? I remember which spells I taught you, Willa."

Willa didn't think she could win, but that wasn't the point. Some things were worth fighting a losing battle for.

She raised her chin. "We'll see."

But before she could cast a spell, a shadow darted overhead. Willa whipped her head around; even the cats took notice. What was it? Suddenly, the Ferula jumble landed on Mrs. Tewksbury's garden fence.

"Step aside, dearie," she said in the voice of a small child. She glared beadily at Willa. "I have some revenge to attend to."

"But how are you speaking?" gasped Willa.

The Ferula jumble smacked her lips. "Stumbled upon a stolen voice bubble and had another witch trap it inside me with a *Sticky-icky!* curse. Not the best solution, but enough to have my revenge on this pompous foofhead."

Gaspard bared his teeth. "I really should have killed you when I had the chance. It was just so amusing to see you as a jumble."

Ferula squawked in displeasure. "I'll show you, you dundering dumfoozle. Bobuggy-doo bibby rabbity!" She waggled her tongue like a dying bug. Thousands of tiny lightning strikes shot from her mouth, screeching the spell words over and over. They turned into fire-breathing bees that swarmed the tutor.

"Don't forget, I can cast Irontongue spells too, Ferula!" Gaspard swatted the bees, hissing in pain. "Jebbity lebbity-jip!"

Magic flew back and forth, cracks of lightning in every color.

But now was Willa's chance.

While Gaspard was distracted, Willa cast a *Reel-me-in!* curse. The golden lasso whistled through the air and wrapped around Marceline. The princess squeaked in surprise as she was pulled toward Gish and Willa.

She collapsed on the grass. Willa removed the yarn with a *Snip-snip!* curse (a spell she had finally taken the initiative to learn).

"I've had enough adventures now," said Marceline. She blew strips of wild, loose hair out of her eyes as she scrambled to her feet. Her face broke into the sunniest smile when Gish handed over Huggin. "Oh, thank you!" She rubbed noses with the little mouse. "I was so worried!"

Ferula cackled as a pair of Mr. Nibler's boots flew out of his house and began chasing Gaspard around the front lawn, kicking him on his behind.

Something butted against Willa's hand. She looked down, expecting Talon. Instead, *The Long and Thoroughly Ordinary Tales of Pearl B. Purcep, an Explorer of Little Note* was floating in the air.

"You again. Unless you're here to help, I haven't got time to play games with you."

Don't be mean, said the writing on the front of the book. *I'm always helpful.* And if it was possible for a book to pout, then that's exactly what it did.

"Then how do I defeat Gaspard?"

The book's front cover shimmered as it returned to the original title. But as soon as it appeared, the title was scratched out and a new one was scrawled below it: *The True (and Explosive!) History of Rab Culpepper.*

Willa frowned. Was it the same book? Had it always been the same book?

But as the battle between Gaspard and Ferula raged on, the new title was scratched out too. A third title appeared beneath it, this one glowing golden: *Rab's Rambunctious Witchcraft for Rebels.*

Was this Rab's spell book? The one from the hiding place?

Holding her breath, she opened the book to the first page.

Sick and tired of the Witch War?

it read in Rab's familiar handwriting.

Do you think Silverclaws stink and Irontongues are Irondungs? Never fear! There is a new kind of magic for witches who'd rather swallow fire-breathing bees than join either coven. Read on to discover how you—yes, you!— can cast spells that aren't a Silverchore or Ironwrong.

Willa gasped. *A new kind of magic?* This was it! Proof! Her chance to avoid both covens. She felt like she was flying again.

The book flicked over several pages on its own. It stopped at a spell that read: The No-bother! curse: For when Things are causing you Great Bother and you'd like them to Stop. The page seemed to shimmer, and her fingers tingled to reach out and touch it.

To cast the *No-bother!* spell, you must:

1. Dance like you're running late for your grandmother's birthday party.

2. Shout an answer to the question "Can fish tell the time?" followed by the words *Ackamarackus fribble fadoodle macaroni schmegeggy squit* (for extra-strength spells, use a silly voice).

3. Think very hard about the color purple.

4. Point at the object causing you bother and wave your finger about like there's gum stuck to the tip.

5. And *poof!* just wait and see what happens!

Willa frowned. Wasn't this just like the modified spells? A loud crack drew her attention back to the warring witches.

"I'm done playing!" shouted Gaspard. His spaghetti hair was wild, his red suit singed, his grin wicked. Magical debris littered the lane. "You're a useless distraction. A fly in my cereal." He flapped his arms, jiggled his legs, and spun in a circle.

"Oh no!" gasped Ferula. Willa watched in horror as the poor creature evaporated and was turned into a cloud, swept away by the wind.

The *Clouds-away!* curse.

Willa was sick to her stomach. She was eleven years old again: helpless, afraid, angry, guilty, watching her parents float away. Magic bubbled and boiled beneath her skin.

You're not powerless, whispered the voice. *You never were.*

Gaspard turned to her with a manic grin. "I see you've stolen your friend back." His laughter rasped in his chest. "Why can't you just be a good little girl?" He stepped toward her, menacing. "If you won't do as you're told, I'll have to teach you a lesson. How about I turn both your friends into clouds?" He took another step but startled as a small tabby rubbed against his ankle. "And for pity's sake *please* do something about your blasted cats. Shoo! Scram! Get away from me, you little menace!"

Willa's rage was so wild, she shook with it. The remaining cats had gathered tightly around her, tails flicking, waiting. Her magic was waiting too. Her magic that fought tooth and nail against being squished into the shape of "proper" spells. Her magic that refused to quack.

"I will not do as I'm told!" she cried. "Not when you're forcing me to be someone I'm not. Not when you only want to control me. My magic doesn't listen to bullies. And if you think you can tell a cat what to do, you've another thing coming."

Gaspard frowned. "What in the Wild are you talking about?"

Willa smiled at her cats. "Do you hear that?" The clerk, the master weaver, the prince, all of them had been right—she *was* a troublemaker. She was wild; she was contrary; she was defiant. And so were her cats. "Mr. Renard wants you to leave him alone. I guess you'd better do as you're told."

The army of cats attacked.

Cats of every color leapt at him, clawing and biting. Talon was at the front, his sharp fangs digging into the tutor's legs. Red fabric flew as the cats struck over and over again. The tutor cried out in pain and fell back, crashing through the fence into Mrs. Tewksbury's front garden.

"Cats will always do the opposite of what you ask them," said Willa with a huff. "Perhaps that's a lesson *you* should have learned."

"Amazing!" gasped Marceline. Gish nodded alongside her.

The Long and Thoroughly—no, *Rab's Rambunctious Witchcraft for Rebels* butted against her hand.

"I haven't forgotten you," she said. "I just have to—"

A magical rope whistled through the air and wrapped around her middle. She cried out as she was tugged through the fence and into the garden. She fell into the rosebushes alongside the tutor and a lot of angry cats. Gaspard sneered at her as she struggled against the rope. "Now do as I say and stay put, okay? I just have to—ouch!—finish off these blasted cats with a— argh!" He inspected his bleeding arm. "That wasn't a cat! That was a rose! It *bit* me."

A rose?

The blood leached from Willa's face. "What day is it?"

Gaspard scrunched up his nose. "Tuesday, but I hardly think—"

"Oh dear," said Willa.

Mrs. Tewksbury's rosebushes attacked.

Thorns pierced their clothes, pinning them in place as the red blooms snapped their hungry mouths. Fortunately for Willa, the bush she'd landed in only had hold of her spare sleeves. She slipped out of the rope and her sweater and crawled to safety. The cats slunk away unscathed too. Gaspard wasn't so fortunate: a rosebush wrapped around his arms and legs, nipping and nibbling everywhere it could reach. Pinned in place, he couldn't cast Silverclaw magic, but he shot an Irontongue *Snip-snip!* curse. Roses began to fall, cut from their stems.

"Take that, you beastly bush!" he cried.

Willa scrambled to her feet. She had to stop him. And she knew exactly which spell to use.

So she danced like she was running late for her grandmother's birthday party ("I don't even have a grandmother," sighed Willa as she pumped her arms and kicked out her legs). She shouted, "Of course they can't! Where would they put their wristwatches?" and then "Ackamarackus fribble fadoodle macaroni schmegeggy squit!" (in a silly, high-pitched voice). She thought very hard about the color purple. She pointed at Gaspard and waggled her finger like there was gum stuck to the tip.

She shivered pleasantly as the magic whooshed from her with ease. Five shimmery, translucent cats shot from her fingertips and danced around Gaspard until the roses transformed into long, creeping vines. They wrapped tightly around him, cocooning him like a *Snakes-alive!* curse.

"Hey! What's—" he cried, but a fistful of rose petals flew up and lodged themselves in his mouth and he could no longer speak. He couldn't move, and he couldn't utter a word—he could no longer cast magic.

"It's working!" squealed Marceline. She clutched Gish and they jumped up and down.

But the spell hadn't finished. Because the biggest bother Gaspard had caused was casting all those nasty spells. The rosebush lifted him until he was standing. He spluttered until every petal had been coughed up.

"Just what do you—*gah!*" His lips stuttered as though he was trapped under the magical contract again. But this time it was the spell forcing him to cast the counter-curse for every mousetrap that had terrorized the city. "What's—*ah!* Undiddy doodiddy dilly dally do!" he shouted. The rosebush made him stomp his right foot, then his left foot. He wiggled his behind and blew a raspberry.

I suppose that's how you cast the counter-curse for Rab's spells, thought Willa.

"Now, you listen here," said Gaspard before another fistful of rose petals lodged in his mouth and he couldn't utter another word. He tried to wriggle and he tried to shout, but the spell had total control over him. The translucent cats vanished.

Willa looked around. Had it worked? How would they know?

There was a long pause—anticipation clenched Willa's heart in a viselike grip. *Please work, please work, please work.*

Finally, there was a gentle whoosh. Willa whipped her head around. *There!* A shimmery golden bubble flew toward them, so fast it was a blur. Gish stumbled back as the bubble flung itself into his mouth. His eyes bulged and he spluttered, grabbing his throat as if choking. His face turned purple.

Marceline thumped him between his shoulder blades. "Breathe!"

"It's okay," wheezed Gish. "It just went down the wrong way for a bit and—" His eyes grew wide. "I've got my voice back!" The brightest grin blossomed across his face. "I've got my voice back!" He jumped up and down. "I've got my voice back!"

Out in the lane, Opalina Starbright re-formed. Her bones solidified and her body filled out like a balloon until she was finally back to normal, rubbing her temples and groaning.

Next, a puffy white cloud floated into the garden and re-formed into the Ferula jumble. "What in the Wild just happened?" she asked in the child's voice. Suddenly she coughed and hacked as though a fur ball was caught in her throat. A golden bubble escaped her mouth and flew away to find its owner. But her own voice bubble soon appeared and dived into her open mouth. Before she could say a word, she was spinning, round and round and round until a full-size Ferula, a rabbit, a crocodile, a chicken, a wolf, a bear, a pig, a baby dragon, and twelve black snakes all collapsed onto the grass in a daze.

"Oh my," said Marceline as the dragon shook itself like a wet dog. Her eyes were ginormous. "Can I keep it?"

Ferula clutched her head and groaned. "Where am I? What happened?"

"Nm mawh," whimpered Gaspard around the mouthful of petals. "Nm mawh!"

"Oh, shush, you," said Willa.

All the critters scurried away as Opalina danced into the garden, long fingernails clacking together. Gaspard tried to back away, but the rosebush held him in place. The Silverclaw queen ran a nail along Gaspard's jaw, drawing blood. He gulped. "The bees are unhappy with you," said the queen.

Gish threw his arms around Willa. "You did it," he said against her ear. "I knew having a witch in the castle would be fun."

Willa blushed. "I had help." Gish pulled Marceline in for a hug too.

Talon trotted up to be petted; Willa was happy to oblige. After all, he was her favorite little troublemaker. "I just hope *The Long and Thoroughly Ordinary Tales of Pearl B. Purcep, an Explorer of Little Note* doesn't expect a hug," she said, scratching the cat under his chin. She grinned and looked around, but the book had once again vanished. "Now why would it—"

Willa looked down.

Her feet were bare.

"Cheese and rice!"

CHAPTER TWENTY-THREE

WILLA STEPPED INTO THE COOL of the castle dungeons. She shivered, but it wasn't the chilly air that crept under her skin. She stared into the shadows; the shadows stared back.

She took a deep breath.

"We're right behind you," said Gish.

"One last adventure," said Marceline. She squeezed Willa's hand.

Willa nodded.

Talon led the way through the twisty passages deep below the castle. The walls were covered in moss and water stains, the ground littered with stone rubble. It was quiet and empty — the jumbles had been unjumbled and the accused witches set free. There was only one prisoner left in the castle now.

Candles burned in sconces, lighting the way. Talon seemed to know where to go, and Willa was happy to follow him. A steep drop of narrow stone steps led them to three cells separated by floor-to-ceiling bars. Guards huddled by the door, casting nervous glances at the figure on his knees in the central cell.

Gaspard.

"Are you sure?" asked Gish.

Willa swallowed down her fear and nodded. She stepped forward.

Her former tutor was a sorry sight. It had only been a handful of days since the fight in Mrs. Tewksbury's front garden, but he had aged a decade or more. His foppish hair was limp and knotted, his skin loose, as if melting off his bones. He still wore the red suit. It was soiled and torn to shreds. Little wisps of smoke curled through the air around him.

So it was true, what Healer Berwig had said. Gaspard was dying.

"He's going to boil away like a pot of soup left unattended on the stove," she'd said, standing in the crumbling remains of the throne room. With the truth revealed and Willa's choice of coven once again set for her thirteenth birthday, everyone had gathered in the aftermath of the battle to make a different choice: what to do with the rogue witch. "All that unorthodox spell casting has decimated his initiation spell, corrupting his magic irreparably. It's seeping through the gaps and poisoning his system. He'll slowly burn from the inside out until he's little more than a pile of ashes."

With her heart in her throat, Willa stepped up to the bars. Talon squeezed between her legs and sat in front of her, his single eye trained on the bowed figure. His tail flicked.

"You wanted to see me?" she said. Her small voice echoed.

Gaspard raised his head. His grin was so familiar it was a punch to the gut. There was nothing fun or sweet and caring about it now, though. "Willa, dear! How lovely of you to visit!"

"I don't have long," she said primly.

"Pity," said Gaspard. He wiggled on his knees, trying to get closer. It appeared his hands and feet were bound, though it wasn't necessary—there was a *Mirror-mirror!* curse on the bars. "It's horribly dull in here. No one visits except Healer Berwig. And she's hardly a laugh a minute." The burns on his cheeks cracked as he smiled. "All she wants to talk about is my impending doom!"

Willa had learned a great deal about Gaspard's past since his capture. He had turned up in Bad Faith aged thirteen and a half, telling folk he was from Bog Hollow, a town as far north as you could travel before you hit the Desolation. He'd found work as a dogsbody for the Academy of Ordinary Studies, where the professor for Magical Understanding had taken an interest in his "unique" knowledge of spells and spell casting. Given access to the academy's vast library of magical research materials, Gaspard had stumbled across Amaryllis Youngblood's forgotten diaries, which introduced him to Rab Culpepper and his controversial ideas. He'd immediately sought out the reclusive former professor to learn more. Exactly how he'd managed to modify the spells and grow his magic beyond the expectation of the Silverclaws was unknown. He wasn't talking about it, all of Rab's work had vanished, and no one could locate Amaryllis Youngblood.

"You asked to see me," she prompted.

Gaspard grinned. "So I did. I wanted to set the record straight. One last chance to teach you something of value." He coughed.

Willa steeled herself.

"I know you dislike the idea of joining a coven," said Gaspard. "But the truth is, there's no other option. Rab Culpepper blew himself up inventing spells. And you see what's happening to me, don't you? Casting Irontongue magic was bad enough, but this pathetic figure you see before you? All courtesy of using Rab's modified spells." He coughed so hard he almost toppled forward.

Willa tried not to pity him, but it was difficult.

"Meddling with the coven spells is dangerous enough," he said once he'd caught his breath. "What it does to your body and your mind . . . Talk to the healer if you don't believe me. But it hardly compares to what happens if you try to make new spells . . . *Ka-boom!*"

"But he *did* invent new spells," argued Willa. "There's a book, and I cast one myself, and—"

Gaspard chuckled. "None of those spells were new, Willa." His tone said *silly, silly girl*. "That last one you used on me? A simple mix of *Do-as-I-say!* and *Busybody!* And that *Pop-goes-the-mousetrap!* spell? A combination of *Bubble-burst!* and *I-see-you!* Rab might have *thought* he was creating new spells, but in reality he was merely mixing and matching the coven spells to create dangerous hybrids."

Disappointment tightened in Willa's chest. She'd had

an inkling, of course. *All that unorthodox spell casting . . .* the healer had said, her shrewd eyes boring into Willa's. She wanted to ask *The Long and Thoroughly Ordinary Tales of Pearl B. Purcep, an Explorer of Little Note*—or whatever it was really called. But the book was hiding and refused to appear, even when Willa dangled her socks in the records room. Ultimately, it didn't matter that casting his spells had been as easy as breathing the evidence was clear: there was no proof of a third kind of magic and Rab's modified spells were a death sentence, just another way to explode—long and drawn-out and painful.

Willa had known this—had accepted this—but still it hurt to hear it again.

Gaspard shot Willa a rueful grin. "Your choices remain the same, Willa. Silverclaw, Irontongue, or explode." He chuckled. "What will it be?"

Willa shook her head. She had accepted Rab was not the answer, but it didn't mean she had lost hope. "I choose me," she said. "I choose my friends and my cats and all the things I haven't discovered yet." She straightened her shoulders. "I choose a different path."

If Rab's spells were too dangerous, she would simply find another way. He hadn't found the answer, but maybe she would. She had time. And she had friends to help her—she wasn't alone.

Gaspard sighed. "Why can't you accept it? All other paths are too dangerous. Just take the choice in front of you, Willa.

The safe option." He licked his cracked lips. "You don't want to end up like me."

Willa looked at the pathetic figure on his knees and let herself pity him, just for a moment. Then she let herself remember all the ways he had done badly by her and the people she cared about. He had nothing left to teach her; he never had.

"Haven't you learned anything?" she said. She raised her chin. "You can't tell me what to do. You'd have a better chance convincing Talon." She turned away before he could argue but drew up short when she spotted the prince sauntering through the doorway.

"What's she doing here?" he sneered at Willa. She moved aside as he marched up to the cage.

There was a permanent ring of guards around the prince these days, and it had nothing to do with witches. The citizens of Bad Faith had a bone to pick with Prince Cyrus. He had turned them against one another, put them on trial, and locked them up. Now they flung fish heads and rotted fruit whenever they saw him. It made him unbearable to be around—he was always in a terrible mood, *and* he stank like the fishmonger's shop.

The clerk, more guards, and quite a lot of witches trailed in after the prince. It seemed it was time for Gaspard to be taken back to Gomerim with the Silverclaws, where he was destined to slowly burn to ashes behind bars.

"Take him away before he blows up my castle," snapped the prince.

Opalina Starbright stepped forward to watch her son being hauled to his feet, her hair cradled like a wedding veil in the hands of the witches following behind her. Eladar appeared at Willa's side. "Do not worry," he said. He picked his nose and flung it at the prince. "We'll take good care of him."

Willa didn't know how to say she wasn't worried. Gaspard had made his choices.

The witches led Gaspard out of the cage. He grinned at Willa as he passed, reeking of smoke. "Remember what I said, Willa Birdwhistle." He almost looked like the man she had first met, flushed with excitement and dragging her away from an angry prince covered in scrambled eggs. But he was a liar. A manipulator. A cruel and heartless man. "Be a good girl, won't you?"

Willa refused to look away, watching with a steely gaze as he was led from the dungeon.

The witches filed out after him, and then the prince, the clerk, and the guards, too. When they were all out of view, Willa finally let out a long breath.

Marceline and Gish rushed to her side.

"He might be lying about Rab," said Marceline. She took hold of Willa's hand and squeezed. "And even if he isn't, we'll find a way."

Gish nodded. "You can stay here with us, where you belong."

Belong. Willa liked that word. In fact, it was high on her list of favorite words, tied in first place with *friend*.

She smiled. The truth was, when you stopped listening to

the voices that crowed about *proper* and *right* and *should* and *shouldn't,* it was much easier to see that your choices were unlimited. It was much easier to honk when everyone insisted you should quack. And Willa had plans to do quite a lot of honking.

"Come on," she said. "I have something to show you."

CHAPTER TWENTY-FOUR

I STILL DON'T KNOW why Father wouldn't let me keep that dragon." Marceline kicked the grass as she walked. Huggin sat in her front pocket, sniffing the spicy afternoon air. "He'd have been better behaved than Cyrus."

Willa led her friends to the banks of the River Disappointment. Three children, a one-eyed cat, and a mouse. She came to a standstill on the river's edge. Talon sat in the grass by her feet.

"Oh, that cloud looks like a jumble," said Marceline, pointing at the sky.

"That one looks like the prince when he's just discovered his spaghetti has been spelled into worms," said Gish with a snort of laughter.

And that one, thought Willa, *looks like my parents.* Perhaps one day she would find and uncurse them, but for now she closed her eyes and made a promise—a new promise—to the clouds: *I might not be who you wanted but I'll always be who I want. I promise.*

A purple frog hopped by them.

"Fart," said the frog.

"How rude!" said Willa. But the frog had already hopped away.

"At least there's still a magical truce," said Gish. "No more frog rain."

"Every cloud has a silver lining, I suppose," said Willa. "Speaking of which, I came here to show you something."

She grabbed both their hands and winked at Talon. The cat winked back.

"Willa?" Marceline frowned at their joined hands. "Don't tell me you're going to do what I think you're going to do. It would be very wild of you. Prince Cyrus will be *livid*."

Gish grinned. "You're out of control, Willa Birdwhistle."

"I am perfectly well-behaved and sensible," she said with a haughty chin-raise. "And I'm sorry you couldn't keep the dragon, Marceline. You could have gone dragon riding. I guess you'll have to make do with the next best thing."

Though Marceline's eyes were wide, they glimmered with excitement. "You're a terrible influence, Willa. I abhor adventures, you know."

"I know," said Willa. "Me too."

With a flick of his tail, Talon leapt into the air, flying.

Willa's magic fizzed and zizzed as she jumped a second later, pulling her friends up with her.

And she was flying too.

ACKNOWLEDGMENTS

Thanks as always to the Line Tamers: Marie Davies, Rosey Chang, Cathy Hainstock, and Sarah Vincent.

Ginormous thanks to Katelyn Detweiler, agent extraordinaire, and everyone at Jill Grinberg Literary Management for your unwavering support and guidance.

Thank you so, so much to Amy Cloud for welcoming me and Willa with such passion, humor, and generosity. A special thanks to Nicole Sclama for being the first to fall in love with Willa and her many cats. Thanks to: Alice Wang, Stephanie Hays, Emily Andrukaitis, Karen Sherman, Taylor McBroom, John Sellers, and all at HMH and Clarion Books. Thanks also to Wendy Tan for the gorgeous cover artwork.

As always, thanks to the Penguin Random House Australia gang: Michelle Madden, Lisa Riley, Marina Messiha, Amy Thomas, Deb Van Tol, Tijana Aronson, Laura Hutchinson, and everyone else.

To Nicola Santilli, Kristina Schulz, Will Kostakis, and Jenna Guillaume: thank you, thank you, *thank you* for helping me brainstorm title ideas.

A big warm hug of appreciation goes to the LoveOzYA and LoveOzMG community: to the authors, book bloggers, booksellers, librarians, teachers, and everyone promoting a love of reading.

Finally, big love to my family and friends, especially Alexis Drevikovsky, Peta Twisk, Mum, Dad, and Fenchurch.